REFUSE

REFUSE
By Elliott DeLine

Copyright © Elliott DeLine 2009
All Rights Reserved
elliottdeline.tumblr.com / facebook.com/politelyrefuse
Edited by Red Thomas and Elliott DeLine
AUTHOR'S NOTE: This novel is a work of fiction. Names, characters, places, and incidents are either products of the author's imagination or are used fictitiously. Any resemblance to actual persons, living or dead is, quite frankly, inevitable.

Printed in the United States of America

*"God, how Sex implores you
To let yourself lose yourself."*

"Stretch Out And Wait." Morrissey/Marr

PART ONE

Growing up, I had a speech impediment. I wish I could tell you that's why I became a writer. I'd admit (after taking a sip of coffee and checking my reflection in the window) I still get tongue-tied in situations like this; it's astonishing I'm even finishing my sentences. You'd confess you're the same way: either excessively chatty or struck mute, with no middle ground. You'd say something else- something calculated, no doubt intelligent, and perhaps even pretty- but I'd be speechless. I ejaculated my words prematurely and can no longer perform. Disgusted and laughing, you'd abandon me. You always do.

Adults always told me to read as much as possible. I imagine this was because they never did. When you're addicted to bookish perfection, you forsake face-to-face conversations, and devalue that which doesn't follow a plot structure. In other words, you hate life. That's the true reason I write. I fancy myself something of a tragic hero. By the end, I hope to beat out Hamlet, Heathcliff, and Holden Caulfield for that special place in your heart.

I was always embarrassed to talk at school. The other kids didn't need more ammunition. I already stood out, due to my crazy curls and oversized glasses. But I endured in silence, knowing my dad would read to me in bed. His deep voice brought the words to life, and those words protected me from harm. With eyes closed, the little brat in footsie pajamas no longer existed. I became the story.

I had two usual requests. The tale I loved was *Peter Pan*; the tale I loved to hate was *The Three Little Pigs and the Big Bad Wolf*. My father thought it very clever to mock me. He would read, *"Then I'll huff and puff and blow your house down!* said the Big Bad Wup." I'd always fall into the same trap and reply "Not, Wup, *Wup!*" I was unable to maneuver my three year old tongue to form the "f" sound but still knew it was wrong. My father would laugh, but to me it was no joke. I imagined huffing, puffing and blowing our own three-bedroom colonial to smithereens. But it was pleasurable humiliation; the habit-forming kind. I reenacted the scene every night, dooming myself to the sticky role of the masochistic toddler.

And so today, if someone should ask why I am what I am, I will point my finger at well-meaning elementary school teachers and the authors of 1980's parenting books. "READ TO YOUR CHILDREN. IF YOU DON'T THEY WILL BE NOBODIES." Oh, what dark times these suburbs have known... Books would only fuel my piousness and gross over-identification with fictional characters. When most kids were settling into their gender roles, I was too consumed in my fairytale crusade. I eventually outlawed that wretched tale of anthropomorphized swine, not because of my inability to pronounce l's or f's, but due to the final page. It described, in a reversal of nature, the pigs cooking the wolf alive, complete with an illustration of a barbeque. I questioned whether this supposedly big and bad wolf ever meant any harm. Maybe he only wanted to meet his neighbors. And were you not supposed to love your neighbors, unconditionally? I was something of a young animal buff, and I knew healthy wolves never harmed people without provocation (they did harm pigs, but I overlooked this). Canis Lupus was a shy species: gentle outcasts, defamed in children's literature. It was human beings who hunted them to extinction in my home of New York State. Wolves were the real victim, and for this reason I brought the book to my mother, ordering she put an end to the injustice by stapling the last pages together. I then scampered off to draw pictures of wolves and pigs holding hands under rainbows.

As an only child, I grew up a prince, convinced make-believe was a serious business and my desires trumped reality. But no matter how many rainbows I drew or how often I praised God's misunderstood creatures, Nature had it in for me. The first harbinger of this reoccurring theme: my original name consisted of an l and two r's- two consonants I always slaughtered. And so, when my father took me to his office cubicle and his co-workers towered over me, asking, "Hi sweetheart, what's your name?" I always replied, in a shy, barely audible squeak, "Yahweh."

A decade and a half later, I would take a college course on the Bible and realize the blasphemy in this utterance. Not only had I broken taboo and spoken God's name aloud, I had unintentionally ordained myself the Messiah. Though maybe I was on to something. In Hebrew, Yahweh translates as "He is." The un-predicated god. Really, even the pronoun is superfluous (aren't they always?). Perhaps my mispronunciation was prophetic. I wasn't "Laura", after all; I wasn't the child they were seeing- not if I didn't want to be. I was Peter Pan, the Big Bad Wolf, even a talking sea lion on occasion- but I was certainly not a little girl. I wasn't anything yet, or maybe I was everything I would ever be.

I am now twenty-two, and I haven't changed much. I do not work and I no longer attend college. On my most productive days, I lounge around the same suburban house, striking bored, artistic poses. But more importantly, what am I? I've been called tomboy, lesbian, bisexual, asexual, it, androgyne, transsexual, transgender, gender-queer, plain-old queer, and the dreaded *tranny-fag*. None of these tags ever sat well with me. You'd assume this heap of titles would indicate many transformations over the course of my life, but you'd be wrong. Yahweh always was and unfortunately always will be. I have given up on any revelation or eschatological coming-out-of-the-closet. Unlike my kindred memoirists, there's nothing I will beg you to believe. You see, I know I'm not a real man. I inject their hormones into my body, I assume their secondary sex characteristics, I play dress up, prowl about and live in their world, but I am not one of them. Nor am I otherwise.

But there is a problem in this dodgy existence, and nowhere more obvious than in the Old Testament. Yahweh provides the Hebrews with a double bind: make no false figures of me, and yet talk about me all the time. How the hell do you talk about something without assuming you understand it? How can you form sentences without predicates? This is the same problem I have encountered deciphering my own meaning, in a world where people force identities down your throat. Appropriately, I stick out my tongue and drop my trousers to the queers and straights alike. "I'm rubber and you're glue," little Lord Yahweh cries, thumbing his nose. "Sticks and stones, stick and stones! I know you are, but what am I?"

Being so disagreeable on top of being a transsexual, how have I possibly functioned in our society? Easy: I haven't. What kind of anti-hero is ever well-adjusted? As I've already hinted, I do nothing but write incessantly, in hopes of easing my anxieties. And I'm willing to bet that's all your fancy prophets and saints were doing as well.

Like I said, gross over-identification. And this is just the beginning, sister.

*

In case you haven't noticed, I suffer from an inflated sense of self-importance (yes, suffer). However, I would not say this is the case of all transsexuals. Just most.

I'll be the first to admit I am vain. Why do you think I have this ridiculous hairstyle? (Pretend you are lucky enough to view me.) Let me tell you, a great deal of research went into this devil-may-care image of mine. I'll cite one source: James Byron Dean.

The 1950's... maybe not the birth of gender stereotypes, but definitely the golden years. At least here in America. And yet Dean spent his numbered days pouting his lips like a pin-up girl. Let it be said: his genius was his ability to be photogenic. Why else would anyone smoke cigarettes? Of course all those famous photos of him are staged. He pretended to play bongos for pigs, to sulk in bars, to have a destination as he walked down the Manhattan streets in the rain. You know he'd been imagining it all along, planning the outfits and the angles, waiting for a photographer to take up his cause, waiting for boys and girls alike to devour him. Even his movies seem like vain, moving photographs; mirrors in which to view himself, not express a director's vision. Luckily this was the pre-Facebook era, otherwise he might have stayed in Hicksville Indiana, the eternal emo kid, overjoyed to discover the timer on his parents' digital camera. "Love me!" all his status-updates would seem to cry. And you'd just have to love him, wouldn't you?

"Alright, alright," my snottier readers are no doubt thinking, "we get it. Your most traumatic childhood memories center on your lisp. You took some classes at a State school and now consider yourself an expert on metaphysics. You have a fetish for James Dean and perhaps a creepy, repressed one for wolves. You are alluding to myriad mood disorders and gender identity issues. Fascinating. Is there a plot in this story or are you just going to keep talking in circles about yourself?" I already explained this, but I maybe if I quote Dostoevsky you'll be impressed:

"I am convinced that fellows like me must be kept under restraint. They may be able to live for forty years and never open their mouths, but the moment they break out they may talk and talk and talk..."

So there you have it, gentlemen. This isn't any old trashy transgender autobiography: I'm an existentialist!

*

It is hard to say whether I've had two homes or none.

I was raised in the vast suburb of North Syracuse- what I always knew as Central New York, but having spent my college years in or around New York City, I have come to know as Upstate. Upstate, I learned, connotes a great deal: provincial, repressed, isolated, behind the times, famously boring, gloomy, and prone to precipitation. These adjectives could also be used to describe my demeanor in comparison to my worldly Downstate contemporaries. But I'm being self-deprecating, or perhaps passive aggressive; it gets hard for me to tell the difference. I will say, Syracuse is forever entwined with the memories of my once female body. They are both, if you will, uncomfortable places of origin.

Upstate, Downstate, and back again. That was my early twenties for you. The details of my life tend to split off neatly in twos. Only appropriate that Colin Mahr should crop up when he did. Only typical that he'd get under my skin, functioning as both doppelganger and foil. Notice I present you with literary terms by which to understand my scatterbrained tale. I imagine for this reason, among many others, this text won't make it into classroom settings. By the end I will have picked over this story to death. There will be nothing left for you hungry vultures to say in your Contemporary Queer Literature Seminars that I haven't made plain in English. Close-read all you want, you philistines. Do a close-reading of this sentence. How did that go? I hate you.

But back to Colin. (Yes yes, always back to Colin!) He attended the music conservatory at our college, studying how to prostitute his art. It made him miserable, but would prove necessary. He worked hard and achieved success doing what he loves. It is admirable, downright American even- I'd be a predictable bore to suggest otherwise. Ever heard of the Brooklyn-based-indie-rock-quintet Owl Eyes? Of course you have; I'd expect only the hippest of readership. Well Colin is none other than their handsome lead guitarist. "That's where I'd heard the name Mahr!" you exclaim. Perhaps. Or, my clever one, perhaps you were thinking of another great guitarist. I know I was the second I heard Colin's surname. But I've been rambling for a while now and I'm unready to cite that particular source (then you'd know everything!). I won't confess the extent of my juvenile projection. Not just yet. Instead I will torture myself with the same old bedtime story. Instead I will step back and play God.

*

One morning in early January, Colin Mahr awoke, as he often did, to the sound of his cell phone vibrating beneath his pillow. He was dreaming again of a shipwreck; of drowning in a riptide. The images of the dark sea, the imagined taste of salt water and his feelings of panic disintegrated as he groped for the source of the buzz. Once he located the device, he squinted his eyes to read the name on the glowing screen. It was Maggie, his girlfriend. It would be the first time they'd spoken in a few days.

"Hello?" he croaked. He ran his tongue over his achy gums, tasting blood. He had a habit of grinding his teeth in his sleep.

"Hey, did I wake you?" Maggie asked.

"No," Colin lied. He sat up and took a sip of the water on his bed stand. "What's up?"

"I just got out of my class. I thought you'd want to know who's in it. It might interest you."

"Who?" he yawned, still too tired to care what she was saying.

"His name is Dean. He's a transfer, and I'm pretty sure," she paused here for dramatic effect, "he's transgender."

Now Colin was interested. "Really?" He pouted his lower lip and released a jet of air upward, blowing his hair out of his eyes. "How do you know?"

"Well," Maggie paused, choosing her words carefully. "I didn't actually talk to him or anything, but I'm almost positive, just from how he looks. He's kind of androgynous and slight, with small hands and feet. I don't think other people picked up on it, but I've developed a sixth sense for this stuff."

"Interesting!" Colin said. "He must have transferred here. Do you think he's on hormones yet?"

"I'm pretty sure, yes. He has sideburns. He passes and all. Like I said, I don't think other people would have suspected."

"Interesting," Colin said again. "Well, I'm sure we'll meet eventually. Maybe we can introduce ourselves sometime."

"Definitely," Maggie said. "Anyway, sorry to wake you. Should we get lunch or something?" Her voice was meek, hopeful.

"Colin hesitated. "Sure," he said, "I'll meet you at the dining hall in like twenty minutes. I've got to shower." He ended the call and decided to lie back down.

His bed was on the left side of the large room, covered in a blue comforter, in the corner of two hospital-white walls. Behind the wall at his feet was the bathroom, and the adjacent was decorated, unenthusiastically, with two small adornments. One was a crinkled show flyer for his band, Owl Eyes. Beneath the headline, there was a drawing of an owl with many eyes, clearly sketched by the hand of someone who possessed a crude, child-like style as well as a Bachelor's degree in Fine Arts. Tacked beside the flyer was a Polaroid photograph of a freckly brunette in a simple white dress. She was holding a bouquet of sunflowers and sitting barefoot on the edge of a dock, indicating the photographer must have been standing in a lake. The young lady had a strikingly genuine smile, and an earthy beauty suggestive of an earlier, more idealistic era. Beneath the photo, Colin had scrawled "Maggie" in Sharpie marker.

It was at this photograph Colin stared, frowning, as he tried to will himself out of bed. He was enjoying his solitude, having just returned from winter break, which hardly constituted a vacation. Christmas at the Mahr house was a whirlwind of wealthy uncles pestering about graduate school and aging aunts who never knew when to leave. Colin kept a busy schedule at school, and knew he would have would little time for introspection, even at night. Soon Maggie would sleep over regularly, as she had every previous semester. Colin was previously the only transgender man on campus, and to avoid legal problems, the college provided a private dormitory and bathroom. Both suited Colin when he was enjoying sex with Maggie, but after the events of the break and the disaster on New Year's eve, he half-wished he had the excuse of a roommate.

But the more time Colin spent alone, the more he began thinking, and the more he thought, the more he wanted a distraction. So he gave in, got up, and headed to the bathroom. He pulled off his boxer shorts and stepped into shower, turning the nozzle full blast. He allowed the hot water to flow from his crown down over his face, not using shampoo. He rubbed soap over his boney body, lingering for a moment on the raised surgical scars on his hairless chest. After about five minutes, he stepped out and dried himself, ruffling his dark, still dingy hair with a baby blue towel that he then wrapped around his hips. He wiped the steam off the mirror and stood only a moment, stroking his stubble. He knew he looked like a man now, and nothing else in his reflection had ever preoccupied him.

He popped in his contact lenses and headed out of the steam to his dresser. He picked out clean boxers, jeans, a white tee-shirt and a navy hooded sweatshirt. He dressed himself and then turned on his laptop, waiting for the screen to load while he tied his boots. When the desktop appeared, he clicked open his email account, typing his password with one hand. He had received a single message over night. He read:

Hey Colin,
There is a new transfer student, a junior named Dean. He is an FTM transgender but since he was listed as female in the system, he was automatically placed to room with a young woman. She has expressed discomfort with this arrangement and wants Dean to move out. But this causes a dilemma. We have no more single rooms available this semester, and due to state policy we cannot place him to live with a male. Would you be interested in allowing him to move in with you? Let me know.
Thanks!
Kathy Brownstein
Residential Life

The timing was eerie. Colin opened another tab to look for Dean on Facebook. After several failed searches, he got up and pulled on his winter jacket, stuffing his wallet in his pocket. As he left his room and locked the door, he decided he would stop by the Housing office after breakfast and talk to Kathy in person. He was anxious to hear more about Dean.

*

Outside, the air was frigid. Colin wished he wore the scarf Maggie knitted for his birthday, even if it made him feel foolish. He walked across the quad to the dining hall, bowing his head against the winds. He stepped inside the heated building, made warmer by the yellow painted walls and smell of coffee. It was around 11:00 and not too crowded. He glanced around, looking for Maggie. He saw her at a window booth, waved, and proceeded to fill his tray with food.

Five minutes later he sat down at the booth with a cardboard textured bagel, orange juice and some questionably fresh fruit. Maggie was dressed in a white wool cardigan with a matching, knitted beret. Her hair was tied back, and her face looked alert and rosy, suggesting she had been awake and productive for hours. She leaned in and gave Colin a dry kiss across the table.

"Good morning," Colin said as she pulled away.

"Good morning baby," she said. "How did you sleep?"

"Alright," he said. "How was your first literature class?"

"It was really good! We're reading *Despair*. I forget, have you read anything by Na*bo*kov?" She emphasized the second syllable, looking pleased with herself.

"No," Colin said, not sure who that was. Maggie always made him wish he were more well-read. It was something he was insecure about, especially around her friends. He wished she wouldn't talk about books and poetry so often. It made him feel stupid. "So I got an email about that kid Dean you mentioned on the phone," he said. "They want him to move in with me."

"Huh!" said Maggie. "Quelle coincidence! That should be interesting. Well, sort of unfortunate. We won't have as much time to be alone together."

"Yeah, that's true," said Colin.

"But I think it's really great," Maggie said. "I think it will be so good for you to spend time with another trans guy. I hope you two end up getting along."

Colin imagined they would. He tended to get along with most everyone, and he felt a bond between two transgender men could be especially strong. They could share coming-out stories, complain about discrimination, support each other through the hard times, compare their surgical scars... They would be like brothers. Or better yet, war buddies. "What did he seem like?" he asked, trying not to appear overly eager. "Was he cool?"

Maggie bit her lip, considering. "Yeah. He's cool, but he's a little awkward. He kept playing with his hair and squirming in his seat. He's got such a pretty face though. He's almost...delicate, in a way." She had a strange, dreamy look that Colin didn't trust. He personally hated the use of feminine words to describe his appearance, and was offended for Dean's sake.

Still staring off, Maggie didn't notice Colin's expression. "He dresses more like a professor than a student, to be honest," she said. "The kind of guy who always wears sweaters, you can tell. Probably takes himself very seriously, reads a lot, you know the type. And he's a twig. About your size, but a few inches taller."

Colin frowned again. His height was another source of insecurity. "I was thinking I would stop by Resident Life after we ate, and just talk to the lady in person," he said. "Let her know that I want to room with him."

"Yeah, that's a good idea," said Maggie. "You should."

They sat for a while, not speaking. They ate their food and then sipped coffee, both avoiding the topic of winter break. In those moments of silence, they reached an agreement. Now back at school, they would pretend nothing happened.

Maggie finally spoke. "Well, I'm going to go back to my apartment momentarily. I've got another class in a half hour. What are your plans for the day? I don't remember what your schedule's like this semester."

"I've got a composition class from four to six," Colin said, "and that's it for Fridays. Want me to stop by after that?"

"Of course!" she said. "I'm going to the store with Jess, but should be back by six. Do you want me to pick you up anything? Wine?"

"Yeah, I'll split whatever wine with you," Colin said, picking up his plastic tray and pushing in his chair. They walked, again in silence, past the lunchtime crowd of students and up the stairs to the main level.

"Well, I'm going to head back home then," Maggie said. "Have a good day, baby."

"You too," said Colin, hating pet names, but he squeezed her hand and gave her another kiss. "I'll see you tonight."

They went their separate ways, Colin with his back to the wind and Maggie bearing its snowy force.

*

Elise Pace had been waiting to use the mirror for nearly forty-five minutes. She needed to fix her make-up for a typical Friday night, drinking and partying in the campus apartments. Once again, her bizarre roommate had locked himself in the bathroom. She tried knocking, but Dean's only response was a gruff, "Yeah, one minute." The *audacity*, she thought. This was truly the last straw. Lord knows he couldn't be taking a forty-five minute shit, and he didn't have to worry about his appearance, seeing as he never went out. So what on earth was he doing? An unpleasant thought occurred to her and she shook her head, banishing it.

"Dean, I'm serious, I need to get in there," she said. "I have to meet my boyfriend at six." No response. She bit her lip. Shouldn't there be a school policy for kids like him? It was awkward enough living with a transsexual, and Dean's behavior made it ten times worse.

He was always around, never giving her time to herself, disappearing only for classes or when she had friends over. He'd scowl as he made a hasty, wordless exit, sighing and letting the door slam, as if he felt himself to be the victim of some great injustice. And he was always listening to that same music; that terrible moaning man over ancient 80's guitar riffs. She could hear it playing from the hall whenever she'd come up the stairs to their floor. He always scampered to turn it off when she entered the room, bothering her all the more. He had a secretive and creepy way about him, and she often found it hard to sleep with him awake across the room, reading by flashlight into the early hours of the morning.

She couldn't take much more. She was about to pound again with her firsts when there was a knock at the dormitory door. "Who is it?" she asked in a singsong voice.

There was a pause. "Uh, my name is Colin Mahr. I'm here to see

Dean?"

The door to the bathroom flung open and Dean dashed to the entrance way, nearly knocking into Elise. "Jesus, relax," she muttered.

Dean ignored her. "What did you say your name was?" he asked in a mumbled baritone, his lips nearly touching the heavy wood door. He kept one hand on the knob and the other with his fingers crossed at his side.

Elise found this all unnecessary. "He said his name was Colin, now just let him in."

Dean didn't make any indication that he heard her. He opened the door a crack and peered out into the corridor. Colin stood rubbing his arm, melting snowflakes clinging to the dark swoop of his hair. "Hey" he said, frowning slightly, unsure why his entrance was being barred. His eyes were large and brown, wide and deep set with long, thick lashes. Most of his features (chin, lips, eyebrows) could be described as thin and angular. His nose was especially prominent, though not bulbous. It gave him a majestic, bald eagle-like quality.

Dean's eye peered through the crack for several more seconds, judging the specimen. "Hey," he said, finally opening the door. "Come in."

"Hey," Colin said again. "Like I said, I'm Colin Mahr. I'm a junior Music Composition major." He held out his hand. Dean grasped it cautiously, as if such formalities were foreign to him. Colin couldn't help but notice he had a feeble grip and avoided eye contact. Admittedly, Maggie was right; Dean was a somewhat delicate. His face was pale, with rosy cheeks and thin, red lips. His light eyes were obscured by dated, horn-rim glasses, and his black hair was styled meticulously in a pompadour of sorts, shaved close on the sides. He was wearing a black tee with faded blue jeans, seemingly ready to slip off his hips at any second. His arms were crossed and his shoulders rounded as he stared resolutely at a hole in his sock. Colin waited for him to introduce himself, but it never happened.

"Hey Colin," Elise said, breaking the silence. "You were in my Women's Studies class last semester."

"Hey there Elise" Colin said with a little wave. "Yeah, I remember. How did you like that class?"

"It was okay," she said. "A lot of it's over my head. I don't get the whole *waves* thing. Was the teacher saying there is a fourth-wave of feminism or no waves at all?"

Colin laughed. "No idea."

"Regardless, we're all drowning," Dean mumbled.

Colin looked to Elise, as if for explanation. She rolled her eyes and shrugged.

"So you're Dean right?" Colin said.

Dean nodded, still staring at his toes.

"Well hi Dean," Colin said. "It's nice to finally meet you." Dean nodded again, the corner of his mouth twitching upward in a would-be smile. No one could see it.

"So," Colin said. "I was wondering if you'd want to go for a walk. There are some things I was to ask you."

"Really?" Dean's head shot up with excitement. "I mean, sure, yes, I'd like that." His cheeks flushed as he brushed past Colin and once again gripped the handle of the door. His hand was trembling.

"Uh, you'll want a jacket," Colin said. "It's snowing out."

"Oh, right," Dean said, blushing again and looking at his feet. "Stupid, sorry." He went to his closet and pulled on an oversized black cardigan and a matching black pea coat. He also removed his glasses, placing them carefully in a case on his bed stand, next to what looked suspiciously like a Bible.

"I mean, you're welcome to talk here," Elise said, curious. Colin was the only other transgender person she knew besides Dean and their interactions interested her, from a sociological standpoint. Maybe Colin could teach Dean some manners, she thought. He at least never made her uneasy. Her friends agreed, Colin Mahr seemed really normal despite his disorder.

"No," Dean said, one-handedly struggling with his Burberry scarf as he opened the door. "Let's go."

*

The sun had set and it was still snowing as they walked down the path away from the dorm buildings. The street lamps glowed yellow, illuminating swirling flakes in the air. The brick academic buildings loomed in the distance, looking castle-like when set against the navy sky. Both boys had their hands balled up into fists inside the sleeves of their jackets as the walked down the snowy path. When they approached the fork between the apartments and the library, Colin turned to Dean. "Where to?"

Dean shrugged. Colin shrugged as well.

"Well, I was going to meet my girlfriend at her apartment, over in Baker," Colin said. "You're welcome to join me if you'd like. That's sort of a hike, you know? She's in one of your literature class actually. Her name's Maggie. I know she'd love to meet you."

"Okay," Dean said, his face still flushed, not sure what Baker was. He followed Colin's lead, taking the path on their right into a grove of pine trees. The lamps were gone, but they could still see one another's faces. The snowfall made everything seem unnaturally quiet. No one else was around.

"So there's no way of addressing this without sounding awkward," Colin said after a moment, "so I'll just say it. We're both trans men."

"Oh!" said Dean. "I uh...well hm. I hadn't realized you were."

"Oh, cool, thanks!" said Colin, smiling.

"Thanks?" Dean asked, scratching the back of his hair.

"Yeah, I don't know. I'm glad I look like a regular guy."

"Huh," Dean said. "Yes. That is the idea, I suppose. Fair enough." He let out a nervous *ha!* his breath visible in the air.

"So anyway," Colin said, "the administration asked me if I'd want to room with you, since you transferred. I've got a double to myself, complete with a shower. I think it'd be pretty sweet if you moved in, since we are the only trans men on campus and all."

"Are we?" Dean said, still messing with his hair. "Well then, yes. Of course. I really don't fit well with uh, uh…"

"Elise?" Colin offered.

"Yes. Her. So okay, we'll be roommates. And that's why we're walking, then? Ah, of course. Got it. Roommates. Transgender. Right." Dean looked disappointed.

Colin wondered if he'd been expecting something else, though he couldn't imagine what. "So you go by Dean," he said. "Are you a James Dean fan?"

"Why?" Dean asked. He narrowed his eyes.

"Uh, I don't know," Colin said. "I mean, you've sort of got his hair style."

"Wow, I hadn't noticed." Dean meant to be self-deprecating, but realized he sounded rude. "I mean, yes I am. A uh, fan. Which I guess stands for fanatic, right? The word actually comes from…well, hm. Frightening. Okay, shut up Dean." His voice trailed off into an indecipherable mumble as he unconsciously sped up his walking pace.

Colin felt like Dean was angry with him about something, though the idea was absurd; after all, they had been talking less than ten minutes. As they neared the steps down to the apartments, he kept sneaking glances at Dean's miserable profile. He wanted to take in every detail of his appearance, mark every masculine and feminine trait and compare it to his own. He absorbed Dean's faint five o'clock shadow, his Adam's apple, his pale, darting eyes. He wasn't sure if he felt competitive or what. It was all very strange. "So where did you come from?" he said. He felt like he was talking over his own thoughts.

"Originally?" Dean said, blinking snowflakes off his eyelashes. "North Syracuse."

"Ah, Upstate. So you're used to the snow."

Dean said nothing.

"Heard they've got a good basketball team," Colin added, reaching. "Syracuse University, right? The Orangemen? Football team's pretty popular too."

"Unfortunately," Dean muttered.

Colin laughed. "Yeah, I'm not a sports fan."

18

Dean smiled. He liked when people thought he was funny, despite himself. *Unfortunately* was also one of his favorite words to say. "What do you like then?" he asked, looking up.

"Well," Colin said, "this sounds cliché, but my real passion is music."

"Mine too!" said Dean. He looked excited but it disappeared in a flash. "Well, I don't play any instruments. And I'm not a great singer. But yeah...music." He silently chastised himself for sounding so dumb.

"Yeah?" said Colin. "What's your favorite band?"

Dean blushed. "Oh...I dunno." He did know. "What's yours?"

"Answering a question with a question, eh?" Colin said, smiling. "Well, I'd have to say *my* band is my favorite, actually. We're called Owl Eyes, and I'll risk sounding like an asshole, but I really believe in what we're doing."

Dean shook his head. "No, I admire your honesty" he said. "You should think you're the best, otherwise why bother?"

"Well, I don't know if I agree with that" Colin said. "I mean, I'd be nowhere without my influences."

"Influences?" Dean said.

"Yeah, you know, like, musicians who inspire me."

Dean was silent.

"Hasn't an artist ever inspired you?" Colin asked. Now he was the one blushing.

Dean bit his lip. "Who inspires you?" he asked.

The truth was, Colin loved all kinds of music. But when this question was posed, he tried to read his crowd and cite something impressive. "I've been really into The Smiths lately," he said, eyeing Dean's hair.

Dean blushed, his tongue poking out as he gave Colin a sideways glance. His eyes seemed disbelieving, but hopeful; almost pleading. Colin turned away. Something about Dean was too familiar. It scared him a little.

Colin lit a cigarette. Dean kept his fingers crossed in his pocket. They didn't talk again until they reached the apartment.

*

Maggie's roommate was gone for the weekend, so Colin slept in her bed that night. By eleven they had finished a double bottle of merlot, and were watching television in their underwear, feeling warm and woozy under the pink down comforter. Unlike her boyfriend, Maggie had taken great care decorating her walls. Every inch was covered in paintings, photographs or posters. They seemed to serve as templates for self-expression. Most of the photographs featured Colin, and two posters were of Owl Eyes.

"I really liked Dean," Maggie said, stretching her thin arms. "I'm glad you brought him over. I want to be his friend."

"He's interesting," Colin said. He stared at the wall, distracted. There was a photograph of him at age eighteen, before he started hormone therapy. He wished Maggie would throw it out.

"He seems shy," Maggie continued, "but it's endearing. He's definitely a cutie."

"Yeah," Colin said. He wished Maggie wouldn't use words like *cutie*.

"I'm not attracted to him, Colin, don't get the wrong idea. I just mean he's sweet."

"I know."

There was silence.

"He reminds me of Morrissey," Maggie said. "Especially with his hair."

"Yeah, he likes The Smiths," Colin said, eyes now on the television. "I'm sure he's going for that."

"Do you think he's gay?" Maggie said.

Colin frowned. "I like The Smiths and I'm not gay."

Maggie blushed. "I wasn't saying there's a correlation. He just seemed sort of gay, didn't he? Is that wrong to say?"

"What? How the hell should I know?"

"I don't know," Maggie said. She hesitated. "Colin, you seem upset. Should we talk about-" "No," Colin said. "Not tonight."

They both knew this meant never.

"I'm sure he'll say eventually if he is," Maggie said after a moment, nodding to herself.

"What? Who?"

"Dean."

"You're still on that? Who cares?"

Maggie sighed. "I don't know. It's just interesting, that's all. I've never met a gay trans man."

Colin didn't respond. Maggie kissed him on the shoulder and then leaned her head against his bare chest. "I love you," she said.

"I love you too, but I've got a headache," Colin said, turning on his side.

"Oh no, I was just...never mind." Maggie said, edging away. She stared at the back of his head, embarrassed. Her throat hurt.

She went back to watching television until she fell asleep.

*

Oh boy, maybe I'm expecting too much of you, reader. Not everyone had the benefit of going to a chic college like me. I'll give some definitions that may be helpful:

1. <u>Transgender-</u> people who feel the gender they were born into is Restrictive and does not Define them. For the most part this term is used to describe people who feel they are the opposite gender inside. But also this includes people who don't feel like anything, or feel like everything, or are just overwhelmed with feelings and genders completely. Anytime

someone calls this an umbrella term I get an urge to take an umbrella and stab them.
    2. Transsexual- these are people who have SEX CHANGES(!!!) or take hormones to alter their body or something. The term is outdated and offensive, and therefore appeals to me. This includes MTF (male to female), and FTM (female to male), but never F2M. That's vulgar, stop it. We are not a 90's boy band, regardless of what tacky drag king performers persuade you to believe. No numbers, no exceptions.
    3. Transvestite- Eh, you know. No one cares about them anymore.
    (Fun fact for Catholics: Similar to the term "God" in the Holy Trinity, "Transgender" encompasses all three categories as well. Nifty, eh?)
    Transgender individuals (trans for short!) like to be called by the Pronouns that go with what they feel on the inside (wherever that is located). So if a person was born a female but grows up to feel like a man, you should probably call him by male Pronouns, regardless of how you feel in your insides about the matter (or how much evidence you have to the contrary). But no one can make you. It's a free country.
    Note: It's alright to admit transgender people are unattractive. Not because they have supposedly deviant bodies, but because they won't shut up about them. You will find yourself wondering, "Does this person ever stop talking about their feelings and their insides? Why does it even matter?" It shouldn't and doesn't. In fact, thinking about any of this stuff is bad for you. I'm bored of definitions though, so if you're still baffled, maybe you should go read some books on Theories. But I'm warning you, you may break out in a rash. Maybe turn on the television. Perhaps Oprah is doing a special.
    But back to my initial point. You might be a little confused seeing as Maggie just said something about *gay trans men.* "Okay," you say, with boundless generosity, "so I accept that females can be men and males can be women. But wait. A female who is a man who is a gay man? I don't mean to offend you, but that's sort of absurd."
    You're telling me.
    And for the record, I am offended by your question. To be transgender is to be perpetually offended. But now, since as the narrator I am God, and God works in mysterious ways, let us jump back in time about five years. After all, it isn't proper if I don't include some whining about my teen years. On your journey towards understanding, you may allow your tears to drop freely upon the pages. As your diversity tour guide, I assure you: it will only enhance the sanctity of this text.

*

    Dean sat in the Tim Horton's across from the high school, drinking black coffee and looking out on the parking lot. Across from him sat Vivian Angeli. She was the head of their class, president of the literary society, and Dean's only friend. They went to this restaurant almost every afternoon, though they despised the place. They longed for a locally owned café, where they would meet artistic teenage comrades and maybe see some intelligent live performances. Alas, that was the stuff of books and indie flicks; this was the realm of Walmarts and hardcore bands.

To avoid going home after school, they'd walk across to a plaza that housed the dreaded restaurant, right next to a tanning salon (discounts for Class of 07 Seniors!) and an Evangelist youth center. There were exactly eighteen American flags leading up the path; they counted. Once inside, Vivian would order them both drinks, since Dean never had any money and her dad was always giving it away. Then they would sit in the darkest corner they could find and do what they did best: complain.

"Michael got the stupidest tattoo." Vivian said. "It's the friggin' Olympic rings."

Dean looked away from the window, scowling. "Are you kidding me? Why would anyone ever, ever do that?"

Vivian shrugged. "He's orange too, have you seen? Been tanning, no doubt."

"Oh Lord." Dean took a snotty sip of his coffee. Neither he nor Vivian approved of her other friends.

"Did you do the English homework?" Vivian said. "You have no excuse to fail this semester. Though admittedly, Mrs. Moriarty can't teach. I swear she gets her notes off the internet."

"She's dreadful," Dean said, tracing the water ring on the table with his finger. "The books have been enjoyable at least. Did I tell you my theory about-- well, later." He glared as two boys in lacrosse uniforms walked in the door. "I can't focus, this place is too ugly. Why are we here again? Want to walk to the cemetery?"

"Later, maybe," Vivian said. "Must we go in the sun?"

They took some time to catch their breaths before Dean cautiously continued. "I skipped gym again."

Vivian groaned. "Dean! You're going to fail." She was preoccupied with grades and following rules. It is hard to say why she was so fond of Dean, as he was oblivious to both these things.

"Well, what am I supposed to do?" he said. "I can't change with the girls. Everyone acts like I'm staring at them. It's so homophobic. Plus I don't take my clothes off in front of people, ever. It goes against my code." He smirked into his coffee cup.

"Maybe you should get a letter from your mom, saying that you're transgender," Vivian said.

Dean frantically signaled for her to lower her voice. Vivian was the only person, outside of his family, who knew his secret identity. Or at least that's what he thought; there were rumors, given his somewhat masculine clothing and hairstyle. Though some assumed he was a lesbian, there was a peculiar air to his timid androgyny most people noticed. It hinted at something far more sinister.

"Yeah right, some good that'd do." Dean muttered, referring to the suggestion of a letter. "My mom would burst into tears if I so much as mentioned it. And do you really think the idiots who teach Phys. Ed. will respect my wishes? Besides, what am I supposed to do, change with the guys? I'm sure that'd go great."

Vivian sighed. "Well, you can't keep skipping."

"Well, technically I can."

"No, you can't." Her dark eyebrows angled with fury as she glared over the rim of her glasses. It was her signature, librarian expression that Dean would one day adopt.

Dean muttered something inaudible. His voice was naturally high pitched; he was seventeen and not yet injecting one milliliter of testosterone biweekly into his body, as was the custom for boys like him. He compensated by speaking in a grumble that was almost impossible to hear.

Glancing out the window over Dean's shoulder, Vivian suddenly looked alarmed. "Wait a minute, is that my mom's car?"

"What?"

"Yeah, it totally is. She's coming inside."

She was. The middle-aged, squat Italian women looked frazzled as she burst through the door and sped-walked to their booth. Her dark complexion, angular eyebrows and reading glasses made her look like Vivian's funhouse mirror reflection. She had a romance novel under her arm.

"Hey mom, what's up?" Vivian asked. Dean waved shyly, but she ignored him.

"We need to go," her mom said, her eyes darting around the restaurant.

"What? Why?" Vivian said.

"We'll discuss it in the car." She looked slightly deranged, staring off over their heads, as if checking for spies.

"Is everything okay? Is it Dad, or Adrienne?" Adrienne was Vivian's quiet, often overlooked little sister.

"We'll discuss it in the car," her mom repeated. "Hurry."

Vivian looked like she might cry. "Bye darling," she said to Dean as she grabbed her purse and stood up. "I'm sorry about this."

"No, no, don't be. I just hope everything is okay," Dean said. "Phone me later!" he called as she made her way to the exit. Her mom shot him a dirty look, and put her arm around her daughter as she pushed through the door.

*

Dear Dean,
   I'm crying as I'm typing this, so excuse me if my writing is not exactly coherent. I don't know how long I have, because my parents come in to check on me periodically. I may have to send this suddenly without finishing. But I'm rambling, let me get to the point.
   When Mom and I got to the car, she filled me in on what was going on. Thankfully no one in my family is hurt (though maybe now I wish they were. No, that's awful to say, I'm sorry). But she told me that I'm not allowed to hang out with you anymore. I kept asking why, but she said we'd talk about it when Dad got home. So I sat in my room fuming and waiting until five o'clock, when we all sat down to talk.
   Recently one of Mom's friends found out her daughter was a lesbian and was warning Mom of the tell-tale signs. Apparently my new liberal attitudes, lack of interest in boys, and friendship with someone who looks like you are all common "symptoms." Mom's friend's daughter had a masculine female friend who ended up being her "butch lover." At this I burst out in bitter laughter. The idea of anyone calling you butch is absurd (no offense dear) and we're both a pair of asexual amoebas, give or take a few occasions. So I tried to explain that we are just friends, and that you are transgender, not a lesbian, while simultaneously attempting to assert that if we WERE girlfriends, they'd have no reason to be angry. It proved disastrous.
   They went from calling you too butch and masculine to suddenly insisting how feminine you are. "Transgender?" Dad said. "What is this crap? That didn't even exist a few years ago. If a girl wants to be a boy and dresses like a boy, she is a lesbian. Tons of lesbians are that way. I'd even venture to say most."
   "If she were a boy," Mom said, "she'd be out playing football or working on cars. Instead she sits around drinking tea and gossiping with you. If she grew out her hair and wore some makeup she'd be a very typical girl."
   "You had me read her writing once," Dad felt the need to add. "It's not linear like a male writer. It's circular and disorganized...overly emotional, like a female writer." Guess he loves MY writing.
   "I don't get the point," Dad said. "She'll never be a REAL boy, so what is the goal?" I then told them about transitioning and your plans for after graduation.
   "That's disgusting," Mom said. "She'll never pass for a man; her features are extremely soft and feminine. She's downright dainty!"
   Dad said, "I don't care how many steroids she puts in her body. Even if she had a full-faced beard and washboard abs she'd still be the gayest man I'd ever seen. I've seen transsexuals on TV. You can always tell. Society will never accept her."
   "That's not true," I said. "And besides, Dean doesn't care what

24

other people think. He's just trying to be himself."
"No she's not, she's trying to trick people!" Mom said. "She's trying to trick good girls like you into sleeping with her."
"I'm not involved with him like that! We're just friends," I said.
"Nonsense, I know how guys are. They only want one thing," Dad said. I pointed out he just admitted you were a guy and contradicted his whole point. He said, "You think you're so smart Vivian but you don't know anything about the world. People like that are bad news. They are bad for society and they are bad for you. You don't hang out with any of your normal friends anymore, and with a transgender around you will never find a boyfriend."
So I said, "Maybe I don't want a boyfriend!"
And mom said, "So you are a lesbian!" There was no winning the argument.
And that's when they planted the news on me. They are forcing me to go to Bishop Grimes. Catholic school, Dean. I can't stop crying. I can't stand the power they have over me just because I am sixteen. I never used to feel this way. I knew my parents were politically conservative but I thought they had my best interests in mind. For the first time I want to do something crazy, like run away from home or get a tattoo; anything to defy them.
I'm so angry I could scream. I just want to see you. This is the worst. How will we ever hang out without going behind their backs? But I promise I won't stop being there for you. You have my word.
I feel awful because I know you're already lonely and depressed. You are going through so much and need a friend now more than ever. I don't want to abandon you but I feel I have no other choice. We will find a way to see one another eventually, I promise. They can't monitor my phone and computer usage forever, and I will make sure to be in touch. But for the time being, I guess this is goodbye. I'm so sorry Dean.

Love always,
Viv

*

Dean made a routine of riding city buses. He would ride aimlessly for hours to avoid going home, staring out the window, listening to music and pining for Vivian. Sometimes he'd stop in the used record store and look at albums he couldn't afford. One particular day in autumn, he was doing just that, when he was struck by a feeling of déjà vu. He stared down at the cover of the CD in his hand, straining his mind; where had he seen this graphic before? The person was lying down, eyes glazed over under heavy brows, hands raised slightly. Their gender was indeterminable. Something about the figure was corpselike, though not repugnant; perhaps it was the frill on the sleeve of the shirt. Though the image seemed to suggest death, there was something unmistakably lively about it. The background was a moldy greenish gray. It stirred something deep in Dean's psyche, like a memory from a past life. It was strikingly similar to the color of his eyes. In pinkish serif text above the figure, it said:

THE SMITHS
The Queen is Dead.

There was simple beauty in both the cadence and appearance of these words. Far away, a child's voice seemed to cry, "Now!" So Dean did something he had never done before. He glanced around before shoving the CD in his messenger bag. He made a hasty exit, the doorbells clanging behind him, and ran to the bus stop.

Outside, it was a warm and hazy afternoon. Red leaves and cigarette buts littered the sidewalk by the bus stop. There were only a few days left of summer before Dean would return to the high school, without Vivian, for the first time. He bit his cheek as he waited under an awning for the bus. His eyes darted around the busy street, and his heart throbbed painfully at the sound of a siren in the distance.

The bus ride home, he was still full of adrenaline. The trees looked greener, the sky looked bluer and even the grays of the abandoned factory buildings appealed to him. He took out the CD and carefully placed it in his walkman, donning his goofy oversized headphones. Putting his bag on the adjacent seat to discourage company, he checked the name of the first song. Ah, the title track. He also caught sight that the album was from 1986 and Manchester, England. This pleased him. He preferred the archaic.

The album started with the faint singing of a crowd, bringing to mind an Irish pub. It sounded like mostly women. They sang this:

"Take me back to Dear Old Blighty
Put me on a train to London town
Take me anywhere
Drop me anywhere
Live or leave Suburbia*
But I don't care."

There was a drum roll. The guitar came in, ringing and wavering at first, but then the beat changed and the instruments came together. It had that recorded-in-a-tin-can, distant, 80's timbre, but it only added to the allure. Dean could feel the music in his bones, but at the same time, he had left his body behind. He was on a misty moor, under an iron bridge, behind a disused railway line. How strange, how strange...The ensemble was soon accompanied by ghostly echoing moans and then, above the sound, like nothing he ever heard before and yet horrifically familiar, more so than his very mirror reflection, a voice began to sing.

*

I may have gotten a little carried away there.

There is no use trying to further describe this in my mediocre prose. I still prefer singing over writing. For the lonely, there is something magical about a voice in your ears, not just your head. And to sing along! Melodic vibrations, from larynx to ear drum to another larynx. Poetic union, celestial alignment, daemonization, mutual damnation. URGECY URGENCY URGENCY! These little black symbols just can't compare.

I succumbed to bizarre hero worship many times in my youth, but this was different. Nothing affected me like The Smiths. This man was singing. Not like a Broadway star or an American Idol, not like the Chemical-Panic-at-the-Fall-Out-Charlotte-Days that plagued the airwaves, not like the emerging plethora of indie DIY jerks who never took a step back and realized they had nothing to say. This was media, the music industry; this came from the *80s*. And yet this man was singing his life, singing poetry. But not the postmodern nonsense or boring European floridity I would later study. It was not poetry because some scholar deemed it so. It was poetry because it came from the heart.

I was in love. I don't say this lightly.

In the Smithology, sulky youth were inherently superior. Abstinence, of all varieties, was noble. The band's reputation and imageless image were almost as consuming as the records themselves. The legend is as follows: Steven Patrick Morrissey, the near suicidal, somewhat sexless poet, is unearthed in 1982 by Johnny Marr, the energetic, guitar-playing wonder boy. Together they take on the hum-drum, antagonistic world, assaulting it with a series of catchy pop songs that sprung forth from their entwined souls.

I get the feeling this tale was embellished, but I wouldn't be a modern writer if I didn't throw in a spicy little, THAT DOESN'T MAKE IT ANY LESS TRUE moment. I believe that Morrissey believed in it. I believe The Smiths were something real, for him, so it's real, for me.

I suppose Morrissey, like most my teenage interests, was just another impediment to my recovery and maturity- oh, but what handsome impediment! The fusion of music and poetry was far more interesting a drug than Prozac, leaving me (yes yes) emotionally invested in my own despair. Don't think I don't see you there, adult intruder, looming over my beloved reader's shoulder, shaking your shaggy, educated head. Kindly go fuck yourself and leave us kids alone. Morrissey made me feel beautiful. Morrissey made me laugh again. My dogma kept me living, much like my Catholic ancestors, in a state of compulsive guilt and confession. But none the less, it kept me living.

Dancing alone in my bedroom, I believed it was only a matter of time before my own Johnny Marr showed up at the door.

*

It took under an hour for Dean to lug his few belongings from his old dorm to the left side of Colin's room. Colin sat on his own bed, absent-mindedly playing his unplugged black Les Paul, watching him unpack. He paused for a moment, deciding to attempt conversation. "So when did you go on hormones?" he asked.

Dean kept folding shirts. "It's complicated." He looked up and realized Colin was waiting for him to continue. He sighed. "A few years ago I suppose."

"That's awesome," Colin said. "I've been on them since freshmen year. Do you go to Callen Lorde?"

"Yes."

"Nice. Me too."

Dean forced a smile.

Getting Dean to open up was an increasingly difficult task, especially when it came to transgender topics. Colin never had a close friend who was going through the same difficulties, and he wanted to discuss all kinds of things. At what age did Dean discover what he was? How did his parents react when he came out? Did he have any surgeries yet? Did he intend to? When? But Colin sensed, without asking, that Dean didn't want to discuss any of it. He just wondered why. He wasn't sure why he did this, but he started playing the riff to "This Charming Man" by The Smiths on his guitar.

Dean didn't say anything at first. "That's very good," he said finally, still staring at his shirts and blushing.

"Thanks man," Colin said, setting his guitar on the bed. "I thought you'd like it. Hey, would you maybe want to come to one of my shows in the city? It's two weeks from now, on a Friday night."

"Let me check my calendar," Dean said, rolling his eyes. "No, I'm just kidding," he added quickly. "I'd love that. Is Maggie going as well?"

"Probably," Colin said. "It'd be really cool. I'd like you to meet my friends."

"Really?" The word slipped out before Dean could stop himself. He blushed yet again.

"Yeah, of course!" Colin said. "I think they'll love you, especially the guys in the band. And we can hang out and get some drinks at the bar afterwards."

Dean nodded. "I've never hung out with friends in the city." This was an understatement. Dean hadn't hung out with friends anywhere in years.

"Don't worry about it, I'm driving in," Colin said, thinking Dean was anxious about getting lost. "Wait, really? Didn't you say you went to that art school for a year?"

"I didn't get out much," Dean said.

Colin laughed. "Well, that's all going to change. I'm making you go out with me."

Dean moved on to folding his pants, smiling slightly.

*

Dean had never gone out drinking on a Friday night. Due to nerves, he kept taking glasses of beer every time Maggie offered to refill the pitcher. He lost count around his fourth. He tried to distract himself from agonizing over the calories by looking around the bar. They were sitting in a small back room with circular tables and booths in front of a stage. The lighting was dim and there were white Christmas lights strung along the wood-paneled walls. On the stage, a wispy blond girl was playing the piano and singing in a pleasant but unremarkable voice. Dean felt happy as the chemicals seeped in.

"How nice," he said to Maggie.

Maggie smiled, tucking her hair behind her ear and revealing a dangling peacock-feather earring. Dean noticed it matched her dark green sweater, which matched her eyes, which also matched his eyes. He smiled again as she took a sip of beer. Maggie was pretty, and he was growing fond of her.

"I want to go out for a cigarette," she said. "I guess I'll just wait. They should be going on soon."

Sure enough, the piano girl announced her last song. Colin came into the room, carrying his guitar case. He was wearing an aviator jacket and tight black jeans tucked into his boots. He sat down on the arm of Maggie's chair, snuggling close. "Decent crowd," he said, looking around, pursing his lips and nodding.

"Are you nervous?" Dean asked, leaning in and nearly knocking over the candle centerpiece.

Colin shrugged his shoulders. "Not really."

"I'd be terrified," Dean said. "I'd be shakin' in my boots." He pointed at Colin's pointed leather shoes and giggled.

"Are you drunk?" Colin asked, raising one of his eyebrows.

"I like how you did that," Dean said, pointing his finger dangerously close to Colin's eye, "with your eyebrow. I liked it. Well done." He giggled again.

"Oh my," Maggie said softly.

The girl on stage stopped playing and people applauded. "Oh shit, gotta run," Colin said. He kissed Maggie on the cheek and took off towards the stage, giving Dean a wink.

"This will be just marvelous," Dean said, folding his hands on the table.

Maggie laughed. "How would you know? You've never heard Owl Eyes."

Dean put a finger to his lips. "Hush. Don't speak. We're in the presence of genius."

A boy came rushing into the room, brushing Dean's back as he passed. He mounted the stage with a single bound, and got to work adjusting the height of the microphone stand. He was tall and lean, dressed in tight black clothing. His hair was short and blonde, and he wore large, circular wire-framed glasses. You could call him a hipster with confidence.

"Good evening, we are Owl Eyes," he said finally, looking around and sounding bored. "This is a song of our latest album. It's for sale right over there." He pointed off stage with his large, skeletal hand.

"One two three," said the muscular drummer, clicking his sticks.

The band started out with a fast paced song. People tapped their feet. Dean wasn't that into it, but he wasn't opposed either. He was a little too drunk to be objective.

"The singer is dull," he said loudly in Maggie's ear. "You can't even understand him and he doesn't move about. Bor-ring."

Maggie frowned. "You think so? Aw, I love Craig though. He's one of Colin's best friends from high school. He lives in Brooklyn."

"Of course he does," Dean said darkly. He suddenly had to use the bathroom. "B.R.B." he said, tripping over a chair but regaining balance.

He descended a flight of stairs and found the restrooms in a dark corner. He pushed the grimy door open with his elbow. He felt uncomfortable in the men's room, as always, even though he was drunk. He waited for the stall, clutching his hair and looking away from a man washing his hands.

"Owl Eyes is good," the guy said to his friend in the stall. This struck Dean as odd; he never heard men talk in the bathroom the way women often did.

"Yeah, they're decent," the other guy said, and there was the sound of the toilet flushing. He came out and Dean rushed into the stall. The two men continued to talk as they washed their hands.

"The guitarist is talented," one of them said. "Colin Mahr. My girlfriend said he was in a magazine recently. He's really young, but he's been asked to play with all these crazy guitarists and shit. He's like a... what's the word? It's a German word."

Dean smiled. "Wunderkind," he mouthed silently. He stood by the toilet waiting for the men to leave, studying crude drawings on the walls. The beer left a gross aftertaste and he felt like he was spinning.

"You know what I heard though?" the other guy said. "He's really a chick."

The sound of the water stopped. Now there was the hand dryer.

"What the fuck? No way."

"Yeah, like, a transgender or whatever."

"That sounds like shit someone would make up. He seems chill, I don't believe it for a second."

"No, seriously, it's true. If you look close you can totally tell."

"So wait wait wait. You're saying he got a sex change to be a girl?"

"No, he got a sex change to be a guy. Or she did, I should say."

"So does he-slash-she have a vagina then?"

"I have no idea. I think so. I don't think that…you know. I don't think like, you can make a dick. It's not physically possible. You can dig a hole but you can't grow a pole." He chucked, and his friend swore under his breath.

"Dude, that's sick."

There was the sound of footsteps and then the door swung shut behind them. The bathroom was silent.

Without warning, Dean puked.

"I'm sorry," Dean said for fifth time on the car ride home.

"Relax, it's really okay," Colin said. "I don't mind missing the other bands. You can't help that you got sick."

"I know, I'm sorry," Dean said, looking out the window, miserable. Also drunk, Maggie had fallen asleep in the passenger seat.

"Did you like our set at least?" Colin asked.

"Oh, yeah," Dean said, listless. "You were great."

Colin frowned. "You can tell me the truth you know."

"Well, to be honest I wasn't a fan of the singer."

Colin sighed. "Yeah. That's what a lot of people say. I can't say I entirely disagree with you. I feel bad, sometimes I think we'd be better off if we replaced Craig. But we started the band together, you know?"

Dean nodded, and then realized Colin couldn't see him. "Yeah," he said, "I mean, the music itself is great. I just think you need a front man with more charisma."

"By the way, this doesn't leave this car," Colin said.

Dean smirked. "Who am I gonna tell?"

"Craig's a good guy though," Colin said. "A little rough around the edges, but I think you'd like him. He comes to campus often- you'll get to meet him."

"Lovely," Dean said, indifferent.

"I thought the show went well though," Colin said. "The only thing was these two guys kept staring at me. It was creeping me out. Did you see them? They were in the corner. They were like crust-punk kids."

"Yeah, I saw them," Dean said, feeling depressed again.

Dean hesitated. "Actually, I didn't know whether I should tell you this, but I overheard them talking about you. In the bathroom."

"Really?" Colin said, "What were they saying?"

31

"Well, first they were saying you were a great guitarist, which was nice. But then the one guy said you were transgender and they were, um... rude about it."

"Oh," Colin said. Dean had never heard him sound so sad.

"I'm sorry, I shouldn't have said anything. I'm still a little drunk. God damn it, I'm sorry."

"No, I'm glad you did," Colin said, "I mean, what did they say?"

"Oh, I don't know..."

"Tell me," he said, starting to sound angry. "What, you don't think I can handle it? You don't think I've heard worse?"

Dean cringed. "Alright, I'm sorry...they said you were... female. And they speculated the nature of your, um... genitalia."

"They speculated the nature of my genitalia? God Dean, just say it. They wondered whether I have a dick."

"So that's why they were staring at me. They were trying to figure out what's in my pants."

"Maybe," Dean said quietly.

"Great. I mean, maybe that's why I even get booked at places. Maybe it's all just a circus act for people."

"I think you might be overreacting," Dean said.

"No Dean, I'm not. I fucking hate being a musician half the time. I hate being in the spotlight. I should just quit. If I'm out as transgender, then that's all I'm known for. I'm always the trans-guitarist, always booked for queer events. And to the straight audience, I'm always seen as a sideshow freak, no matter how open minded they pretend to be. Trust me, I used to be very vocal about being queer. It's such a fucking boys' club. Anyone who isn't a dude gets treated like shit in this business. I want to just forget about it, move beyond it, be known for my talent and not some stupid identity I never even wanted in the first place. So I don't mention it. And then what? People find out anyway. Queers call me a coward, and straight dudes comes to my show and laugh at me, thinking I hide it because I'm ashamed. It's fucking bullshit."

"It is unfair," Dean said softly, "I'm sorry I said you were overreacting. I only wanted to calm you down."

Colin sighed. "I probably should be open about it. I just don't want people knowing, is that so wrong? I don't want people thinking about my body. I guess I am ashamed. That's so politically incorrect to say. I guess I want to be stealth half the time. Other trans people would call me a coward."

"It's okay," Dean said, "I'm ashamed too. We've got every right to be. Who cares what people say?"

Colin laughed. "Is that supposed to be comforting?"

"I don't know, I'm awful at this," Dean mumbled.

Colin reached behind the seat and messed up Dean's hair. Dean felt as if his entire body was blushing this time.

"You're right," Colin said, laughing. "We're entitled to our self-loathing. Who are they to take that from us?"

"Without my guilt and my hair I'm nothing," Dean said, rearranging the latter in the reflection of the dark window.

*

"That's because you have INTERNALIZED YOUR OPPRESSION," says an imaginary activist. I stab hir with a trans umbrella.

I've had some awful days lately, but today was one of the worst. I didn't leave my room all day; instead I lay in bed and stared at the ceiling, thinking. I really have no excuse for this behavior anymore. I am twenty-two years old, still waiting for a miracle to snap me out of this stupor. It never comes. Forcing myself to relive all these memories certainly isn't helping.

It's a wonder my parents don't kick me out. My father thinks I haven't heard him suggest it. I don't think my mother would really have the heart, but they might get stern. They might say I have to go out and start trying. I don't even know where to begin.

"Everyone hates working, Dean."

Yeah, yeah… so why do they do it? And yet I know this is nonsense on my part and I want to puke with self-hatred. Why can't I bring myself to do what other people do? That is growing up, they say. Learning to do things you hate. Well, I just can't.

"You could."

No, I'd rather just lie here. When I think of taxes and rent and resumes and cars and tool sheds and retirement funds, I lose my will to live. You can't catch me and make me a man.

"But isn't that all you ever wanted?"

No. I wanted to be a boy.

And in today's world, what I'm saying is linked to latent pedophilia, but I've already admitted I'm a transsexual so what's a little more? What I wouldn't give to be Peter Pan!

The cockiness, the detachment, the surplus of energy, the appetite for adventure. Peter Pan is a myth; actual males his age never behave as beautifully. Peter Pan is so pleasing because he is truly, one hundred percent sexless. His interest in Wendy is purely make-believe. Peter Pan cannot love. And because of this, he is wild.

Nowadays, I believe sex only tames us. It is just another activity where we lose ourselves; where we surrender our individuality for approval. We grow insecure and needy. We compare ourselves to what we are told is sexy; we begin to believe our various body parts are too big or too small and we beat ourselves up over it. We seek in our reflections that which will please others, not what pleases us. We begin to do everything in order to attract a mate. Graduate school, business classes, indie rock bands, writing novels: all done for love- for sex. Marriage is a supposed assurance of it. The very nature of copulation ensures we act out our petty roles, whether hetero or homo. As far as I'm concerned, there is no such thing as harmony between two human beings- especially not physically. Sex is a means to possess one another, like objects, and my interest in being owned is about as strong as my desire to own someone else. Far too much concentration involved. Far too much responsibility.

And so I'm a heartless, impotent jerk. Fine. But know I am my own worst critic. Yes I stand in front of my mirror, disgustingly self-aware, for I have chosen to know myself inside-out over getting to know someone else. That is my choice. But don't think I am recommending this to others. Quite the contrary. Have your sex, make your love; if it makes you happy, good for you. I realize there is something terribly wrong with me. And there are times when I want to scream at myself,

"Just who do you think you are? You have invested so much time and energy into your body, and for what? For who? You say you have no interest in sex, but you're a dirty liar. Your whole self-worth comes from trying to look desirable when your clothes are on and your depression comes from feeling repulsive when they are not. Do you have the audacity to believe you are the only human who struggles with these feelings? You are sick, and the fact that you even call yourself sick is self-absorbed and sick. You are everything that is wrong with youth, everything that is wrong with our culture. You are the very spirit of Twitter, of Facebook, of this disillusioned sickening future where every isolated egotist in front of a computer screen thinks they deserve to be a celebrity; you are the reason that every new product must be prefaced with i ! Stop pretending to be a snobbish author and audition for a reality TV show already. You think testosterone injections will save you? You think surgery will save you? You think there is anything you can do to your body that will save you? You think any outside appearance will make you more you? There is no you. You are not unique, you are not beautiful: everything you are is plagiarism. What don't you understand about this? You are living a borrowed life on borrowed time. Your physicality means nothing. Your gender means nothing. You mean nothing; you might as well have never even existed. Your body, your very self will decompose. You will age and become ugly and eventually you will die, just like everyone else, and no one will miss you."

But that is quite the mouthful, so I usually settle with knocking my head against my wall and repeatedly muttering "Idiot, idiot, idiot..."

*

One spring afternoon, Dean was sitting in the campus café with Maggie and her literature friends. His eyebrows were so furrowed they appeared to touch his eyes. He glared at one particularly loud boy who was dominating the conversation, insisting Kierkegaard had saved his life. After about five minutes, Dean stood up and left, abandoning his salad. He stood outside and lit a cigarette, rudely visible to the others through the glass.

Maggie came out to meet him. "I didn't know you smoked," she said.

Dean shrugged. "Neither did I."

"You don't really like them, do you?" she asked, nodding towards her friends inside.

"I'm sorry."

"No, it's okay," Maggie said. "I mean, they are a little much. I just think it's good to build relationships with people in your major, you know? Networking is so important for people our age. I thought it might be good for you."

Dean scowled, toying with the button on his jean jacket.

"I'm sorry, does that offend you?" Maggie asked.

Dean took an awkward drag of his cigarette, his shoulders hunching. "No," he said after a moment, sounding slightly defeated, "it's just... I feel like you and Colin have got it in your heads that I need help making friends. I'm perfectly capable of it on my own, you know. I just choose not to."

"I'm sorry," Maggie said. "Wow, I feel like a jerk. I really was just trying to be helpful. You're new at the school, and I thought you'd want to be introduced to people."

Dean shook his head.

"Oh, okay." Maggie picked fuzz balls off her yellow cardigan, feeling very awkward. "Well, I don't really need to hang out with them today. I just thought since Colin wasn't around...well, never mind. Do you want to go for a walk instead?"

Dean couldn't help but wonder why Maggie and Colin bent over backward to please him. But he agreed to a stroll around campus. The air was cool and windy, pleasurable on his skin. The trees were beginning to bud, and if he got nervous, he could always watch the sparrows dart along the brick walk. He lit another cigarette.

"I sort of thought you would like to talk about literature," Maggie said as they passed the library, getting out her pack as well and popping a cigarette between her lips. With uncharacteristic suavity, Dean flicked open his silver lighter. Maggie leaned in towards the flame, blushing.

"Eh. I do like talking, sometimes," Dean said, pocketing the lighter and blushing as well. "But not when it feels disingenuous...no, that's not the word I want. I don't know. It felt competitive." He kicked at a stone. It soared, almost striking a girl reading in the grass. He didn't notice.

"So you don't like competition?" Maggie asked. "You don't think it's important to debate?"

"No, that's not it exactly. I'm not some sort of hippie." He said the

last word loudly, making a passing boy with bongo drums scowl. "I don't know. There's just something about most academic discussions that nauseate me. Or most discussions, for that matter. Especially with men."
"Hm," Maggie said, "perhaps you feel threatened?"
"Yeah, I'd say that's accurate. I'm easily threatened."
"Well, I admire your honesty."
"Thanks." Dean snorted. "I figure it has something to do with my astrological sign."
"Really?"
"No, I don't believe in that. I tend to be skeptical of mysticism. It's a Leo thing."
Maggie smirked. "Ah, so you're a Leo man. That explains why you were uncomfortable. You need to be the constant center of attention."
"Maybe. I mean, we have been talking about me for this entire walk."
"Alright, so let's talk about something else," Maggie said. "Aren't you going to ask me what my sign is?"
"Well, no, I wasn't, but tell me if you must."
"I'm a Virgo," she said, with feigned, feminine annoyance.
Dean nodded. "That means absolutely nothing to me."
"It means I am practical and pure."
"Well, that's nice for you. Like I said, I don't believe in that stuff. It just gives people the false sense that they know things about one another."
Maggie rolled her eyes. "Yes, I suppose. I just find it fun. Have you heard of fun, Dean? It's a crazy concept."
"I think I read about it once."
"Maybe you just didn't like what astrology had to say about you," she said, eyeing him slyly.
"Maybe. I find I have a tendency to rebel against anything predetermined."
"How profound!" Maggie exclaimed. "An idea no one has thought of!"
Dean felt embarrassed and began to pout. Maggie had beaten him at his own game.
"Dean, I'm just teasing you," Maggie said, elbowing his gently in the ribs. "You're totally rebellious. You're the epitome of punk rock. You're terrifying."
Dean rolled his eyes. He wanted to go home.
"Ack, you're bothered," Maggie said, shaking his shoulder. "I'm sorry. I think you're awesome, really. I'm sorry." She hugged him from the side. He winced, his skin prickling.
"No, it's fine. I'm just a brat," he said, edging away. He hated how sensitive he was. He felt tears. What was going on?
"You are not. You're just too serious." Maggie offered him one of her

cigarettes. Dean shook his head. Who was he trying to fool?

"I don't know why we have to be this way with one another," Maggie said. "It's like we're constantly trying to be sharp. We're friends, aren't we? Maybe we could try to have a real conversation, without sarcasm."

"Maybe," Dean said.

"It's a Saturday evening. Let's have some drinks."

"Alright."

It was starting to rain, so they headed towards her apartment. By the time they got there, it was coming down in sheets. Dean was stressed about his hair.

*

Several drinks later, the conversation had turned back to literature. Maggie was sitting cross-legged on the dingy sofa, leaning in and gesticulating as she spoke. Dean was leaning away, hiding behind his mug, in shadow. Maggie had been talking for a half hour about her passion for Flannery O'Connor and planning her thesis. Dean half listened as he sipped his vodka, watching the storm outside. The room was dimly lit by a buzzing, yellow lamp. He wondered how many calories there were in vodka.

"So who is your favorite author?" Maggie asked. "No, no, wait, I bet I can guess."

Dean groaned. "I bet you can too. Must we talk about this?"

"Yes we must, lighten up. Heaven forbid I try to get you know you." She took a gulp of her mug, her cheeks flushing. "Hm, let's see. Definitely someone European. Someone classic. I feel like you like Dostoevsky."

Dean laughed. "Am I really that dreadful?"

"No? Maybe J.D. Salinger then?"

"You think I'm a joke."

"Stop it, no I don't!" She hit him on the arm.

"It's okay, I am a joke." He was ashamed to love both those authors as much as he did.

Maggie sighed playfully. "Come on, tell me! Who is the dearest to your heart?"

"The dearest to my heart?" Dean laid his hand on his chest. "Bah. Well, give you a hint: his gravestone gets a lot more action than I ever will."

"Oscar Wilde!" Maggie exclaimed a little too quickly. Oh, of course. Of course Oscar Wilde."

Dean blushed. "Well just what is that supposed to mean?" he said with a hand on his hip.

Maggie didn't answer and instead went to the refrigerator to get a beer. When she returned, she had removed her sweater. Her shirt was a sheer pink, low cut, revealing her color bones. Dean, though normally oblivious to such things, could not ignore her partially exposed bosom. He bit his lip, eyes cast down at the dingy gray carpet.

"Dean, can I just ask you something?" Maggie sat back beside him, tying back her hair as she spoke. "I wouldn't normally ask, but I'm a little drunk and we're friends, right?"

"Yes." A loaded question, he noted with unease.

Maggie put her hand on his knee. "It's just I've known you for few months now. And you haven't made any indication as to whether you're attracted to men or women or ...what." She tried to stare into his eyes, but Dean wasn't having it. He edged away, blushing.

"Well, no," he said, "I mean, yes. I was afraid this might come up. I guess the easiest answer is I don't know."

"You don't know?"

"No. And I don't really care to. I don't honestly think there is anyway for me *to* know."

"I don't follow."

"Well, maybe it'd be easier if I just told you a story," he said. "I've wanted to tell it to someone for awhile. Mind if I have another shot first?"

Maggie nodded and handed him her bottle.

"Ah, more vodka," he said in a poor Russian accent. "Perfect. Funny you should mention Dostoevky, because I came up with this story of mine after reading *The Brother's Karamazov* last summer. It's obnoxious, but I guess I fancied myself something like Ivan."

Maggie rolled her eyes. "Of course you did. So I take it this isn't going to be about actual sexual experiences but rather some sort of depressing metaphysical allegory?"

"That's what she said," Dean said. He threw back his head and downed a big swig of liquor.

*

"I'll start by mentioning that I intended this as something of a Biblical story. I see no reason why those shouldn't still be written, except for the fact that the stories of the canon were already chosen. So maybe it's more like Biblical fan fiction, ha ha ha. I must sound crazy to you right now. For the sake of this story, God is real, and so is Jesus, and so is Zeus and werewolves and fairies and the fountain of youth, for all practical purposes. I guess I might as well add that this could be considered an alteration of a Greek myth as well. So enough disclaimers, I will begin.

Once there was a beautiful boy named Narcissus. Simply put, he was perfect in every way. He had many talents but his favorite past time was admiring himself. He'd stare into the pool of water all day, in love with his reflection and wanting for nothing and no one.

"Have you seen my creation Narcissus?" Yahweh bragged to the angels in heaven. "Why he is the most beautiful human yet! I've really outdone myself." He heard someone laughing. It was the Satan.

"Where have you been?" Yahweh asked.

"Prowling about on earth," the Satan said. "Roaming around there." He always said that.

"Did you notice Narcissus?" Yahweh asked, "Isn't he just lovely?"

"Yes," the Satan said. "He is quite lovely. But have you noticed he has never once thanked you for making him so? Never once has he admired your power. Why, it's as if he believes himself to be his own creation!"

"I never thought of that," Yahweh said darkly. "You are right, and I cannot stand for it! I shall take away his beauty and make him ugly."

"If I may be so bold," the Satan said, "he will grow ugly in time, as all people do. That is what it is to age. I have a more interesting experiment in mind."

"Go on," said Yahweh.

"Excuse my vulgarity," the Satan said, "but I couldn't help but notice while observing the boy, there is a certain body part he admires more than the others; more than even his own face. I suggest we leave his youth intact, but take away the particular extremity he holds most dear; the very attribute of his masculine self-love."

"Are you suggesting we make him a eunuch?" Yahweh asked.

"What's more," Satan said, "I'm suggesting we make him female."

*

When Narcissus awoke the next morning on the bank of the pool to discover the changes, he cried out in panic. "I must still be asleep!"

"No, you are awake," said a voice from the bushes. Out stepped the Satan.

"The Satan!" Narcissus cried. "Why, it is your doing then! I will pray to God to be restored."

"God won't hear you," the Satan said. "Your only choice is to cut a bargain with me."

Narcissus didn't hesitate. "Deal. Anything to get back what I've lost."

"Anything?"

"Anything," Narcissus repeated.

"Could you not learn to love yourself this way, as women do?"

"I am not a woman!" Narcissus shouted.

"Is it such a bad thing to be a woman?" The Satan asked, "I, who am not human, do not understand such trifles."

"It is not a bad thing for a woman to be a woman, but I am not a woman!" Narcissus shouted, tears forming in his eyes.

"Very well, very well," the Satan said, disgusted by the boy's obvious prejudice, "My, you humans are strange creatures. But we shall strike a deal. You must tear yourself away from this pool and go out into the world. You must try with all your might to find a lover who will love you the way you are and see you as you wish to be seen. If you cannot find someone by your eighteenth birthday, than I shall restore your manhood, and you may return to gazing in the pool. But if you do find someone who accepts your body and wishes to love you, you will stay this way forever."

"Deal," Narcissus said, for he was youthfully impulsive and hadn't entirely been listening. He had been distracted by his face reflected in the Satan's dark eyes.

"And either way, your soul now belongs to me," the Satan added.

Narcissus shrugged. "Whatever."

*

And so Narcissus began his search for love and acceptance. He started with the bathhouses in town; there he knew he could find men who welcomed boys his age as lovers.

As he entered, he felt the eyes of several bathing men upon him. He suddenly felt shy. "Remember," the Satan said in his head, "you must try with all your might."

So Narcissus approached one man who was tall and muscular with a well trimmed gray beard who was lounging out in the water.

"Would you take me as your lover?" he asked.

The man burst into laughter. "You are blunt, my boy! But yes...I would. First, join us in the bath."

Narcissus hesitated, and then began to undress. When he had removed every garment, he turned around to face the man.

"Why, you are no boy! Everyone, this is a young girl!"

"No, no, I am not!" Narcissus said, "I am a boy, I swear it."

All the men began to laugh. "What would we want with a skinny little girl who looks like a boy?" they said.

Narcissus blushed crimson. He hastily collected his clothing as the men continued to laugh and throw food at him. "Get out of here, girly!" they shouted. "No women allowed in the bathhouses! Freak!"

Narcissus snapped. He pulled his dagger from his pocket and charged at the man with the grey beard. He plunged the blade straight into his heart, blood spurting everywhere. He continued to stab him, again and again, all over his muscled torso, creating gaping wounds. The man screamed in agony and then fell backwards into the water, twitching. Another man came forward and Narcissus stabbed him in the face, gouging out both his eyes. He too screamed, writhing all over the place. Narcissus held him under the water until he drowned. The other naked men ran away, terrified.

Narcissus calmly walked away, leaving the blood red bath water behind him.

*

This continued for several fortnights. Men would take Narcissus back to their chambers only to insist he was an ugly woman after he removed his clothes. Narcissus in turn would stab them to death. It was becoming addictive. He collected their body parts and burned them at the village altar as sacrifices to Yahweh. He particularly liked burning foreskins, as there was something charmingly Hebraic about it. Sometimes he would attempt this while his victims were still alive. Because the Satan was on his side, he was never caught.

He even tried women, young and old, all to a similar effect. However, unless they were particularly cruel he tended to spare their lives, making them promise at knife-point never to speak of him to anyone. He was something of a gentleman.

Finally the day of his eighteenth birthday drew near. Narcissus was exhausted and cold inside from slaughtering and wanted nothing more than to return to his former self. What did he care if he could not find a lover? He never wanted one in the first place. Then one evening, only hours before midnight, he saw a beautiful boy. He was walking down a path in the forest by the pool where Narcissus once dwelt. He was tall and lean with beautiful black curls and smooth olive skin. Narcissus sighed. He did promise he would try with all his might.

"Hello," he said, catching the boy's attention, "I am Narcissus. What is your name?" He felt the weight of the dagger in his pocket and it reassured him.

"I am David," the boy said, "It is a pleasure to meet you, Narcissus. Would you care to walk with me?"

They walked among the trees until it grew dark, talking about trivial topics such as birds and the seasons and great works of art.

"You know," said David, "I feel as if I know you so well, although it has only been a few hours. You are so handsome and clever. May I kiss you?"

Narcissus hesitated, and then nodded. Both boys leaned in and their lips touched. The kiss was true. Narcissus felt something stir inside of him. He didn't trust it.

"I must tell you," he said, "I am not the man you think I am."

"What do you mean?" David asked, stroking his cheek.

"I will show you," Narcissus said, and he promptly removed his garments. He held the dagger at the ready behind his back and stood naked before him. David didn't say anything.

"Well?" said Narcissus, "Aren't you shocked? Aren't you repulsed?"

David looked him in the eye. "Why should I be repulsed? You are the most beautiful boy I have ever seen. I love you."

Suddenly the bushes beside them burst into flames. David let out a yell. Narcissus bowed his head.

The Satan stepped out. "So it has happened," he said, smiling wickedly. "You have found someone who loves and accepts you for what you are. And therefore, forever in this form you shall remain." And with a wink, he vanished.

Narcissus collapsed to the ground weeping. David attempted to comfort him.

"No, do not touch me! Just go away! Leave me!" Narcissus shouted, shoving the boy off of him, "It cannot be me you see! It cannot be me you love! I wish I'd never met you! Now it just hurts all the more!"

David was so confused that he began to weep as well. Eventually he retreated and disappeared on the path, never to see his beloved again.

Narcissus wept on the forest floor for several days, and finally, with nothing better to do, resumed his place on the bank of the pool. He would continue to stare for the rest of his life, obsessed with the hope of glimpsing the beauty he once saw in himself. He never would see it."

*

"...And all hope was lost, the end," Dean concluded. He had broken out in a sweat and felt slightly feverish. The room appeared to be spinning. He looked at Maggie for the first time since he started. Her expression was difficult to read.

"I'm sorry, you must think I'm awfully stupid," Dean muttered after a moment, "and sexist, and wallowing, and repressed, and frightening, and..."

Maggie took his face in her hands and kissed him on his lips. Dean cringed and recoiled, as if burned.

"That's plagiarism," he said, his eyes screwed shut. "Literary theft."

"I knew you'd say that," Maggie whispered, and leaning back against the couch, she passed out.

*

"What do you see?" The psychiatrist asked me, holding up a symmetrical inkblot picture. Oh come on dude, are you for real?

"I see death," I said, yawning. He wrote something down in his notepad. "What about for this one?"

"More death," I said.

He wrote down that down as well, this time pursing his lips.

I responded to the subsequent inkblots as "Murder, more murder, Jeffrey Dahmer, a phallus, another phallus, Jeffrey Dahmer eating a phallus, and finally, a butterfly."

"You know miss, if you aren't going to answer me seriously there is no point in you being here," the doctor said.

"Then there's no point in me being here," I said, scowling and hiding behind my hair swoop (remarkably similar to Colin's). I was fifteen and my parents were forcing me to go, as to get a second opinion. My regular old head shrinker said I was failing in school and behaving like a jerk because I had Attention Deficit Disorder (albeit the more reserved, feminine version.) This shrink suspected something more sinister. Like most unruly females, the diagnosis I received was Borderline Personality Disorder. From what I've read, I reckon if I had been a male it would have been Oppositional Defiance or Antisocial Personality Disorder.

He told my mom that people with Borderline have unstable identities, are self-destructive, prone to moodiness, anxiety and impulsivity, and most importantly, have reoccurring suicidal thoughts. Another name for this diagnosis could be American Teenager. Bah hum bug.

To be fair, if the doctor knew I was "male inside" (play along) perhaps the diagnosis of Antisocial would have proved illuminating. Though I'm pretty sure sociopaths often have histories of torturing animals, not crying in the deli aisle of the supermarket. And I'm pretty sure they can't even feel remorse, let alone become paralyzed with it. But I've always had a morbid fascination with serial killers and cult leaders. The charm, the detachment, the sadism: it's strangely appealing to a bumbling masochist like me, and I find such criminals almost admirable. That's not something you're supposed to admit, unless you are fourteen and wear Marilyn Manson tee-shirts. It's not as cute when you're unemployed, going on twenty-three and living in an upstairs bedroom of your parent's house. Of course, implying a connection between transgender people and psychopaths is probably as politically incorrect as saying *Boys Don't Cry* was about a dyke who had it coming (please don't send me letters). But I'm going there anyway.

The crying mother of the serial killer: when on the television, what does she always say?

"I don't know what went wrong. He used to be a sweet boy."

"Could he have been molested?" the reporter asks. "Did you coddle him? Did you neglect him? Could it have been the divorce?"

"I don't know, I don't think so," the mother says through tears. "We raised him right, took him to church. There were no signs. Sure he was shy, sure he was sad, but we never imagined this would happen. Never in our wildest dreams."

"And so," the TV host says to the camera, "the age old question: what makes a monster? Is it nature or is it nurture? Is there a genetic code for evil?"

I munch on kettle corn and turn up the volume. Lucky murderers. Fame was just handed to them. We folks with consciences have to do shit.

What makes a monster a monster? Everyone is just dying to know. Maybe then they'll understand what makes normal men and women so damn normal. But when I say everyone is dying to know, I really mean everyone. You're the crazy one if you think Jeff Dahmer, me, or either of our moms knows the secret.

Morrissey b-side track, "Sister I'm A Poet," 1989 (same year Dahmer hollowed out the skull of a kid named Anthony he picked up at a gay bar):

> *"I love the romance of crime.*
> *And I wonder,*
> *Does anybody feel the same way I do?*
> *And is evil just something you are*
> *Or something you do?"*

Even the old tranny Ed Gein, dressed in suits made out of women's flesh, just shrugs his shoulders.

*

The clock radio read 8:03 PM. Dean was lying in his bed, staring at the dorm room ceiling. He was watching a small brown spider, thinking about Maggie, when there was a knock at the door. He got up, pulled on some jeans, and crept over in his socks as quietly as possible, buttoning and zipping his fly. He peered through the peephole and saw it was the blond, spectacled lead singer of Colin's band. His name escaped him. He sighed. He figured as much as he didn't want to, he had to let him in.

He opened the door. Craig stood about three or four inches taller, making him around six foot. Up close he appeared lanky and worn out, with bags under his dark eyes. He was dressed all in black again, except his light blue skinny-jeans.

"Hey," he said, "I'm Craig, you must be Dean. Is Colin around? He isn't picking up his phone."

Dean was glad he didn't try to shake his hand. "No, he went to get food with Maggie at the dining hall. He was supposed to be back by now."

"Oh. Hm, weird. Well, mind if I come in?"

"Oh, right, sure, make yourself at home." Dean stepped out of the way, wondering if he sounded sarcastic.

"Nice room," Craig said. He had a flat, bored tone with everything he said.

"Yeah thanks," Dean said. "It's one of the better ones. Perk of mine and Colin's conditions." He laughed nervously.

Craig dropped his duffel bag on Colin's side and sat down on his bed. Dean sat in his desk chair. Neither one knew what to talk about. Craig eyed the James Dean and Morrissey posters on Dean's wall. Dean wished he could take them down. He felt his armpits sweating and his throat going dry. He tried to think of a way to distract Craig. "Maybe we should try to find Colin," he blurted.

44

"I'm sure he'll be back soon." Craig said, eyes still on the posters. His gaze lingered momentarily on Dean's hair, then back to the wall again. Dean's heart was pounding. He wanted to hide under his desk.

There was the sound of the key turning in the lock and Dean exhaled, relieved. Colin stepped into the room with a large paper bag in his arms, struggling to hold the door open. He looked furious.

"Hey buddy, what's the matter?" Craig asked.

"It's Maggie," Colin said, setting the bag at the foot of his bed. There was the sound of glass bottles hitting linoleum. "She just broke up with me, out of nowhere."

"Oh no," Craig said in that same, unconvincing tone.

Dean scratched his arm, recalling the prior weekend. "Did she give a reason?"

"No," Colin said, sitting down on the bed next to Craig, "I mean, we got in a stupid fight again, but I wasn't expecting her to dump me. She said she thinks its better this way, whatever that means. She was being annoyingly vague. She said we'd been dating for too long and were holding each other back."

"Well, maybe there's hope you'll get back together then," Craig said. He was clearly indifferent, but no one could take it personally. Dean coveted his emotionless mannerisms, like he would a well-tailored overcoat.

"I don't even care," Colin said hotly. His cell phone vibrated in his pocket. "Fuck, it's her." He looked stressed.

"Go ahead," Craig said. "It's fine, really. I can hang out here. We have the whole weekend to catch up."

"Okay," Colin said, getting to his feet, "if you're sure. Dean, you don't mind?"

"No," Dean lied. "Not a problem."

"Okay, thanks you guys. I'll see you later. Help yourselves to some beer." He gestured towards to the paper bag on the floor and then left.

There were a few moments of silence.

"So," said Craig.

"Weird they broke up," Dean mumbled.

"Yeah," said Craig, "Colin's been dating her since way back. They were high school sweethearts."

"Seriously?" The disgust was apparent in Dean's voice.

"Yeah, sort of gross, right? Well, Maggie actually lived in Connecticut, but they met at a Mirah concert and started dating their senior year, despite the distance."

"Huh. So you knew Colin in high school?"

Craig shrugged. "Yeah. He was kind of the same. I mean, I knew him before he transitioned, back when he identified as a lesbian and all. But he was always kind of the same. You know. Laid back. High energy."

Dean wasn't sure if those two traits were reconcilable but chose not to say anything. "I didn't know he once identified as a lesbian."

"Yeah, don't most trans men at some point? Before they hear about being trans?"

"I've never identified with much of anything," Dean said.

"That's interesting," Craig said, not actually sounding interested. "I've known a lot of transgender guys and most of them identified as lesbians at some point or another. Or at least tried to."

"I've never really tried at anything either."

Craig blew air through his nose and smiled slightly.

"So how do you know a lot of transgender men?" Dean asked. "If you don't mind me being nosey."

"No, why would I mind? Colin and I used to be really involved in queer activism kinds of stuff. We played benefit concerts and did marches and rallies and workshops... crap like that. I made a lot of trans friends that way."

Dean nodded. "Ah. So how long have you guys had the band?" He wondered why he was suddenly so interested.

"Oh, since we were teenagers," Craig said, "but we didn't really get any attention until a few years ago, when we both left Long Island and it was easier to do gigs in New York."

"Huh."

"Yeah. After Colin got into the music conservatory here he had a lot of ideas about changing the band. We're a lot less political now, and focus more on decent songwriting rather than having a message. We added two other guys as well, and it's really benefited us. We used to be this like, horrid queer-folk-punk duo." He shuddered.

"So then you write the lyrics? And sing?"

"Yeah."

"That's my dream," Dean said, immediately wishing he hadn't.

"You should do it," Craig said.

Dean laughed. "It's not that easy."

"Why not? You can find people who will start a band with you, especially on a campus like this. You just have to put yourself out there."

Dean rolled his eyes.

"What?" Craig said.

"Nothing." He remembered how he had insulted Craig the night at the bar. He hoped he never found out. He also recalled Colin calling Craig 'rough around the edges.' He wondered why he said that. It seemed inaccurate.

Craig took off his cardigan and placed it in his bag. Dean noticed his tattoo beneath the sleeve of his tight v-neck shirt. "*The Great Gatsby*," he said, pointing.

"Yeah," Craig said. "I mean, I regret it. I guess I identified with it when I was younger. Pretty stupid, huh? It's not even great literature or anything. At least it's not *The Catcher in the Rye*." He laughed.

Dean didn't respond. He was thinking about both books and feeling sad. "The green light," he murmured, staring off into space and shaking his head.

Craig pretended to need to clean his glasses, feeling uncomfortable. "Yeah, well, anyway."

Dean snapped out of it. He was suddenly in a good mood. "Well Craig, old boy," he said, "Let's have some beers, shall we?"

*

Colin came back around midnight to find his two friends lying on the carpet with the lights out, listening to Patti Smith. "I knew you two would like each other," he said, rolling his eyes. He flicked on a light. Both the boys on the floor groaned.

"Don't speak, don't speak," Craig said, "I need to hear this part." He closed his eyes and mouthed the words. "Suddenly…Johnny…gets this feeling…he's being surrounded by…"

Dean was curled up in a fetal position.

Colin shook his head. "You two are wasted."

"Horses, horses, horses, horses!" Both the boys spun around and faced each other, lying on their stomachs, their eyes gleaming, holding still for several seconds. When the fast-paced music kicked in they leapt to their feet and began to prance around the room and dance.

"Do the Alligator! Do the alligator!" Dean began to wave his arms and stumble backwards. He then stood on one leg, twisting his body back and forth, his hand balled up by his lips, indicating an invisible microphone.

"Like your baby sistah!" Craig did what people call a Russian dance. He squatted down and kicked out his legs to the music. It was impressive until he fell on his ass.

Colin paused the ipod. Dean and Craig groaned again.

"I'm sorry," Colin said, "but you guys drank all my beers and are using my ipod dock without asking. It's starting to piss me off."

Both of them looked ashamed.

"I'm sorry," Dean mumbled.

"I'll give you some money," Craig said.

"It's okay. I've just had a really bad night and I want to relax, alright? No more drunk dancing."

Dean smirked despite himself. He hadn't been reprimanded for rowdiness since he was probably twelve.

"Of course," Craig said, "let's watch a movie or something."

"Yeah, alright," Colin said. "First I'm gonna take a shower." He went over to the hamper and stripped down to his boxers. Both Dean and Craig watched him intently as he grabbed his towel. Colin was too stressed to notice their gazes. He closed the door to the bathroom.

When Craig heard the water turn on, he turned to Dean. "I really like you," he said. "I haven't had stupid fun like this in years."

"I really like you too," Dean said, "It sounds like I'm just saying this, but I haven't either. Seriously, in years."

Craig groaned. "It's just I'm always working! I should just set things right with my parents but I'm too proud. But now I'm running out of money."

"Set things right?"

"Long story, forget it. How about you? You're always working too?"

"I've never had a job," Dean said. "I've got plenty of free time, I just don't have fun."

Craig raised his eyebrows. "Wow. Never had a job." His tone was judgmental and he smirked as he looked over at the bathroom door. "This is a great night," he said, turning back smiling again. "I'm so glad Maggie dumped him."

It was Dean's turn to raise his eyebrows and judge.

"Can I tell you something?" Craig said. "I'm drunk and I'll probably regret this, but oh well."

"Go ahead if you want," Dean said.

Craig took a dramatic breath. "I'm in love with Colin."

Dean felt his face flush. His mood turned sour. "Maybe you should tell him?" he said, not focusing on the conversation anymore.

"Maybe," said Craig. "Sometimes I think I will."

"Huh," said Dean. "Well I'm starting to feel a little sick so I think I'll just lie down."

"Okay," said Craig, "I'll set up my sleeping bag if I can manage it. I'll talk to you tomorrow Dean."

"Yeah. Night." Dean crawled into bed, but instead of closing his eyes stared at the wall. He reminded himself Craig was not a very good vocalist and even Colin said so. He felt slightly better and was asleep before Colin even turned off the shower.

*

Craig woke in his sleeping bag to the sun shining through the windows. He was still drowsy but wanted to take a shower. Standing and stretching, he couldn't help but notice Dean sleeping. His usually gravity- defying hair lay flat against his forehead and his face was slack and serene. He looked younger and more feminine, despite the trail of dark stubble on his chin. Craig would never say this, but he could tell what he must have looked like as a young girl. Dean twitched and frowned. The spell was broken.

He looked around the room for a clue to Colin's whereabouts. He found a note on Dean's desk.

Going to get bagels -Colin

Craig noticed more hand written papers beneath the note. They looked like poems. He heard Dean snoring softly and his curiosity got the better of him. He picked up the papers and began to read.

"What are you doing?" Dean was awake and horrified. He leapt out of bed and snatched the papers out of Craig's hands.

"I'm sorry," Craig said. "They were lying out. I know I shouldn't have, it just caught my eye."

Dean cursed.

"I'm really sorry," Craig said. "I only read the first few."

Dean didn't say anything. He was scanning the papers. "Where did Colin go?" he asked, not looking up.

"To pick up some bagels," Craig said. "Look, can I just say, you don't need to be embarrassed."

Dean ignored him. "I wrote these awhile ago. When I was less mature," he said. "It's not supposed to be poetry. I'm not stupid. They're song ideas."

"I thought they were brilliant," Craig said. "I'd love to hear them."

"Well, there are no real songs, just a sort of tunes in my head- wait, you liked it?"

"Yeah," said Craig, "It's really funny, the way you kid about wanting to be a criminal. I loved it."

"Oh, I was serious," Dean said, but something about Craig's face made him add, "No, I'm just joking. I'm glad you liked it, I was worried it would come off wrong."

"I really did like it. A lot." Craig fiddled with his sleeve. "I hope this isn't weird to ask, but could you maybe show me how to write like that?"

Dean stared at him, confused. "I wouldn't really know how. I mean, really? It's just a stupid song I made up when I was miserable one summer."

"But it's very well done. My lyrics are so stupid. I know everyone thinks so but just doesn't want to say it."

"To be fair, I rhymed breath with death," Dean said, pointing to the page. "I am no poet."

"Will you help me anyway?"

Dean shrugged. "I guess I could try. There's nothing to really say. If you want to write like me I guess just...well, gee, I don't know. Why would you want to?"

"Could I read some more of your stuff?"

"You mean lyric ideas I've had?"

"Yeah. Or other stuff."

"You must be easily impressed," Dean said, shaking his head, "but alright. You can borrow the rest of the papers on the table if you want. Just don't read it in front of me, okay? It's humiliating."

"No problem," said Craig, taking the papers and putting them in the front pocket of his messenger bag. "I think this will really help Colin and me with the band. I appreciate it Dean."

Dean shrugged, jealous again. But he hadn't time to dwell, because Colin was back with bagels and, surprisingly, Maggie.

*

The four of them took their breakfast outside to eat, as it was a sunny and the temperature was perfect for a picnic. Craig and Colin wore matching black retro sunglasses and Maggie, rose-tinted aviators. Dean was the only one squinting and scowling at the sunlight as they made their way to the quad.

Maggie laid out the picnic blanket under an oak tree and they all sat down. Colin kicked off his shoes and Maggie laid her head in his lap. Craig and Dean didn't dare ask what changed since the previous night. The former looked a little grumpy as he rummaged through the brown bag for a cinnamon raisin bagel. Dean leaned back against the tree, relieved to be in the shade. He munched on his bagel plain, as he was too impatient to deal with cream cheese.

"Thanks again you two," Craig said, slicing his bagel in half. "These look delicious."

"No problem," said Colin. He seemed in a better mood than the previous evening. "So what did you guys want to do today?" he asked, "I've got the car, we could go somewhere off campus."

"Hm," said Craig, "it's really up to everyone else."

"I've got a lot of reading to do," Dean said, his mouth full of bagel.

"Do it tomorrow," Maggie said. She gave him a deliberate look. "We could go to a museum in the city or something," she suggested.

Dean didn't say anything. He really couldn't afford to be going into the city again so soon. The only money he had was the couple hundred dollars his parents gave him each semester for supplies and emergencies. He felt ashamed.

"I just left the city," Craig said. "I'd rather not. Oh, I have an idea."

"Yeah?" said Colin.

"We could visit my friend Sheila," Craig said. "She lives in an apartment not far from here. The ocean is within walking distance. We could take Dean to see the pier."

"I'd do that," Colin said. "I've always wanted to meet Sheila. She's the photographer right? I thought she lived near you."

"She did. She moved here to be closer to her girlfriend who goes to school at Saint Matthew's."

"Oh, yeah, that's practically right next door," Maggie said, "I've got some girlfriends there."

"I'd love to go to the ocean," Dean said.

"Perfect then!" Maggie said. Colin nodded.

"Great," Craig said, "Let me just call her up."

50

They didn't end up leaving until around four, but the car ride only took about twenty minutes. Maggie rode shotgun, knitting a hat, and Craig and Dean sprawled out in the backseats. The windows were down, blowing wind in everyone's faces. Colin blasted his ipod. It sounded like the Pixies. Craig hummed quietly to himself under his breath. Dean tried to preserve his hair arrangement and gnawed at his nails.

"Alright, take a left up here," said Craig suddenly, leaning forward and pointing. Colin obeyed.

They parked on the street and put coins in a meter. Sheila lived above a pizza shop in an apartment, so they went around back. They made their way up the black metal stairs, Craig leading the way. He knocked on the door.

After about five seconds, Sheila appeared. She had a thin face and large dark eyes. Her hairstyle was similar to Colin's. She wore a blue work shirt, with the sleeves rolled up, revealing her olive arms. A gold necklace somewhat feminized her appearance. Like Craig, she was very fashionable. She was smoking a long cigarette.

"Hello!" she said. "Welcome to my humble abode." She emphasized the last word with a fake accent. With a grandiose gesture of her hand, she bowed as they stepped inside. Dean grinned like a skull.

"Wow, nice place Sheil!" Craig said, looking around at the plush furniture and the framed photography on the wall. "Are these originals?"

"Some are, some aren't. But enough about that, come 'ere you!" She pulled Craig into a hug, patting him roughly on the back. "How have you been, chum?" she asked, putting her cigarette butt in an ashtray on the glass coffee table.

"I'm good," Craig said, "and you?"

"Never better. And who are your friends?"

"This is Maggie and Colin. I've mentioned them before. And this is my new friend, Dean. He's Colin's roommate at college."

"Well, hello to you all," Sheila said, nodding. "Are you hungry? I made pancakes. Also, come meet Viv, fresh from the shower."

Another girl had just entered the kitchen. She had dark, sopping hair and an equally dark expression. She was wrapped in a bulky men's bathrobe, but her curvy figure, much like her thinly-veiled frustration with Sheila, was still evident.

"You didn't tell me we were expecting-" She stopped short. "Jesus! Dean?!"

Dean's eyes widened. "Vivian?"

"Oh my god!" She ran forward and embraced him.

"I can't believe this! What a small world!" Vivian cried as she clung to him. She knew better than to be hurt when he cringed and squirmed

51

away."

"Ah, the legendary Dean," Sheila said quietly to Craig. "I've heard a great deal about this one."

"Wait, how?" Dean asked as Vivian released him. "Huh?"

"You always had such a way with words!" Vivian exclaimed. "I go to college near by. Saint Mathew's."

"You go there?" Dean said. "I had no idea, all this time. I go to RC."

"Oh wow!" Vivian said. "Heck, I wasn't even sure you got into college."

Dean made a face.

"No offense, I didn't mean that." She ruffled his hair. "Aw, look at you!" she said in a high register. "You look so manly and grown up! And look at your hair! It's all…different!"

"Yes, well spotted," Dean said, rearranging it. "You look great as well. Uh, a little…wet. But great."

"Thanks!"

"So wait, let me get this straight," said Colin, "You two are old friends?"

"Old best friends," Dean corrected.

Vivian grinned. "Oh I missed you!" She grabbed him again and squeezed his abdomen.

"Break my ribs why don't you?" Dean said, wriggling free once more. "If you missed me so much, why didn't you ever answer my emails or phone calls?"

Vivian's face turned red. "Well, it wasn't that I didn't want to…"

"Why don't we have some pancakes!" Sheila said a little too loudly, gesturing towards the table. The five of them sat as she went to get the silverware. Dean looked miserable.

"Let me go change," Vivian said. "Go ahead and start eating without me."

The other four took their seats. Sheila finished setting the table as Vivian returned, in shorts and a blue tee shirt. She took a seat next to Dean.

"About the emails…" she said. "As I was saying, it was complicated, Dean. At first I was afraid my parents would know I was responding somehow. Then after awhile, I admit, I tried to um…well…forget you."

Dean smirked. "I see."

"I'm really, really sorry," she said. "If it's any consolation, it was difficult! You're very memorable."

Dean rolled his eyes.

"I'm sorry," Vivian said. "I was so young, and I started to feel guilty about my feelings."

"You can feel?"

Vivian sighed.

"Seriously," Dean said, "what feelings? What are you talking about?"
"I don't know, I don't know." She blushed. "I felt really bad. You have no idea. I started to miss you so much I couldn't stand it. But by then I figured you were mad at me so I thought it was better to let you be." She looked down at her plate, ashamed.
"It's okay," Dean said softly, "It was a long time ago." He gave her a reassuring smile as Craig handed him the plate of pancakes. He took a small one and began to eat it plain with his hands.
Vivian took a sip of her water, still feeling guilty.
"So," Sheila said, sitting down at last on the other side of Vivian, "I'm dating Viv, who knew Dean in high school, who is…"
"Colin's roommate," Maggie picked up, "who is dating me and is best friends with Craig from high school, who is friends with you."
"Wait. You're dating her?" Dean said to Vivian, pointing his fork at Sheila.
"Yes, I am," Vivian said.
"Ha!" Dean said.
"Why is that funny?" Sheila asked, her expression cold.
"Oh, no, I'm sorry," Dean mumbled. "I just figured it must make her parents miserable."
Vivian shrugged. "What they don't know can't hurt them. Besides, they don't run my life anymore."
"Good," Dean muttered to his pancake.
"They've got their hands full with my sister anyway," Vivian said. "She's almost as terrible in school as you were."
"Gee, thanks. Make me look impressive in front of my new friends, why don't you?" Dean said.
Vivian stuck out her tongue. Dean gave her a thumbs down. It was like they never parted.
"These are great," Maggie said to Sheila, meaning the pancakes.
"Why thanks. They're from a box."
"After dinner, I was thinking we could go to the beach," Craig said.
"Sounds perfect," said Sheila, pouring a massive pool of maple syrup.
"Let's do it."

*

The six arrived at the ocean around dusk. They walked past the closed hot dog stand and seafood restaurant, out onto the pier. A rusty rollercoaster loomed in the distance. Dean saw a great blue heron fly by. After the walk they hopped the fence, planning to relax in the sand while the sunset. The air was cool and breezy, but Colin insisted he was going swimming.
"Baby, that's crazy," Maggie said, trying to zip up his red track jacket.

Colin pulled way. "Come on men, who's with me?" he said, rubbing his hands together. "Dean?"

"No." He was on all fours, stuffing seashells in his pockets.

"Craig?"

"Must I? Alright." Craig sounded indifferent as usual, but his smile gave him away.

Dean scowled as they stripped down to their boxers and headed towards the water. Craig stepped in and immediately and stepped back out. Colin ran in, yelped, but kept going until it was up to his waist. He splashed Craig on the shore, making him screech and splash him back. Colin chased him up on the beach and tackled him. They began to roll around in the sand, trying to pin one another.

"I'll be right back, I left something in the car," Dean muttered, getting to his feet and brushing the sand off his trousers.

"It's locked, take the keys," Maggie said, tossing them. Dean caught them and then shuffled towards the parking lot, going out of his way to avoid the fragile sand dunes.

The three girls stretched out on a blanket, removing their shoes and watching the sun set behind the homoerotic buffoonery. Maggie started knitting again. Vivian watched her, frowning.

"Is Colin always so hyper?" Sheila asked. "Because I've never seen Craig like this."

Maggie rolled her eyes. "Eh, he gets like this. I think he's just trying to impress everyone. He had chest surgery last summer and now he looks for any excuse to show off his body."

"Chest surgery?" Sheila asked.

"Yeah, he's transgender. So is Dean. He had chest surgery. That's what trans men do."

"Oh, gotcha," Sheila said, rubbing her arm. "They removed the…uh…the uh…well, right. That's great for him then."

"Yeah, definitely. He's so much happier now," said Maggie.

Sheila yawned and leaned back on the blanket. "Cool." She noticed Vivian frowning in her peripheral vision. She closed her eyes, waiting to hear what she said wrong this time.

"I don't mean to reprimand," Vivian said to Maggie, "and I'm not sure how Colin feels about the matter, but you shouldn't tell someone you just met that Dean is transgender without his permission. It's personal."

Sheila opened her eyes, relieved she wasn't the target.

Maggie looked affronted. "Personal? I suppose. I mean, it's nothing to be ashamed of. It's just how he is. It would be like pointing out that you are Italian."

Vivian raised an eyebrow.

"You are Italian, right?"

"Yes. 100%. But I think that's different. I agree it's nothing to be *ashamed* of, but I still say it should be up to Dean when and if people find out. You're talking about the nature of his body."

Maggie shrugged. "There's no need to be argumentative, we both love Dean. Let's just watch the sunset."

Vivian opened her mouth but Sheila gave her a look. Vivian sighed and nodded, scowling to herself.

Dean was back. He sat down on the blanket next to Sheila.

"What did you forget?" Maggie asked.

"Huh?"

"What were you getting from the car?"

"Oh, um, I forgot."

Vivian laughed, thinking he was telling the truth. "You're as absent minded as ever."

Dean didn't respond. Craig and Colin were trudging back, bare-chested and covered in sand. He averted his eyes.

The six sat in silence for several minutes, watching the low orange sun and listening to the ocean waves.

"That was lovely," Maggie said when it was finally dark, "The dunes, the smell of the sea...it's all so picturesque."

"The sea smells terrible," Vivian said, "Like salty puke." She was playing solitaire on her cell phone, her face alight in the glow.

Maggie glowered while Sheila and Craig rolled up the blanket and Colin looked in the sand for any forgotten belongings. Dean sat on a large driftwood log, off to the left. His face was solemn as he gazed at the heavens, lost in thought. Against his better judgment, he made a wish on a star.

*

It's July, if you cared to know. The rain is falling outside. My blinds are drawn, so I can't see it but I can hear it. The lights in my bedroom are too bright. I sit clutching my hair, shifty eyed, certain I'm being watched. I around turn and see our old Siamese cat, lounged out on my bed. He mews when I look at him, as if to say, "relax dude."

But I'm running out of time, Cat.

For starters, my supply of testosterone is nearly depleted. I'll need to return Downstate to the clinic, and I don't have the funds or willpower to do so. My mom will maybe help me out again, if I don't mind making her cry and listening to another round of "where did I go wrong?" But when I turn twenty-three in a month, I will have to pay for my prescription out of pocket. I'll be too old for their teen program. In other words, I will need a job. To obtain a job, I need to legally change my name to Dean. To change my name I need two hundred and ten dollars, and a ride to the county clerk office. Somehow I never managed to take care of all this. Why do the little things seem impossible to me?

On top of needing testosterone, my doctor in New York City called today. My blood work results are in. Something might be wrong with my liver and they need to check it out. I should be planning a trip Downstate as we speak, but instead I sit still, panicking. The back and forth of yore has ceased. I'm immobile, resigned to my Northern fate. Maybe I'll let my liver inflame. Maybe I'll let my prescription run out. The curves will come back, my period will start, and I'll stop getting called "sir" when and if I ever go out. Self-destruct, or rather, go au natural. That'll show 'em.

Yet I wonder, why don't I just get a job if this is so important to me? Why don't I make the changes I need to ensure my transition is complete? Change my name, start saving, have chest surgery (it's not like I don't want it), get a place of my own in the city; start living like a man instead of a mouse. There are plenty of transgender success stories. I could be a banker, a lawyer, a teacher, anything. This is America! Just need to pull myself up by the bootstraps. Get 'er done. Manhood is something to be earned, bought, just like everything else on this miserable continent.

Do I really believe what Morrissey has been feeding me through my headphones?

*"If you must go to work tomorrow,
well if I were you I wouldn't bother."*

Thanks pal. I know you weren't talking to me, but it was sure what I needed to hear. Fame saved you from the abyss; I won't be so lucky.

When I get dangerously depressed, I hate my distant be-quiffed idol like anyone else. I scowl at my reflection in the dark, framed poster, our expressions equally dour. "In the days when you were hopelessly poor, I just liked you more," I spit. Of course this doesn't make any sense because: one, even in my anger I am paying homage to his lyrics; two, I am talking to a photograph and three, I only feel more alone. But no, it's not my music preference. I'm willing to bet I don't bother to try because, like James Dean photographed in that coffin, I already know how this will end. Why pretend otherwise? I'm the most selfish of cowards, what do you expect? As Peter Pan says, to live would be an awfully big adventure. If only I wasn't so tired.

*

Dean sat in a navy plush chair, on the top floor of the college library, a book of Greek mythology sitting open in his lap. It was his typical Sunday morning ritual to watch the sunrise, visible through the large glass windows, and sip coffee, his nostrils filling with the scent of dust. As he observed the empty campus below, his mind wandered to the previous evening at the beach. He was preoccupied with visions of Colin. When pretending to go to the car, Dean had wandered down a path and discovered a wooded marsh, not far from the sea. He sat on a stump for several minutes, collecting his thoughts among the cattails. He had difficulty understanding what he could feel for another man, physically or emotionally; it was always shrouded in envy and insecurity. Colin, though transgender, was no exception. His shirtless horseplay filled Dean with multiple desires, each more excruciating than the last. Although he was alone, Dean blushed, rubbing his graying temples. He did not want to deal with this.

"Dean?"

He turned to his left. Maggie had just come up the stairs. He resisted the urge to curse. "Oh hey," He closed his book and set it on the table. "What brings you here?" He was avoiding meeting her one on one for a while now.

"Nothing." She coyly tucked her hair behind her ear. "I actually stopped by hoping to find you. I wanted to talk." Her cheeks were slightly flushed.

"Here?" Dean asked. There was no one else around.

"Yeah, I don't see why not," Maggie said.

"Okay, well, pull up a chair I suppose."

Maggie dragged another armchair over from the corner. Dean watched her strain, chivalrously stifling a yawn. Finally, she arranged her chair and sat down across from him. Dean suddenly felt like he was on a talk show.

"I wanted to talk about that night, when you slept on my couch," Maggie said, crossing her legs and leaning in. "I want to apologize for kissing you like that. I was drunk; I don't know what came over me. Now I realize that you're gay-"

"I'm not gay," Dean said, angry. "When did I ever say that? Did you even listen to my story?"

"Yes, of course I did. I thought it meant you wanted men but were conflicted. I was drunk, I barely-"

"Well, I'm not gay," Dean said. "I can't be."

"What do you mean?"

"There's a prerequisite."

Maggie looked confused.

"Gay men have gay sex," Dean said, crossing his arms and looking at the ugly carpet.

"And why can't trans men have gay sex?" Maggie said, folding her arms as well.

Dean sighed loudly. "Because it involves cocks. There, I said it, happy?" He glared at her with startling hatred. "And I know what you're thinking. Those silicone things aren't body parts, they're chew toys. And don't give me any bullshit about transgender men just having small cocks. Using that logic, you have a tiny cock as well, and so do most women. Why, we all have cocks! We're all gay men!" He laughed.

"You're being really offensive," Maggie said quietly.

Dean rolled his eyes. "To who? Myself? I can handle it."

"To other trans men," Maggie said, trying and failing to meet his eyes. "This sort of talk would really hurt Colin."

"Well, I didn't make the rules, I just enforce them. Now leave me alone." Dean took a sip of coffee, hoping Maggie would leave. She didn't.

"You're conflating gender and sex," she said. "Gender is a social construction-"

Dean snorted. "Are you kidding me?" he said. "You think I don't know the deal, Maggie? Come on, name one thing that isn't a social construction. Talking is a social construction. Cows are a social construction!"

Maggie ignored him. "So you're telling me transgender men have to be straight? I don't get you, Dean. A gay man, as I understand it, is attracted to people who have the male gender."

"Then why is it called homo*sex*uality? Why is it called *sex*? Forget it, you're right. If females can be men, then they can go ahead and be gay men. They can call themselves turtles for all I care. I'm not saying they should be heterosexual. That's equally stupid. I'm just saying I'm not your and Colin's little novelty-gay-tranny, alright? So back the hell off."

"Why are you being so rude to me?" Maggie asked, her voice cracking slightly and her eyes tearing up. "What did I do, seriously?"

Dean cringed, feeling guilty. "You called me gay," he muttered.

"So? I made a mistake. There's nothing wrong with being attracted to men!"

"I never said there was."

"So why are you so mad?"

Dean gave her a haughty glare over the rim of his glasses. "Because you made a careless assumption. I'm just trying to enjoy a Sunday morning alone without someone telling me what I am. You should just tell Colin what happened instead of talking to me. I'm sick of feeling guilty about it. I want to be left alone."

Maggie stared at him, shocked. "Okay. I'll just go then. I'm sorry. I hope we're still friends."

"We are. Just leave me alone."

Maggie looked at him cautiously, as if he were losing his mind, and then exited down the staircase. Dean took a sip of coffee and leaned back in his chair, sighing and closing his eyes. When he opened them, tears streamed down his cheeks.

"Oh come now," he whispered to himself, wiping his eyes viciously with the back of his hand. "No need to get hormonal."

Tear ducts fairly dry, he returned to reading about dead boys transformed into flowers.

*

Dean returned to his room around noon to find Colin sitting at his computer in the dark, still in his plaid pajama pants. Craig had evidently packed up and returned to Brooklyn.

"Hey," Colin said turning around as Dean locked the door. His eyes were red and his face was puffy. He'd clearly been crying. "Maggie and I talked," he said. "She told me what happened."

Dean froze. "At the library?"

"No. About kissing you, when I was away."

"I'm really sorry Colin," Dean said, wincing. "Seriously, I understand if you want me to move out. I can start packing right away."

"No!" Colin said. "No, relax. I mean, sure, I'm upset, but I'm also a little relieved. Things weren't working out. And Maggie doesn't like you like that or anything. She was just drunk, she says, and I believe her. Still, she and I are through. It's for the best. I'm so over it." His bloodshot eyes and runny nose said otherwise.

Dean didn't move. "I'm still awful for not telling you." He looked at his feet, clinging tightly to his ratty book.

"Seriously dude, it's okay," Colin said. "I don't blame you at all. You didn't ask her to come on to you. I realize you were in an awkward situation, and I'm not mad. I swear."

Dean sighed, cautiously taking a seat on his bed. "Well, I still feel bad. But I'm glad it's out in the open. I felt so guilty these past weeks."

"You shouldn't have," Colin said, kicking off his slippers and revealing small, porcelain feet. "I know you don't like her like that. I mean, I was mad at first, but now I just hate Maggie. She's a fucking tranny chaser."

"Mm," Dean said, frowning.

"So yeah, I'm single," Colin continued, moving to his bed. "I haven't been in years. I don't even know what to do with myself." He let out a nervous laugh, leaning back against a pillow. "Honestly, I've been feeling pretty anxious. I might go to this trans support group back home. It usually helps me to vent."

"Mm," Dean was tracing the embroidery on his pillowcase with his pointer finger.

"So I was thinking I'd go home next weekend," Colin said. "And I mean, you're welcome to come with."

Dean held his breath for several seconds. "Yeah, I'd go," he said, attempting to sound indifferent.

"Awesome!" Colin said. "My parents are vacationing, but I should let them know. I'll email them right now actually."

Dean exhaled and then went at it again with the embroidery, biting his lip. Colin went back to his computer.

"I used to go to a support group in Syracuse," Dean said.

Colin turned away from his computer again, surprised. Dean never spoke of his past. "Really?" he said. "Did you like it there?"

"No," Dean said.

Colin nodded, waiting for him to continue. When Dean didn't, he turned back to his computer.

"I only went a handful of times," Dean said a half-minute later.

Colin turned back. "Yeah? Anything interesting ever happen."

Dean grinned mischievously at his pillow. "Yes." He inflected, so it almost sounded like a question.

"Yeah? Wanna tell me about it?" Colin took a gentle tone, swerving and just missing condescension.

Dean itched his hair with both hand like a beast, scattering dandruff. He was very caffeinated and wanted nothing more than to tell a long story. He looked up from his pillow, his eyes wild, as if brought back from the dead.

"Well, it was me, this older transgender fellow named Will, this younger guy named Ethan, and... two tran women, one named Melissa and... the other woman's name escapes me. But they were both in their twenties at the time, and Melissa and Ethan had also brought their girlfriends with them. That was the usual crowd I guess. So we were all sitting in this room with this stupid rainbow mural on the wall. Oh God, don't get me started! I was about eighteen, definitely the youngest person there. We were introducing ourselves when there was a knock at the door." Dean knocked on the bed-stand, supplying a redundant illustration. "Will thought it was the pizza man, who had actually been giving us trouble and acting weird. Even though it was super secretive, we suspected he knew what our meetings were about. In fact, it was so secretive you had to actually call this number to find out where the meetings were located. Syracuse is weird. But anyway, Will answers the door and in walks this guy with a leather jacket and a pompadour, but in a cool, rockabilly way that wasn't sleazy. I think he was Hispanic. He was really handsome, like a model. He was probably in his late thirties. In any case, most people would say he was too old to dress like that, but he pulled it off confidently." Dean narrowed his eyes, as if daring Colin to challenge this. Colin didn't.

Dean continued. "So he sat down on a bean bag looking rather out of place. He introduced himself as Hunter and shook all our hands. He had a really big hand. He smiled at me and winked. I think it was because I had this hairstyle. Maybe he was a creep, I don't know. Everyone else introduced themselves, and then Will told Hunter to tell us a bit about himself. Hunter said he was a car mechanic, owned a motorcycle, and recently adopted a border collie. He really loved Elvis. Everyone nodded politely, as they clearly were expecting him to talk about his transition like everyone else. Someone asked if he preferred male pronouns and he said, Sure.

Melissa then went on to talk about how she had scheduled her vaginoplasty with some surgeon in San Francisco. Hunter waited until she finished talking and then said that was where *he* went as well.

Melissa told him that was unlikely because the doctor only did male-to-female surgeries. Hunter said that was what he got.

Everyone looked confused, and someone asked if he was a transgender woman. He said no, that he identified as a transgender man, but that he was born in a male body. I remember Will and Ethan's eyes nearly popped out of their heads. Hunter went on to explain he never felt comfortable in his body and that he hated his genitalia. He had wondered if he wanted to be a woman, but that wasn't it. He felt like a man, he just didn't want his genitalia. He said he read about transgender men in a book, and he related to them instantly. He said he wanted more than anything to be a part of their community. He said everything suddenly made sense; he was a man who was a transgender-man inside. So he had surgery to get female parts and started injecting testosterone, since his body could no longer produce it naturally. He said he finally felt like himself.

So of course everyone just stared, dumbfounded. Someone asked what kind of surgeon would let him do that. And Hunter repeated that it was the same surgeon Melissa mentioned, apparently not realizing it was a rhetorical question. No one spoke for a long time.

Finally Ethan said that he though that was incredibly offensive. Hunter said he didn't understand. Ethan asked how he could mutilate his body like that. Doesn't he know that trans men would give anything to have what he had? How could he be so ungrateful? What did he mean he felt like a trans man on the inside? Didn't he realize how absurd that sounds? He made the rest of us look like jokes, Ethan said.

Will said he agreed. He said Hunter could do what he chose with his body, because it was a free country, but that maybe he should have seen a therapist instead and worked out his issues. How did he know he wouldn't end up regretting this?

The woman who wasn't Michelle added that Hunter could never truly be a part of the community, because he hadn't had the same experiences as transgender men. How could he ever relate? He was socialized as a man, grew up a man...How could he know how hard it was for these men who had been denied that?

And then Hunter looked around the room, looking amused. Finally he said that he made it all up, that he didn't have a vaginoplasty. But he said he thought he should go, and it was nice meeting everyone. And he just got up and left without saying another word. We heard his motorcycle rev outside. It was incredible. Just like a movie." Colin was sitting with his mouth open. "Wow! What did everyone else do?"

"Well, we sat in silence for awhile. Then, at almost the same moment, Melissa, her girlfriend and I got up and left. What else could we do?"

"Jesus! That's so weird. Did you ever find out what he really was?"

"No, I never saw him again."

"Wow," Colin said again. "Why would he do that?"

"What do you mean?"

"I mean, what was the point? Seems kind of stupid, doesn't it? Was he just trying to get a rise out of people?"

Dean stared at Colin. How many nights had he laid awake thinking about Hunter? How could he put into words emotions that evening stirred in him? He felt like he grasped something for the first time that he didn't want to accept: maybe Colin didn't want to understand those kinds of emotions. And if not Colin, who did? He felt a pang of loneliness, as if he were the last remaining member of an endangered species.

He didn't have to wonder if Colin would have walked out of the room.

"Yeah, I guess it was just to get a rise out of people," Dean said. "I'm going to go take a shower."

*

It's 11:30 on a Thursday night here in the present tense.

I injected what was left of the testosterone into my right thigh two days ago, and tonight I find myself in a barely controllable rage. It's a noted negative stereotype that transgender men get aggressive from their hormones. And so my enemies no doubt will say, "Ah, Dean champions offensive opinions! He will insist it is fact, as he loves to offend us elgeebeetee plebeians." You think you've picked up on my strategy, but the jokes on you because I never had one. You give me too much credit.

I wonder on nights like this, why wage war at all? I am insatiable- a savage beast. I want to break everything down, I want to kill, I want to destroy, leave the world a bloody pulp. Is this how many teenage boys feel when these androgens start naturally secreting? Do I dare risk biological essentialism? Do I dare ask: what is going on inside this body of mine? What concoction of chemicals and genetics and synapses are making me feel like I want hurl myself into traffic and take you with me?

I didn't, thankfully; not this time. I walked along the sides of main roads, my fists literally clenched, digging my nails deeper and deeper into my palms. When there were no cars coming, I burst into short sprints. I wanted to kill this feeling, exhaust it with force, exhume it from its ancient burial plot, exorcise it from my frail and feminine chest, etc etc. Running, I nearly crushed a dead blackbird with my tennis shoe. I stopped to observe the tiny wreckage in the dim glow of the streetlights. Looking up, I could see into the windows of homes, where there are trophy rooms and kitchenettes and household appliances galore. Is this my inheritance? I felt more akin to the bird.

My dad says I catastrophize. It's time to move on, he said to me in the car the other day; time to get a job, make some friends, cut back on the caffeine. It was one of the first things he said to me in months. I have made the choice, he said, now I need to live with it. He doesn't make his heterosexuality the focus of his life. I don't respond. My nails dig, my jaw clenches. Every minute I slip deeper inside myself. A perpetual, painful tight fit.

On nights like this I can't help but get nostalgic in my hatred and wonder what combination of events brought me to this present. If I could, would I go back and undo the damage, blow out the consecutive candles that lead me down this dark path? Or was it written in the stars, and by this I mean programmed in my mutated genes? Or, dare I say it; was it someone else's influence?

Well, was it?

If I could go back in time and change that, would I? Could I? No piercing penetration, no stifled terror, no wondering "this is it?" There would be no whiskey or pills in my stomach that night, and so my tongue and lips would be able to form the shapes they required, my pubescent female larynx would be able to utter the vital sound. "No," I would say, "No, no, no, no, no, no, no."

I would not be discarded.

This is a cop-out. This isn't relevant. I never want to talk about this again.

I'm full of shit, but please don't hate me. I don't know what I am but I am yours. Please reader, I implore you, please, please, please, love me. Is it too much to ask? Try to climb on stage and embrace me, I'll reach for you with arms outstretched, only because I know you won't make it. Put a picture of me on your wall; scrawl my name on your arm: D-E-A-N. Please make love to me somehow without touching me or making eye contact. Reinvent the whole game. Rescue me from my tower, but don't you dare come anywhere near.

I'll take anything I can get. Heck, I'd even look to Jesus if I weren't so envious of his international success. Or maybe I just figure he'd never like me back. No, that isn't it either. For starters, he's too mainstream; finding God, how typical a solution. But mostly, it's the hair. The horrible, hippy hair. It simply must go.

Some more advice for your second cuming, Jesus: try singing your sermons. I might as well add, put Johnny the Baptist on guitar; after all, without him you would have been stuck in that Northern nowhere of Nazareth. Your other working class ruffians can make up a well disciplined rhythm section. Now that's a reunion tour I can get behind!

*

Today I went for a walk through suburbia with my headphones and an ancient portable CD player. When I'm not hiding in my room, I try to keep moving. Now, when on these walks, I send off as many signals indicating I don't want anyone to acknowledge my presence or make me acknowledge there's. This non-spoken yet simple request was violated twice in less than forty-five minutes.

First, some pimply idiots, rattling by in their rusty car, felt the need to slow down and inquire as to whether I "like balls." When they rolled down the window, the air reeked of marijuana, Axe, and body odor.

I gave them a sideways, exasperated glance and kept walking, but they persisted, repeating the question. I sighed. I was half expecting one of them to be- well never mind, never mind.

"Show us your ass!" one suggested.

It's amazing how being harassed by straight boys can sound awfully similar to being propositioned. Coincidence?

"Show us your ass, Jew-fag."

This was a new one, and I couldn't help but laugh a little. But admittedly I was nervous. There were four of them and one of me. I continued to avoid eye contact. It was getting dark.

"Are you a dyke or a fag?"

I have refused to answer this question when posed to me by far less apelike individuals and I certainly wouldn't answer it then.

"I said are you a dyke or a fag?"

Alright, I caved. "Hm, I seem to have forgotten. Will you check my ass and let me know?"

This was a mistake. One of the cretins got out and advanced on me. I ran like the coward I am. Luckily, he noticed there was a family outside on their lawn watching us. He got back in and they sped off, making sure to swerve at me as they passed.

"Fag!"

I guess they made up my mind for me.

Even though I was probably safe, I still ran all the way home, with the hopes of burning off lunch. When I got around the curve of the cul-de-sac, much to my dismay, another local had taken notice of me. It was my mom's friend Janet, our neighbor from across the street, and she was waving. "Oh Loooora!"

I cringed and walked over, wishing I weren't wearing shorts, as my curly dark leg hair was blatantly visible, even at dusk.

"Hi," I said in my best falsetto.

"Let me take a look at you!" Janet said, stepping back. I slouched and tried my best to disappear.

"You look so much older!" she said. She was more than full of shit; she was overflowing with it. This is my third summer home since I've been on hormones. Granted, the first summer I hadn't changed much, the second I was away most of the time, but come on. I have low self-esteem but not that low. I know I don't still look the same as I did three years ago. I have sideburns, hairy limbs, a baritone voice, a five o'clock shadow. She knows. Everyone in the neighborhood has known for a while, they just pretend they don't.

"So what have you been doing this summer, girlfriend?" Janet asked.

"Gotta go," I said, not answering her question and taking off at a run up my driveway before she could object.

Finally I was back home. I sat alone on the couch and watched TV for awhile, but it was a poor distraction. I cleaned up and put on a bathrobe while I waited for some tea to boil. I poured myself a cup and went upstairs to write.

*

Dean was distracted all through his literature class. He wanted more than anything for it to be four o'clock so he could leave campus with Colin. He was usually on the edge of his seat during lectures, scribbling illegible notes (*ex: Poetry is Condensation. Something about Camus, Sartre, France, blah blah blah... Liminal identity. Ha. Laceration. Why Commit a Crime? Is Suicide a Crime? I hope so. Is this text a polemic? Is Christ the Feminine then? We condemn but are secretly drawn to It. Well duh. Sex=Murder, Horses, Insects, obvious imagery here...revolution or submission? The fanatic personality. Note to self, read The Anxiety of Influence*) But today his notebook lay open to a blank page as he gulped coffee and watched the clock. He tapped his feet and chewed his pen, only-half listening as the aging professor gave her same lecture on Kafka and dream analysis.

The usually responsible Maggie was absent for the second time that week. Dean hadn't spoken to her since the day in the library, and he wondered if someone should check on her. He tried to avoid texting, but he decided he would send her message after class and make sure she was alright.

At four o'clock, he sped-walked out of the Humanities building and back to his dorm. A warm breeze blew back his hair as cut through the soccer field and jogged up the gravel path. It was hard to believe it was already May. In a week he would be back Upstate for the summer. He didn't want to think about it. For the first time, he was starting to enjoy college.

When he got to his dorm, Colin was waiting with his suitcase already packed. He was dressed in shorts and a tank top, his scrawny, hairless limbs visible. "Ready to go? We've got to hurry, the support group starts at six."

Dean threw a tee shirt and some underwear in an empty pillowcase. Colin laughed.

"What?" said Dean, grabbing his CDs.

"You are so strange."

Dean shrugged his shoulders as always. He remembered he wanted to text Maggie. "How are you?" he typed slowly into his phone, lagging behind Colin as they made their way out of the building and towards the parking lot.

"You're shot gun for once," Colin said with a weird smirk when they reached the car.

Dean climbed into the passenger side. "Yeah, should be, uh, interesting."

He didn't really know what to say. His phone vibrated. It was a text from Maggie. "I'm ok. What are you up to?"

Dean didn't respond. He pocketed his phone.

There was really no reason for Dean to bring his CDs because Colin had a huge selection of music on his ipod. They didn't talk for a while, instead listening to boring Grizzly Bear songs. There was traffic. It had been poor planning, and they kept stopping and starting. Dean was about to doze off when Colin spoke.

"Have you ever had a girlfriend?"

"Not really," Dean said.

"What do you mean?"

"Well, I mean, not really. No."

"Well," said Colin, "it's really difficult." He looked ahead, his foot still on the brake and his face miserable. Dean decided it would be polite to encourage him. "How is it difficult?" he asked.

"Well, maybe you'll understand this," Colin said. "I feel really inadequate, and it always hurts the relationship. I mean, my first girlfriend was a lesbian, and when I told her I was trans, she still got really upset. She tried to talk me out of it. She like, wanted me to be a butch woman. So that was rough, because I felt like I was letting her down. But then I started dating Maggie who is queer and all *now*, but before me she'd only been with regular men. And that was almost worst, because I just felt... dysfunctional, or deformed or something. No matter how she protested, I felt like I must pale in comparison. It's almost like I can't win. Even if the girl is bi, I just feel like there's twice the amount of ways for her *not* to be attracted to me. That doesn't really make sense, but that's how I feel."

"I get what you mean," Dean said.

"And what's worse," Colin said, "even if a girl is attracted specifically to trans men, then I just feel like I'm a fetish. I mean, look at Maggie for God's sake, kissing every trans man in sight."

Dean cringed. "I'm really sorry Colin."

"No, no, it's not your fault," Colin said. "I was jealous before, but I'm okay now. Forget her. But seriously, where do I go now? I really can't win. I mean, I've considered dating men before, but I think that would just make me feel worse. I'd be so envious I wouldn't even be able to enjoy it. Plus, a gay guy wouldn't want me, because of my body. At least I'd always worry he didn't, just like with straight girls. But for some reason, the rejection would feel almost worse. You know?"

Dean nodded, his heart pounding.

Colin rolled his eyes. "Well I wouldn't want them anyway, so what do I care? It's pointless speculation. I'm not into dudes." He laughed. "Honestly, I just feel nervous with most everyone. I feel like that's why I stuck with Maggie so long, you know? It was comfortable, even if I worried."

Dean smirked as the traffic finally cleared. "Well, I mean, there is one obvious solution isn't there?"

"What do you mean?" Colin asked, pressing down on the gas pedal little too quickly. They jolted forward.

"Never mind," Dean said, scratching the back of his ear and blushing.

"No, what? Tell me. If there's a solution I need to know it."

Dean hesitated. "Well, you, uh, could date other transgender... people."

Colin lowered his eyebrows, considering. "Huh," he said after a minute. "This probably sounds stupid to you, but I honestly never thought of that."

Dean could feel his face getting hotter. He hoped Colin didn't look away from the road. "Well, I have," he said quietly. "Trust me," he added, speaking up some, "I've thought of all those issues, even if I haven't experienced them first hand."

"Relationships are the worst," Colin said. "Do you ever think you'll have genital surgery? Even if it's risky?"

"No," Dean said, harsher than he intended.

"Huh. I'm sorry."

"No," Dean said, "I'm sorry, I don't mean to be prude. We can talk about it."

Colin nodded. "Do you feel bad about that though?"

"What?"

"You know. Having female... parts."

Dean sighed. "The truth is, that's one thing I can't intellectualize my way out of. Heaven knows I've tried. But yes. I am dreadfully preoccupied with that. Bah, beyond preoccupied. For whatever gross reason, I'm tortured."

Colin glanced over at Dean's face and knew he was earnest. "Yeah," he said softly, "Yeah. Tortured. That's a good word for it. I am too."

They met each other's gaze. Dean's tense expression softened. "Well, we should be there soon," Colin muttered, even though they wouldn't. He fumbled around to find a different album on his ipod. Dean bit his nails, wishing he'd used a different word.

*

Colin and Dean arrived at the community center around dinnertime. "Go ahead without me," Colin said. "I have to use the bathroom." He turned down the corridor to his left. "It's the seventh door on the right," he added, gesturing towards the adjacent hall. "You can't miss it."

Dean stood alone, hesitant. He took several deep breaths as he walked down the hall, his wingtips tapping on the linoleum tiles. He could hear voices, but they sounded far away. He counted doors until he reached the seventh room. It sounded silent inside. Multi-colored flower leis and Mardi Gras beads trimmed the entranceway. A sticker on the door proclaimed it a "Safe Zone!" It didn't make him feel any better. Still, he turned the doorknob and stepped inside.

The room was small, with several bulletin boards and posters of smiling, same-sex couples nailed to the lime green walls. The back wall featured an amateur mural: a rainbow composed of multi-colored handprints with the word "ACCEPTANCE" painted beneath. Dean gave it a moody glance over the rim of his glasses. He took a seat in one of the orange plastic chairs, spreading his legs and slouching. There were three other people seated across from him, all sneaking looks in his direction. Feeling self-conscious, he sat up and crossed his legs. His right foot jiggled. He avoided eye contact.

In the circle there were, presumably, two other transgender men and one transgender woman. The woman wore a sack dress, a cardigan, and combat boots: all in black. Rings and bracelets covered her large, boney hands and her nails were speckled with chipping black nail polish. She hid behind the curtains of her dark hair, hunching her shoulders and resembling a large bat.

The boy to her right was wearing a tie-dyed tee shirt with cargo shorts. He had dirty, beaded dreadlocks and a patch of blonde fur growing on his chin. He was listening to his ipod, bowing his head gently with the beat. To his right sat a second boy. He was physically androgynous but had a macho style and general aura. His red hair was shaved military-style, his ears were gauged with black plugs, and there was a tattoo of a nautical star, among many freckles, on his left forearm. His tee shirt said, "Check a Box: Male, Female, Fuck You!" Naturally, there was a check mark in the third box. He kept looking at Dean, and eventually crossed the room. "Hey man, what's good?" he asked, taking a seat beside him.

Dean scratched his left sideburn. "Oh. Hi. I don't know, nothing is especially good." He bared his teeth, attempting to smile, and lowered his head like an omega wolf.

The kid nodded. "Word, word. I'm TJ. 'sup."

Dean wasn't sure if *sup* was rhetorical. "Sup," he said, hoping, it functioned like *ça va* in French.

"What's your name, bro?" TJ asked.

"I'm Dean...comrade."

TJ didn't seem to pick up on the mockery. "Word, like Jimmy Dean! Cuz you're rockin' a pretty sweet pomp!

"Excuse me?"

"Hair," TJ said, reaching out his small freckled hand.

"Yes. I have hair." Dean covered his head, flinching.

"I'm basically obsessed with James Dean," TJ said, putting his hands back in his pockets. "I base my philosophy for life off of him. Live fast and die young! I should get a tattoo of that next. I watched this movie about him once, it was epic. I think I was James Dean in another life."

Dean gave him a queasy smile.

"Hey TJ!" Colin had returned from the bathroom. He strutted across the room, his hands in the pockets of his zip-up sweatshirt.

"Colin!" TJ said. They slapped hands, clasping and releasing. Dean couldn't help but admire their synchronized, fraternal grace.

"How've you been, man!" Colin exclaimed. "It's been ages!"

"Tell me about it," said TJ. "Hey, nice shoes!"

Colin looked down at his white high-tops. The large tongues covered the ankles of his dark skinny jeans. "Oh, thanks! I like yours too. And your piercings, your hair, everything! You look awesome, dude."

TJ blushed. "*You* look awesome. The hormones sure did the trick. Made you really...manly, you know?" He blushed even redder, his face nearly matching his hair. "I mean, I don't mean that in a *gay* way."

Colin laughed, patting him on the back. "I know, I know. Thanks man. That means a lot."

Dean scowled, but no one noticed.

"So how's college?" TJ asked.

"Oh, you know, decent," Colin said. "How's high school?"

"Just finishing up. It's the shit, man."

Dean wondered if this was good or bad. He wished TJ would go away, forever.

"So you met Dean?" Colin said, placing his hand on his roommate's shoulder. Dean felt warmth spread through his body.

"Yeah! *James* Dean," said TJ. "I'm going to call him Jimmy."

"I'd rather you didn't," Dean muttered. His body was buzzing with warmth. He slipped off his black cardigan and rolled up his shirt sleeves.

"You even look like him!" TJ said, pointing at Dean's face. "When you came in, you were all brooding and shit. Blaze, doesn't this dude look like James Dean?"

The boy with the dreadlocks paused his ipod and gave Dean a look up and down. "Sort of," he said. "Actually, he looks more like...what's his name." He snapped his fingers repeatedly, his face scrunched up in thought.

"That's okay, don't bother." Dean mumbled. His heartbeat was racing. The more he tried to stop blushing, the hotter his cheeks burned. The girl in black was looking now as well.

"Robert Smith!" Blaze blurted. "That's the guy. You look like Robert Smith." He looked pleased with himself.

"No he doesn't," said the girl, not bothering to mask her disgust.

"Yes he does," Blaze said. "He looks just like him."

"No, he doesn't. Trust me, *I'd* know." She smirked. "You mean Morrissey. That's who he looks like. Sort of."

"No, I mean Robert Smith," Blaze said, "the guy from The Smiths. You know, the flaming British guy, with the crazy hairdo. No offense, dude."

"None taken," Dean said, looking at his feet. His ears were ringing. *They're onto you,* said a cruel voice in his head. "But she's right." He pointed at the girl without looking up. "Robert Smith is from The Cure."

"Well same thing," said Blaze.

"*Not* the same thing," the girl said, narrowing her eyes.

Dean smiled at her. She looked confused and started cracking her bejeweled knuckles and chewing on a strand of her hair.

A fifth guy entered the room and closed the door behind him. "Alright, let's get started," he said, sitting down and crossing his legs. He was dressed in sportswear and looked like he'd come from the gym. His sneakers looked comical on his tiny feet. "Welcome to TransPride," he said, nodding around. "We are a discussion group for gender-variant youth, age fourteen to twenty-two." He smiled briefly, rubbing his goatee. "Go ahead and sign yourself in." He handed the clipboard to Blaze. "It looks like we've got some new faces tonight, so let's do a go-around. Everyone say your name, pronoun preference, a little introduction and um....your favorite candy." He cracked his knuckles and neck. "I'll start us off. Name's Ethan. I'm twenty-two. I indentify as a straight trans man, and I prefer male pronouns. I'm a personal trainer. My favorite candy bar is Butterfingers." He nodded to Blaze. "Your turn, dude."

Blaze nodded stoically. "Hey. Blaze. Male-pronouns. I'm in high school. I play guitar. I'm an FTM. And yeah, Butterfingers are good."

"Thanks Blaze," Ethan said. "Teddy?"

The girl in black smiled halfheartedly. "Yeah, I'm Teddy. Female pronouns. If you feel the need to address me at all." She laughed, staring at the ground. "I'm trans....ish. And I dig Swedish Fish. I think. They're so much better in theory." She licked her lips, flicking lint off of her cardigan.

"Right," said Ethan. "Thanks Teddy. Next?"

Colin brushed his hair out of his eyes. "Hey, I'm Colin. I haven't been here in a few years, but I used to go as a teen. That was before I transitioned and all. But yeah. I'm twenty years old, and I'm a college student. I'm also in a band called Owl Eyes. I play guitar and write all the songs and stuff."

"No shit!" said Blaze, "For real?"

"Yeah," Colin said. "You've heard of us?"

"Everyone's heard of you," Teddy said.

TJ grinned. "I went to the shows *before* they were popular."

Colin smiled. "Yeah. You uh...sure did."

Dean smirked. He straightened up in his chair.

"Owl Eyes is sick, dude," Blaze said. "I've seriously got you right here on my ipod."

"Awesome," Colin said. "Thanks guys. I'm glad you like us. But anyway, yeah. I indentify as a trans guy. Male pronouns. And I really like Snickers. Especially the ice cream ones."

Dean felt his empty stomach rumble. Everyone turned towards him. He blushed, wondering if they had heard it. Then he realized it was his turn. "Oh," he said. "I'm Dean."

Everyone waited.

"I forgot the questions," he muttered.

"What did you say?" Ethan cupped a hand to his ear.

"He forgot the questions," Colin said.

"Oh," Ethan said. "Pronoun preference, identity, and favorite candy."

"Male pronouns," Dean said, sounding as if it were a shameful admission. He frowned for several seconds, staring at the mural. "I don't really like candy," he concluded.

TJ forced a skeptical cough. "You *don't* like *candy?*"

"I don't know," Dean said, adjusting his glasses. "Maybe. I like chocolate."

"That's candy!" TJ said.

"Okay."

There was silence again.

"Why don't you tell us about yourself?" Ethan said.

"I don't know," Dean said. "What do you mean?"

"Are you in college?"

"Yeah, he's my roommate," Colin said.

"What's your major?" Ethan asked.

"English," Dean said. "For now."

"And how do you identify?"

"I don't."

"Oh come on," Ethan said. "Of course you do! You're queer, right?"

"No."

TJ looked confused. "You're not? So you're straight? Wait, are you even trans?"

"Yeah, he's a trans guy," Colin said.

More silence.

"Yeah. That's it," Dean mumbled.

Ethan nodded. "Okay, go ahead TJ."

"Okay," TJ said. "Sup. I'm TJ. I'm a radical queer, pre-t, straight-edge, vegan-anarchist trans guy. I prefer male pronouns, local music, and femme girls with tattoos." He grinned.

"Awesome," said Ethan, clapping his hands together. "Short and sweet. So, let's start the discussion by sharing two good and two bad things that happened this week. Colin and Dean, you're our guests tonight. Why don't you go first?"

The boys looked at each other. Dean shrugged passively.

Colin nodded. "Right. Well, I'll start off with the bad. I'm really stressed about final exams at school. And to make matters worse, I broke up with my girlfriend." He glanced to his right, but Dean was staring at the floor. "So that really sucked. But good news is, I got an email from this guy who wants to manage my band. It seems legit, and it's a great connection. He's well known in the industry, and that will save me a lot of stress. Other good news is…well, I've got my friend Dean here. It'll be nice to spend the weekend just hanging out at home. And I'm gonna take him to the ocean tonight."

Dean smiled, picking at his nails. He could hardly wait to get out of this place.

"Great!" Ethan said. "Thanks Colin. And what about you Dean?"

"Oh. Um, pass."

"No, no passing!" said TJ.

Dean scowled. "Well, okay. Um… I'll start with good things."

"Speak up!" Ethan said.

"I'll start with the good things," Dean said, not much louder. "I'm glad to get off campus with Colin. Yes. Also…I had a good breakfast."

"What was it?" TJ asked.

"A tangerine," Dean said.

"That's all?" TJ exclaimed.

"Yeah," Dean said.

"And the bad stuff?" Ethan said.

"Um…" Dean stared at the wall again, thinking. "That mural for starters." He laughed. Teddy smirked but no one else reacted.

Ethan looked around the room. "Well thanks guys. Who wants to go next?"

"Me!" said TJ, quite literally on the edge of his plastic seat. "Bad: I had to work all weekend. Super lame. Also, I haven't been passing in public places, so that's bad for my ego. If you know what I mean. But good: I got my second tattoo." He pointed to the star on his arm. "And best of all, I finally start T in a week!" He was referring to testosterone injections.

"Congratulations!" Colin, Ethan, and Blaze said at different times. Dean nodded. Teddy didn't look up from her hands.

"Yeah I'm totally stoked," TJ said.

"Well good for you, buddy!" Ethan said. "You've been waiting so long." He turned to his left. "Your turn, Blaze."

"Nothing really happened," Blaze said. "I don't know. I got this new ipod." He showed it to everyone.

"Cool!" Ethan said. "That's alright, let us know if you think of anything else. Teddy, do you want to go next?" His voice was soft and he looked uneasy.

Teddy shrugged and sighed. "I don't mean to sound negative," she said, still looking down, "but nothing noteworthy *ever* happens to me. That's the thing. Maybe I can get some support. That's why we're here, right?" She snorted. TJ and Blaze shifted in their chairs, but Teddy continued. "I'll try to make it... brief. I know I've been criticized in the past for, um... ranting." She snorted again. "So anyway...here's my issue. Like many of you, I used to read transgender memoirs, almost obsessively. I'd sneak into the Gay section when my mom was at Barnes & Noble. I basically read them all. And every author says they feel like themselves once they transition, right? That they *finally see the woman in the mirror.*" She made quotation marks with her large, white fingers. "So I've dreamed of that day since I was a kid. And I don't regret my decision, but I'm telling you, I've been on estrogen for almost five years now. And when I look in the mirror, I still don't see the woman I want to see. The thing is, I can't see anything. My eyes look dead, my face is unexpressive... It's like I'm wearing a mask. It's almost more mysterious to me now then it was before. It's beyond freaky." She snorted again, but didn't smile. "Has anyone else experienced this?" She looked up, her pale cheeks tinged pink.

Ethan shook his head, staring down at the clipboard. Blaze was playing a game on his ipod. TJ was the first to speak. "I don't think that's normal," he said. "You should talk to a therapist-"

"Of course it's normal," Dean said, interrupting. Everyone turned, startled by his acerbic tone. He hesitated for second, scratching his head. "I mean, I feel that way."

Teddy pressed her palm to her forehead, grimacing. "But then what's the point?" she nearly yelled, her voice hoarse. "I was waiting for that shining moment, where I'd look in the mirror and finally see myself. I feel fucking cheated." She pounded her fist against her bare thigh.

Blaze and TJ made eye contact, holding back guilty smiles.

"Yeah," Dean said, looking at Teddy's bowed head. "Yeah, that moment is a myth. I'm sorry."

TJ frowned. "I mean, not really...from what I hear-"

"So then what the hell am I doing?" Teddy said, ignoring TJ and looking into Dean's eyes. "Why the hell am I putting myself through all this shit? Years of therapy, invasive questions, electrolysis, voice lessons, tons of medical tests, losing my family and friends?"

"I can't answer that," Dean said quietly.

Teddy attacked her tears with the back of her hand. "I guess there is no point. I'm just sick." She smirked. "They were right about me. I don't know what I want."

"*No*," Dean said. "No. You are *not* sick, and you *do* know what you want. You want to feel at home in your body, like anyone else."

"But I never will," Teddy said. "It's my brain that's fucked up, that's why. It's my attitude. My goddamn personality. Why can't I just be happy now, like everyone else? Why am I so ungrateful?"

"I agree with TJ," Ethan said. "This is something best left for therap-"

"Because to feel comfortable in your body, you can't think so much," Dean said. Teddy glared at him. "Don't give me any Zen bullshit," she said. "Trust me, I've heard it all." She nodded at the mural on the back wall. "Acceptance? Never." She laughed. "The day I accept *what God gave me* is the day I'm dead."

There were several moments of silence. Ethan cleared his throat. "Teddy, I'm truly sorry you're upset, but you know you can't say things like that here...we've been over this. There's a hotline you can call, listed on the bulletin board. But we really need to get on with our discussion."

Teddy gripped her hair with both hands. She didn't say anything.

"We can talk later if you want," Ethan said, "but not now. We have to move on. We only have the room for an hour."

She nodded, not looking up. Her hair formed a curtain and she disappeared.

"Okay," Ethan said, pulling a stack of papers out from under his clipboard, "on to today's topic. I want to discuss the petition going around Facebook. Many of you have probably seen it, but in case you haven't, I'll explain. This Australian trans man was asked to take down shirtless photos of himself, because they were deemed *too graphic*. So the petition asks that all us guys pose shirtless in our profile picture, as a gesture of support. Transphobia will not be tolerated on the internet. It's time to show the world that we exist, and they just have to deal with it."

"Word!" said TJ. "I'm totally down."

Colin nodded. "Yeah, I'd do that for sure. That's really fucked up of Facebook."

"I mean, to be fair, the Facebook staff apologized," Ethan said, "and they let the guy repost his photos. But I still think we need to make a point. Dean, Blaze, you in?"

Blaze nodded. Dean didn't say anything. He was still looking at Teddy.

Colin shook his head at Ethan, making a slicing gesture across his neck.

"Oh," Ethan whispered loudly. "Right. Sorry I assumed. Well Dean, if you get surgery soon, you should really do it with us!"

Dean wasn't listening. "I'm not saying you shouldn't struggle," he said.

"What?" Ethan said.

Teddy looked up from her lap. "Then what are you saying?"

"Oh God, we're back on this?" Blaze said.

Ethan sighed. "We have several topics to cover tonight, so I'd appreciate it if we-"

"I'm saying you should keep struggling anyway." Dean said. "Maybe...I don't know...maybe you're getting closer. All I'm saying is, it's not as easy as waking up one morning and looking in a mirror. But so what? Who needs it? The whole transgender cult is stupid. What do they know about you or me?"

"Jesus Christ," Blaze said. "Let me know when this is over." He put his headphones back on.

Colin cringed. "Dean," he said, "you're getting really intense, man. This is how you offend people."

Dean looked into Colin's eyes. "I'm sorry," he said. "I'msorryI'msorry."

"It's alright," Colin said. "Just, like, think before you speak. You know?"

Dean felt his throat tighten. "I'm sorry." He folded his arms across his chest and hunched his shoulders.

"I mean, for some of us, it really is that simple," Ethan said. "I'm pleased with my reflection, and it's all thanks to testosterone. Granted, I don't stare. I'm not *vain*." He laughed. "I'm a proud transgender man, and I'm proud to be queer. Is that wrong or something?"

"Maybe you guys need surgeries," TJ said. "It can do wonders. Sure helped me. There are lots of ways to earn the cash. My friend started a website so people could donate to him."

"Just takes a good old fashion work ethic," Ethan said. "If you want it enough, you'll find a way."

"Sure." Teddy nodded to Dean. "Hey," she said softly. "Don't feel bad. I appreciate your honesty."

"I'm sorry," Dean said.

*

Colin stuck around for awhile after the group ended. TJ had discovered a new website for sex-toy reviews, and he wanted to share it with the other men. Dean felt awful, so he went outside for air.

The sun was setting and the lights in the parking lot were illuminated. The sky was streaked with orange and purple strati, and birds were singing their last songs of the evening. Teddy was standing alone against the brick wall, hunched over in a leather jacket and sucking on a cigarette. Dean approached her, thinking that she resembled a cross between Patti Smith, Joey Ramone and a Halloween witch.

"I don't know why I bother," Teddy said before Dean could open his mouth to say hello. "I'm not like other transgender people. Those men all think I'm a crazy cat-lady before I even speak."

Dean sighed. "I'm sorry."

"Stop saying that!" Teddy said. "Look at me, kid."

Dean looked up at her. She was almost six feet tall, with heavy eyebrows and a sculpted, angry jaw. Her eyes were large and black, so the iris looked like two giant pupils. Her lips were raw and chapped, bloody red. "Don't ever be sorry," she said.

Dean could smell alcohol on her breath. He looked away, shy.

Teddy exhaled smoke, sighing. "Don't start thinking it's a guy thing, either. It's no different when trans women show up. Getting their hair done, facial reconstructions, breast implants…that's all they ever talk about. And sure, I'm a hypocrite. I mean, hey, I've changed my body with pills and what not. But I've never tried that hard to *be* anything. I just am. I'm not a real woman and I never will be. Yet people look at me with pity because I don't pass and don't have the cash for surgery." She snorted. "Well, that's the best case scenario. This girl Jen posted about me on her blog, knowing I'd read it. She said I'm a *fetishist*, not a *real* trans woman. I mean, are you kidding me? What does that even mean? They think I masturbate in high heels or something? And so what if I did? What does that have to do with who I am?"

Dean said nothing. He was suddenly very tired.

Teddy ashed her cigarette with a violent flick. "It gets so you don't trust anybody," she said. "People who call themselves radical-sex-positive-queer-feminists still hold me up to this plastic ideal. They think I don't *know* I look like a guy in a wig? They think I haven't tried?" She laughed aggressively. "Well, I don't give a fuck anymore. I wasn't meant to blend in. If I cared about that, I wouldn't have transitioned in the first place. Half the time I wish I didn't. Back then I wasn't expected to belong to some stupid-ass community. At least back then I was invisible."

Dean stuck his hands in his jean pockets and leaned against the wall beside her. There were several centimeters between their shoulders, but he sensed her body seizing up. He sympathized, and took a step to his left. Looking at the sky, he said, "Oscar Wilde said that when the gods wish to punish us, they answer our prayers."

Teddy smirked. "That fat pedophile had an answer for everything, didn't he?"

"Sometimes I really think so."

Teddy smirked and blew smoke through her nostrils. "Listen Dean," she said, "you're alright. I don't use the internet anymore, and I definitely don't do phone calls. But take my home address." She unearthed a crumpled receipt and a pen from the deep pocket of her jumper and scribbled a few lines. "Write me sometime," she said, handing it to him. "I've always wanted a pen pal.

"I will," Dean said, folding the paper. "I definitely will. Thanks Teddy. You're pretty alright yourself."

Teddy took a silver flask out of her pocket. "If you say so, kid." She snorted, and took a big swig of liquor. As she wiped her mouth on her sleeve, she glanced down at the top of Dean's hair. It was dark and voluminous, much like hers, but because it was cropped, it stood straight up, leaving his face exposed. Still, one could get lost in such things...

Dean felt her stare, but he didn't mind. He wondered if she preferred The Cure or The Smiths, but couldn't bring himself to ask. He kept his head bowed, toying with the buttons on his cardigan. They stood still for several moments, listening to the birds in meditative silence, until

Blaze and Ethan came bursting out the door. Colin and TJ followed soon after, arm-in-arm and discussing testosterone injections. "You probably won't see changes for a few months," Colin said, "Except after a few weeks you'll get *a lot* hornier."

"Fuck yeah!" said TJ, pointing his left finger like a gun. "Look out ladies!"

Colin laughed. "Yeah, eventually you'll learn to control it. But for awhile, you'll want to fuck every chick in sight." His eyes flicked towards Dean, as if daring him to speak. Dean didn't notice. He'd just seen a bat dart across the sky.

"Unless it makes me want dudes!" TJ said. "It can do that to some guys, did you know that? T turns them gay!" He laughed at the absurdity of it all.

Dean and Teddy met eyes, their expressions equally dour. Despite himself, Dean started to grin. Teddy couldn't help it. Behind her hair, she smiled as well.

*

A few hours later, Dean and Colin dropped off their bags at the Mahrs' house and walked down the road to the beach. The sun had set and they were alone under the stars. The only noise was the lapping of waves and the occasional car horn in the distance.

Colin pulled out a bottle of merlot from under his track jacket. "Care to share this with me?"

Dean nodded and smiled politely. They took turns drinking from the bottle as they walked along the rocky shoreline. For a long time, neither of them spoke. Observing the summer homes along the coast, Dean thought of wealth. There was a light in the distance but it was yellow not green. Did this mean yield? Having eaten little, the wine had gone straight to his head.

"You have a beautiful home," Dean said, breaking the silence. From his brief visit, he already noticed that the Mahr's mini-mansion had a spiral staircase, pond populated with Japanese koi, and a private pool and hot tub. He now understood the extent of the Mahrs' fortune; he had only suspicions before.

"Thank you," said Colin. "I'll give you a tour later. I think you'll like some of the rooms. The place has a really interesting history."

Dean envied Colin. He would love to spend his summer in an historic house with statues and fountains and the ocean down the road. His parents' cramped colonial, surrounded by its clones, could not compare. What a difference scenery alone could make.

As if reading his mind, Colin said, "So what are your plans for the summer?"

Dean sighed. "I don't have any. Going back home I guess."

"You should come stay here," Colin said. "We have plenty of room."

Dean's eyes lit up. "Really?"

"Yeah, totally. I mean, I'll have to ask Mom and Dad when they get back from Nice, but I can't see why they'd mind."

"That's where your parents are? France?"

"Yeah. We go often. Dad has friends on the coast, and my sister goes to a fashion institute in Paris. Didn't I tell you?"

Dean sighed, longing. "Well, I'd love to stay here for a few weeks or something. I'd pay rent of course."

"No, I wouldn't accept that. You'd be my guest."

Dean shook his head. "You know something Colin? You're too nice. Why are you so damn nice all the time? You make me feel mean."

Colin wasn't sure how to react to this. He took another sip of wine and realized, from the small amount remaining, Dean was drinking faster. He took swigs to catch up.

"Well, I think that you're very nice," he said, unconvincing.

"Yeah right. I'm a troll."

"A troll?"

"I dunno. It made sense in my head. But really, you're popular at school because you're so nice. And everyone liked you so much at that support group. Plus, did you know that when people at school find out I'm transgender, one way or another, they always say 'talk to Colin, talk to Colin, he's the best.' The *best*! And I say that I do. I do talk to you, don't I? And and and, you know why you're going to be a famous musician? Because you're so dang nice, and everyone will like you! Because you're talented and nice and, might I add, own a car. A *nice* car. And you have nice hair. Nice, nice, nice, everything about you is nice. Ha, even your parents are in Nice. And I bet they are nice too. Nice parents in Nice, how nice! And you are certainly nice looking, to put it lightly."

Colin laughed, blushing. "I'm keeping this wine," he said, mostly because he wanted to get to Dean's level.

Dean covered his face with his hands. "Ahh! The word 'nice' isn't real anymore! It has no meaning. I said it too much and now it's just a sound! Nothing can be nice ever again!"

Colin laughed. "I hate when that happens."

"Reality is crumbling around me! I'm going down, down..." Dean fell over in the sand.

Colin plopped down beside him. "Come on, you're getting all sandy," he said.

Dean continued to lay face down.

"Are you okay?" Colin asked, shaking his shoulder, "Hello? Dean? You in there buddy?"

"Maybe it's better this way," Dean said. "Leave me. Leave me for the seagulls. Leave me for Poseidon." He pretended to weep.

Colin raised his eyebrows, looking around to see if anyone was coming. They weren't. "You are so strange," he muttered.

"Is it really so strange?" Dean sang into the sand. "Is it really soooo straaaaange? Oh is it really so, really so strange?"

"Yes," Colin said, suppressing a smile, "Yes, it is."

"But you will change your mind!" Dean sang in a muffled, would-be British accent. He lifted his arms in the air and wagged his fingers back and forth like windshield wipers, still on his stomach. His face was covered in sand.

"You are such a lightweight," Colin muttered.

"Light as a feather and stiff as a- well, never mind. A boxer and a fighter by my trade!"

Dean sprung to his feet and began punching the air. He ran down the beach, yelling. "I am leaving, I am leaving! I'm gonna be a contender!"

Colin rolled his eyes and ran after him. "You're nuts!" he yelled, jogging behind.

"I can't help the way I feel! I can't help the way I feel!" Dean began to leap in the air. "Hey, Colin?"

"What?"

"I think I'm in lurv."

"What? Stop skipping and come talk to me."

"Can't! Okay, I can." He did.
"Now what did you say?" Colin asked, panting.
"I said I killed a nun."
"No you didn't."
"Well then my dear Watson, what do you think I said then? I certainly didn't say I was in love with anybody."
"Um."
"Or did I?"
"You know alcohol doesn't usually make people this weird."
"I'm not a person, that's why. I'm a myth. Tiresias! A berdache! Two spirits! Three spirits! Infinite amounts of spirits!" He began to make ghost noises. "Some misplaced Joan of Arc!"
"I have no idea what you are talking about," Colin said.
"Hm, indeed that makes two of us, daddy-o."
"Maybe we should start walking home. I could make you some tea before bed to calm you down."
"There you go again, being nice! Well la dee da. Tea would be splendid, Johnny. Let us retire to Pemberly!"
Colin took Dean by the arm and led him towards the street before he could take off skipping again.
"Lord Alfred, you little charmer!" Dean exclaimed in falsetto as they trudged slowly over wet sand, "you have proven positively gallant, dear boy!"

*

Back at the house, Colin watched the flame as he waited for the water to boil. He felt woozy. Dean was in high-ceilinged living room, lying on the leather sofa, his head hanging over the edge. He was still singing softly, hugging a throw pillow and studying a beetle on the wall. Colin could see the outline of his ribs through his gray tee shirt, beneath the line where his chest-binding undershirt ended. The bones were accentuated with the rise and fall of his chest as he breathed. His shirt was riding up slightly, and the lower half of his stomach was visible. Colin couldn't help but notice the shadow of his pelvic bones and the trail of hair that ran down his abdomen. Giving himself a little shake, he went back to staring intently at the stove.
"Hey Colin, stop watching that teapot. You know what they say." Dean wagged his finger and frowned, his face upside down. He went back to singing, the blood rushing to his head.
Colin came and sat on the couch opposite him. "You have a pleasant voice," he said.
"Do I?"
"Yeah, it'd probably be even better if you sat up straight."
Dean flopped onto his stomach. Colin found himself tracing the slight

curve of his backside with his eyes.

"Well, thank you," Dean said. "No one's ever told me that."

"Were you in chorus in high school?" Colin asked. He leaned over the glass coffee table and adjusted the pink gladioli in a vase to distract himself.

"Nah," Dean said, cuddling up to the pillow. "Wanted to be, but they made girls wear skirts to the concerts. No exceptions."

"Ah, yeah, that's rough."

"Nothing could be rougher."

Colin leaned back from the flowers and closed his eyes, attempting to sober up. He forgot he left the wine bottle next to his jacket on the couch. The little remaining spilled onto his lap.

"Shit!" he said, jumping up. He unbuttoned and kicked off his gray jeans. Dean looked up at him, a smile twitching in the corner of his wine-stained lips. Colin stared back, standing in his boxer shorts. Drunken eye contact was maintained a little too long, and it was suddenly very obvious.

The teakettle whistled. Neither of them moved.

*

Colin's bed was queen sized, in the far corner of his room. The window was open, and perhaps it was his imagination, but Dean thought he could smell the ocean on the breeze. There was no illumination but for moonlight, no posters on the pale blue wall. The sheets were cool, the comforter was padded with down. The mattress was firm, high off the ground, perfect.

Dean let Colin take the lead, his body seizing up with nerves as his friend drunkenly mounted him. He allowed kissing, but when Colin tried to undue his pants, he rolled onto his stomach, facing the wall.

"Come on," Colin said.

Dean shook his head. "Not yet."

Colin sighed and sat up. He took a swig from the mystery concoction on the bed stand. "You don't trust me?" he asked.

"That's not it," Dean said, his voice muffled by a pillow and slurred with alcohol.

"I won't do anything you don't want," Colin said. "I just want you naked."

"Well, that would fall under the category of something I don't want."

Colin shook his head. "You can't live like that. I used to be stone, before Maggie. I wouldn't let anyone touch me. It's no way to be. Let me help you." He pressed his pelvis against Dean's behind, kissing the back of his neck.

Dean edged away. "I said no."

Colin sighed. He was beyond drunk. "I read this play once, and it changed my whole outlook on sex. It was like *Vagina Monologues*, but about trans vaginas."

"If you are to repeat those last two words I will lose the capacity to ever be aroused again." Dean said.

Colin scowled, hurt. "See, that's your problem, Dean. You hate yourself. You need to embrace being trans. So your body is different than other men. So what. You're still hot." He leaned in again and wrapped his arms around Dean's waist, whispering, in a misguided attempt at seduction. "You need to *celebrate* your differences."

*

Here's a proposal. Instead of celebrating our differences (genitals), let's just forget about them. Please trans men, I implore you: stop bringing it up.

"Oh dear, we have no word for them!" you cry. Well, good. When something has no name, it isn't real, and I don't want it to be. Stop trying to shove it in normal people's faces. They do not care. At all. They have finances and puking babies and ride-on-lawn-mowers to worry about, and good for them. All you are doing is making people aware of what I look like naked, and I don't appreciate that. I'm a private person, perhaps one of the few left on the planet. That is why I didn't title this *The Mangina Manifesto*. I'm not brain-dead like most you queers who base your entire lives around what's between your legs and the legs you fuck.

Instead of coming up with atrocious names like "cockpit" or "dicklet" (Christ, no wonder no one wants to touch us) let's start a revolution where we pretend everyone is Barbie and Ken beneath the waist. I'm sick of being preached the importance of "sex positivity." Negativity is never the problem. The problem is thinking some types of sex are better than others. They are all equally negative, not to mention boring.

I have no goal to ever embrace or celebrate my genitals. At the end of the day, I strive for respectful indifference, thank you very much.

Oh my. I wanted to write to get things off my chest, but I think all I'm succeeding in is elevating my blood pressure. Bah, if I wanted to get the real perpetrators off my chest, I would have to go under a scalpel. Why am I really churning out this crap? Because experience shows me that poor entertainers become famous by writing, and transgender people achieve success via whiney memoirs.

God, already I've said too much. It's such a pity sublimation has gone out of fashion.

*

Dean woke. He was hot, headachy, and alarmed to feel someone's hand on his waist. He scooted away from Colin and in the process roused him from his sleep. He turned before they made eye contact, but Colin knew he was awake.

"Morning," he said to Dean's back.

"Morning."

Neither of them spoke for minute.

"You uh, feel okay about last night?" Colin asked, "I didn't do anything that made you uncomfortable, did I?"

"Yeah, it's fine," Dean mumbled. "You?"

"Oh, I feel fine."

"Cool."

More silence.

"I don't think we should be room mates next year," Dean said.

"Oh, okay," Colin said, folding his arms behind his head and looking at the ceiling. "It's not because you want to stop being friends, right?"

"No, I just don't think it'd be a good idea."

"Right, right."

As Colin stretched, Dean wondered why he felt miserable. Hadn't this been what he wanted?

"Along those lines," Colin said. "I don't think there's any reason to mention this to anyone. Particularly Maggie. I wouldn't want anyone getting the wrong idea."

"Ah. Yeah, I didn't plan on saying anything."

"Cool."

Dean got out of bed. He was still wearing his Levis and tee shirt. He found his cell phone on the floor and, intending to check the time, he saw he had one missed call from Vivian. Pleased to have a distraction, he called back, sitting on the edge of the bed.

She picked up on the first ring. "Dean?"

"Hey Viv, you called?"

"Yes, thank goodness it's you. When are you coming back to Syracuse?"

"Well, I can leave any time. I'm done with finals early, but I was planning on staying another week."

"Can you come home now?"

"Wait, you're already back?"

"Yes," she said. "I hate to ask this, but I really need you here."

"Um, I could come back a few days early. Maybe tomorrow. Why, what's up?"

"It's Adrienne," Vivian said, "She- uh, Adrienne ran away from home."

Dean could tell she close to tears. "Oh wow…are you going to be okay?"

"Yeah I'm just freaking out a little and I know this is ridiculous to ask and I don't deserve it because we've hardly talked in years but I need your help if you don't mind, I'm sorry." She said this all without taking a breath, as was her typical manner.

"Of course," Dean said, "Don't be sorry, I'll pack tonight and catch a bus in the morning. Any idea why she would do this?"

Vivian was crying now.

"It's okay," Dean said, feeling awkward, "Don't...cry."

"That's just the thing. That's why I need you. Adrienne ran away because, well..." She paused, seemingly careful to choose her words, and then said, "Adrienne is having gender problems."

*

Dean and Colin stopped at a roadside diner on their way back to campus. They were still yawning and bleary eyed when the waiter took their orders. Dean tried to hide his scowl when Colin asked for bacon. He ordered oatmeal. For a while they sipped their coffee in silence, on opposite sides of the booth. Dean stared at a poster of Marilyn Monroe, his head throbbing.

Finally Colin spoke. "Everything is okay at home, right?"

"Yeah, it's just Viv," Dean said. "She needs my help with something. No big deal."

"Oh, okay," Colin said. "But you'll come back to visit soon, won't you?"

Dean looked away from the poster. "You still want me to?"

"Of course!"

Dean stuck his tongue out the corner of his mouth, thinking. "But what about...you know." He blushed.

Colin shrugged. "Well, let's just see what happens, alright?" He smiled sheepishly.

Dean stared. "Okay," he said at last, "I'll come back as soon as I can."

"Great," Colin said, "I can't wait."

Dean began to toy with a saltshaker, anxious. He poured a small hill on his placemat.

"So we're both going to be seniors," Colin said, eyeing the salt with suspicion. "Crazy, right?"

"Oh," Dean said, now cutting salt-lines with his knife. "Yes. I forget."

"You have any plans for after graduation?"

"Not in the slightest." Dean said. He added some pepper to the mix.

"Well, what do you want to be when you quote unquote grow up?" Colin asked.

Dean frowned. "I don't really plan on growing up," he said.

The waiter returned with their food, lowering their dishes onto the table.

"Thanks," Dean muttered, brushing the mess of spices aside.

"No seriously though," Colin said, immediately seizing and

chomping on the greasy pig flesh, "What do you want to be?"

Dean shrugged, crinkling his nose. "I dunno. Morrissey?" He wished that hadn't slipped out. He began to eat his oatmeal slowly.

"Be serious," Colin said.

"I am! I am a very serious person, Colin Mahr, and don't you forget it." He took another sip of coffee. "Besides, that's how people become successful. Look at James Dean. He was obsessed with becoming Marlon Brando. Even Jesus was ripping off earlier prophets."

Colin snorted. "Yeah, great. James Dean and Jesus. Those stories end well." He smirked fondly, shaking his head.

"Yes, I agree, they do," Dean said. "It's like how there was this poet. I forget his name, but he said as a young man he didn't want to be *like* Yeats, he wanted to *be* Yeats. And look, he became a poet."

"But you don't even remember his name," Colin said, "And do you know how many more people aspire to be like famous people and don't succeed?"

Dean frowned. "Yeah, well, actually I do remember. It was Robert Lowell, and I'm sure a bunch of other successful poets. That's how it works. It's uh, literary…inheritance." Dean trailed off, realizing how stupid it sounded out loud. Why was he admitting these crazy ideas? Was he starting to trust Colin?

"That's how it works?" Colin said, "You wish hard enough and it just happens?"

"Why are you giving me a hard time?" Dean asked, "Mister guitar virtuoso over there. You talked about your influences the first day we met. You're telling me you don't have big dreams?"

Colin shrugged. "Yeah, but I know it's unrealistic."

"How's it unrealistic? You've already got a band and you've even been in magazines and stuff. Fancy musicians are asking you to play with them."

"Yeah, but that'll fade," Colin said. "And besides, it's one thing to be a star in a college conservatory and play sessions. It's another to actually have people relate to your work and really love it. I don't care that people think I'm technically skilled as a guitarist. It takes more to be great."

Dean crossed his arms. "And you want to be great, don't you?"

"Well, deep down, yes."

"See? We're not so different." Feeling especially courageous, he brushed Colin's leg with his own under the table.

Colin blushed. "No, I guess we're not," he said. "We're both secretly attention whores. Or not so secretly."

Dean leaned back and took a sip of his coffee, considering. "Our kind need an inordinate amount of attention," he said wisely. "It's been proven in various medical journals."

The next morning Dean waited with his bags at the White Plains bus station. He didn't have much luggage: he brought most of it home over spring break. Ticket in hand, he leaned against the brick wall, watching for the Greyhound bus to pull around the corner. He amused himself with the activities of the pigeons. The males seemed to be doing some sort of mating ritual, puffing out their chest-feathers and strutting in circles around the females. He watched intently, taking no notice of the other humans around him.

Finally the bus pulled up. After checking his luggage underneath, Dean climbed aboard and found a seat by a window. He was one of few passengers and had room to himself to stretch out his legs. He began listening to his CD player and leaned back, preparing himself for the long ride.

He felt a tap on his shoulder. He paused his music and turned away from the window, startled.

Standing in the aisle was a short boy who couldn't be much older than twelve. He had light, almost greenish skin, black hair, and pale, wide eyes. He looked like he hadn't eaten in days, and his baggy clothes were wrinkled and sagging on his emaciated frame. He wore a metal ball necklace and two sweatbands on his wrists: the accessories a preteen would purchase in his first steps of rebellion against his suburban upbringing.

"Hey Dean," he said in a high voice.

Dean wrinkled his nose. "I'm sorry, do I know you?"

"Yeah," he said, "you came to my house a few times. We ate pizza." He looked slightly hurt. "I'm Adrienne Angeli. Viv's my big sister."

"Jesus Christ!" Dean grabbed the Adrienne's thin wrist, "You're here? Your sister is worried sick about you. I'm calling her right away." Dean could have sworn she was a boy. Gender problems indeed.

"No, please don't," Adrienne said, looking panicked. "She'll tell Mom and Dad!"

"Well, too bad."

Adrienne crossed her arms. "I'm just going to go then."

Dean sighed. "Alright, I can wait a bit. Just stay, alright? But you should really call home soon. Viv is a wreck."

Adrienne nodded, rolling her eyes. She plopped beside Dean, slouching, her knees pressed against the seat in front of her.

The bus started to move and the driver's voice rang out over the PA. "Welcome folks, thanks for choosing Greyhound. Please keep all electronic devices at a level where only you can hear them. Keep cell phone calls short and quiet, and make sure to pick up all your trash...I aint paid to babysit. We'll be making a brief stop in Kingston, and then in Albany..."

Dean waited until the woman had finished her memorized speech and then turned to Adrienne. "This is absurd. How on earth did you end up at the White Plains bus station of all places? I thought kids ran away to circuses."

"Well, it's really a coincidence that I ran into you." Adrienne said. "I took a bus the other night, and then I wasn't sure where to go. It was late, so I slept under the bridge."

"You slept under a bridge?" Dean's eyes widened.

"Yeah," Adrienne said, "I wasn't sure how to get to Rye College from here. I was thinking of going to New York City instead, to start a new life, but I wasn't sure how to get there either and I was really tired."

"First of all, start a new life? How old are you?"

"Sixteen."

"Exactly. Also, why were you coming to my school?"

"Viv said they're nice to gay people there. And well," Adrienne's greenish cheeks flushed, "I was also hoping to find you."

"Me?" Dean said. "Why me?"

"Never mind, it was stupid," Adrienne said, looking like she might cry.

Dean softened "It wasn't stupid," he said. "When I was your age, I always wanted to run away. Still do, actually."

"Really?" Adrienne looked up at him.

"Sure," Dean muttered, turning away with embarassment. "I just never got much further than Taft Road."

Adrienne smirked with satisfaction. "I guess I went a little far."

Dean smiled. "Maybe. But you made the right choice to go home."

Adrienne shrugged. "I wasn't going to. I just saw you from across the street, ran and bought a ticket, and followed you onto the bus."

"Ah." Dean looked at his phone, thinking that he should really text Vivian, but decided he could wait a little longer. "So what was your reason for running away? Not that anyone needs much of a reason to flee Syracuse."

Adrienne kicked mindlessly at the footrest, smacking on gum. "Well, I've been having a lot of problems at home."

"Yeah?"

"Not just recently," she said, toying with her wristband, "but, well, since I can *remember*." She shook her head with theatric flair. "Viv was always the perfect daughter, you know? Mom and Dad loved everything she did. She could write, she could do science and math, she won spelling bees, she got straight A's, her artwork was hung up all over our friggin' house... and what was I good at? Nothing, that's what. I couldn't even read until like third grade. And my parents always took me to therapists to try to determine what my learning disability was, but the truth is, I'm just not smart like Vivian."

"That's not true," Dean said. "You've always seemed intelligent to me." He barely knew Adrienne and hadn't seen her since she was eleven, but he continued anyway. "I'm sure you've got plenty of talents. What is your favorite thing to do?"

"Well..." Adrienne smacked her gum a few times, thinking. "I like to write songs on my guitar. And I make techno music on the computer. But Mom and Dad don't think that's anything special. They think I'm wasting my time and I should join orchestra or choir like Vivian. But kids in those groups are stuck up. Plus I only like playing my own songs."

"That's great," Dean said. "Guitar is a great instrument. My friend Colin is studying music in college, and he's a guitar player. He writes his own songs too. You can definitely get places with that skill." Dean felt weird. He avoided thoughts of Colin since he left school, afraid to get his hopes up. He also felt dishonest, talking about the value of getting places with skills. It was something he knew nothing about.

"Well, it's more than just that," Adrienne said. "I've never fit in at school either. I was never like the other girls. I've felt this way forever, even when I was really little. I always make-believed I was a boy. Well, usually I make-believed I was a dog, but a boy dog. And I always wore boy clothes and I even wanted boy's hair, but I was too scared to ask Mom. She always told me I should dress nice like Vivian, that I was embarrassing the family. And Vivian isn't like the girls at school- she's nice to me at least. But if I dressed like her and acted like her, I'd feel really sad all the time. Not that she's bad. Does that make sense?"

"Yes," Dean said. "You're different than her. Your parents should accept that."

"Thanks." Adrienne looked down at her converse sneakers. "I'm sorry. Am I talking too much?"

"No!" Dean said, and he meant it. "No, please continue. Did you go to Catholic school? I know they sent Vivian there."

"Yeah," Adrienne said, "I did for awhile, but now I go to the regular high school because Mom and Dad can't afford it. It wasn't as bad as they say it is. I didn't mind, but Viv didn't speak to them for months. So instead they'd always complain to me. Mom would blame it on you and say it was because you told her you were transgender and mixed up her brain. And I'd just keep my mouth shut, because how could I tell them? I didn't even know that girls *could* become boys until my parents told me about you."

Dean experienced an emotion for which the English language has no word. He felt guilt and pride simultaneously, mixed with a sense of irony that almost made him believe in fate. "So is that why you ran away from home?"

"Yeah. They freaked out because I cut my hair short without permission. And then I figured that was that. I was done. I had read a lot on the internet about stuff and I felt more confident than usual. So I left them a letter saying that I am a boy, and that as soon as they text me 'we accept you,' I would come back home. Meanwhile, I wanted to find you and ask you some questions, since you're the only transgender person I've ever known."

"Did they ever text you?"

"Yeah, and left voice mail, but only ordering me to come home. They didn't say they accept me."

"Wow," Dean said. "By the way, do you want me to call you by male pronouns? Like *he*, instead of *she*?"

Adrienne looked excited. "You would do that?"

"Of course."

"Well, then, yes!" He grinned. "Also, I've heard people change their names, but I like my name just fine. I just want to start spelling it A-d-r-i-a-n."

"Sounds good."

Adrian cracked his knuckles and leaned back. "Sweet," he said. "Now can I ask you some things?"

"Sure, go ahead." Dean looked around to make sure no one was listening, for safety purposes. The only other passenger near by was a sleeping old man.

"How do you become a guy anyway?" Adrian asked. "Do you take a pill?"

"Well no," Dean said, certain he was not the best person to explain this. "Generally speaking, pills are not encouraged. What I do is inject testosterone into my body. I have to stick a needle into my thigh."

Adrian looked sickened. "Does it hurt?"

"Sometimes, if I'm tense. It's a big needle, it almost always stings. And you have to be careful to get it in the muscle, not a vein or artery."

"And you do it all by yourself?"

"Yes, but a nurse trained me."

"Wow. And what does the testosterone do?"

"Well, only so much," Dean said. "It lowered my voice, made me get hairier all over. It also made my fat and muscle patterns more masculine, and just changed my general appearance some. You need surgery to change your chest, unfortunately, and that's pricey. But yeah, I've got stronger bones and a faster metabolism, but I've got to watch my cholesterol. And there are other…small things." He blushed, not wanting to say.

"And do you have to pay for it?" Adrian asked.

"Some people do. Mine is free, since I go to this place in New York City and I'm under twenty-three."

"How old do you have to be to get it?"

"Eighteen," Dean said.

"Oh," Adrian said, looking crushed.
"Were you hoping you could start?"
"Yeah. I was going to ask for your help. That was one of the main reasons I ran away."
Dean nodded. "I know you'll hate to hear this, but maybe it's better you have to wait. It will give you time to think, and make sure you really want to make this change. It's a big commitment." Was this really him talking? Wasn't this exactly what people used to say when he was this age?
"Three years is forever," Adrian said. "If I have to go another month, I'll kill myself." He said this calmly, but with alarming teenage gravity.
Dean bit his lip, feeling very strange. "That's no way to view it," he said finally. "You don't have to change your body to be a boy. It's mind over matter." He stopped. How could he live with himself? He shook his head. "No, you know what? I'm not going to lie to you." He dropped his voice and leaned in. "People aren't going to treat you how you want to be treated. To the outside world, it doesn't matter what you say you are: they want physical proof. But they're all fucking idiots. You have to make sure you do it for yourself, and nobody else, even though that can be impossible to tell. Even after you start hormones, many people still won't respect you. And maybe you'll wonder if you want to be a man either. You're just at the beginning of the bullshit- it gets worse. But I will say, there is a world outside of our hometown. There are people who will accept you, hormones or not. Maybe not in that perfect way, but nobody understands anyone if you really think about it."
"But are you happy now?" Adrian asked. He looked quite small in the seat.
Dean sighed. "No. Not at all. But I like to believe I'm getting closer."
Adrian nodded, looking grief-stricken. Dean felt like he destroyed his only sliver of hope. He sighed. Why was he always such an asshole? He pulled out his cell phone. "Here. I want to give you someone's number, alright? Are you ready?"
Adrian nodded and held out his iphone.
Dean rattled off the digits. "I want you to call him sometime. I'll tell him ahead of time, he'll be more than willing to talk. His name is Colin, and he's transgender and a musician, just like you. He's really successful and happy now, and he'll have some great advice. Better than I could ever give."
Adrian stared at his phone for a while. Dean went back to listening to music. After about a half hour, Adrian tapped him on the shoulder again. Dean scowled and paused his music. "Yes?"
"You know, I'm not a baby. I don't want to call your friend and have him sugarcoat things for me. I want to hear the truth, and that's why I came to you. Vivian always said you were honest. Almost too honest, she

said."

Dean smirked. The comment made him, momentarily, feel good about himself. He frantically looked both ways before leaning back in. "Alright," he whispered. "The real deal? Damned if I know the real deal... But I'll tell you this: your gender shouldn't matter. I really don't think men and women are different at all, deep down. I really, truly don't. This shit makes everyone miserable, but it will persist, so long as there is sex and bodies and reproduction. Don't bother with utopian dreams. Gender is everything; it is the human experience, all of history, every culture. It poisons everything. Hormones and fancy identities can only do so much. The way I see it, I should just accept my natural body, but I can't, because deep down I must hate women. I am weak. No, not weak: power hungry, actually. I'm just bad. Fuck, I'm too stupid to figure all this out, alright? Try to forget about it. I don't want to hurt you." His voice cracked. He felt car sick and disoriented.

Adrian shook his head. "No," he said, "It's more than that, Dean. I still believe in some things, and...well, maybe you're right, gender shouldn't matter. Maybe men and women are the same. Maybe *everything* is the same, and *nothing* matters. But I don't think it's bad to feel like it matters for you, since we're stuck with it. You can't carry that weight on your shoulders. You're talking in circles. If it doesn't matter, then it doesn't matter."

Dean didn't comment. His throat was constricted. Nothing felt real.

"I think you're the one who doesn't give himself enough credit." Adrian said.

Dean swallowed and inhaled deeply through his nose. "Oh trust me...if I gave myself any credit, I'd never be able to pay off the interest."

Adrian stared blankly.

"Credit card joke," Dean muttered, "Probably too young to...well, actually, no, it just wasn't funny..."

"You know," Adrian said, "I think you make jokes because if you mock yourself, you can beat other people to it. It's called a defense mechanism. I learned about it in Psychology."

"Well, thank you Dr. Freud...tell me something I don't know. I wonder, do you think I subconsciously constructed my hair as a phallic symbol?"

"Sarcasm," Adrian said, "is also a defense mechanism."

Dean opened his mouth and then closed it again. He crossed his arms and turned away, scowling at the seat in front of him. "Boy, you're just like your sister. You both can see straight to the heart of me."

Adrian shrugged. "No offense, but you're kind of obvious."

Dean laughed. "Yeah? Well la dee da."

*

After several rests tops, they finally reached their destination. Dean gave his mom a call and then waited in the main foyer with Adrian. The Syracuse bus station was more slightly more modern and less shadowy than the one in Albany. Adrian ordered himself a pastry from the Dunkin Donuts.

"Where did you get all the money for this trip anyway?" Dean asked when he returned. He wondered whether the massive Boston Crème would even fit in the tiny kid's stomach.

Adrian shrugged, chewing.

Dean nodded. "Right. Well, anyway, even if your plan didn't work out, you're welcome to come visit me at school in the future. I can show you around. Just call me ahead of time, and let your parents know you're coming."

"I don't think mom and dad are going to let me do much of anything for a long time," Adrian said.

As if on cue, Dean saw a familiar man walk in through the automatic doors.

"Addie!" Mr. Angeli bellowed, walking quickly towards them. He was tall and overweight, with black hair just like his children. His skin was slightly darker, and he had a mustache. His gait was masculine and assuming, and his presence disruptive. He pulled Adrian into his meaty arms, his face stern despite the loving gesture. When he noticed Dean, his veins began to throb in his temple. "What are you doing here?"

Although he was half a foot shorter and much much narrower, Dean held his ground. "I ran into Adrian on the bus back from White Plains, and I made sure he got home safely."

At the sound of the male pronoun, Mr. Angeli's eyes narrowed.

Vivian came rushing in the doors. Dean couldn't help but smirk, watching her try to run with her massive purple purse.

"Oh thank goodness!" she said, pulling Adrian into her arms just as her father did, but with plenty more emotion on her face. "Don't ever leave my sight again!" she said. "I was so, so worried." She wiped tears from her eyes.

Adrian said nothing, looking ashamed.

"Dean, thank you so much," Vivian said, and she reached out to hug him as well.

Her father grabbed her roughly by the arm. "No," he said, "We're going home. Now."

"Dad," Adrian said, "he didn't do anything. It was my fault, I wanted to go find him. He had no idea I was coming."

"I don't want to hear anymore," Mr. Angeli said. "Girls, go to the car."

"No," Vivian said, "I'm not leaving Dean after all he did. Do you have a ride, dear?" she asked, turning to him.

"Yes, I do," Dean said. "Thanks Viv."

"I said go to the car," Mr. Angeli said for a second time, raising his voice. "Don't test me, girls. Don't make me say it again."

Both children hesitantly obeyed and cowered off, not daring to say good bye. Barely a second after they disappeared, Dean's pocket vibrated, with what he imagined was a text from Vivian.

"What's wrong with your voice?" Mr. Angeli asked.

This hadn't been what Dean was expecting. "What?"

"You can't trick me, I recognize you. You used to be Laura."

"I don't know what you mean, sir," Dean said. "Are you implying I used to be a woman? That's highly offensive, not to mention a biological impossibility."

Mr. Angeli leaned in close, his veins still throbbing. "You always were a little liar. I was nice to you, you hear? I let you in my house, I fed you pizza, I gave you rides places when your own dad couldn't be bothered. And how do you repay me? By first corrupting one of my daughters and now my other. I swear, if you ever come near either of them again..."

Dean stared back. His sarcastic smile evaporated and was replaced with a look of cold hatred.

"We clear?" Mr. Angeli asked.

Dean said nothing, although he had a strong and offensive desire to shout "Capiche?" in the Italian-American's reddening face.

"I said are we clear?"

Dean didn't respond.

"Forget it. I'm going home to my family," Mr. Angeli said, and he stormed off, leaving Dean alone in the florescent light.

*

Dear Teddy,

I said I would write, didn't I? If nothing else, I keep my word. I don't even know anything about you or if I'll ever see you again. With that in mind, I suppose it is safe to be honest (if it's ever safe to do such a ghastly thing). What do we have in common? Possibly very little. We are both supposedly transgender. Is that common ground? Some would say so. But do you want to talk about that? I certainly don't. Either that or I want to talk about nothing else. I just never can decide.

I must say, your hastily stated anxieties certainly mirror my own. Most the time I'm convinced people don't see me at all. I wouldn't say I felt you saw me, as much as saw through me. I felt translucent instead of invisible, which is a small improvement. Not to imply you saw who I really was, but I'm pretty positive you got the gist of my body armor and the function it serves (you, at least, did not think I was Robert Smith).

See Teddy, I've been told transgender people are trying to just be themselves.. But the truth is, I've never felt I had a self, and I'm guessing from your mirror comment that maybe you feel similarly. It always frightens me that the few people who are close me to seem to think I have a strong personality (eccentric, blunt, quirky, that sort of nonsense). It makes me feel like I've played some awful trick; I'm pretty sure all they're picking up on is over compensation for my actual emptiness (you wore black nail polish, so I'm trusting you won't judge me for my melodrama). I don't really feel like I'm trying to be myself, so much as constantly inventing myself, or rather stealing other selves and adding them to my repertoire. And when you're so focused inward, you have little time for external stimuli, except when you're looking for more idols to emulate. Female-to-leech.

Maybe being a man comes naturally to some, but for me, it's constant method-acting. Even when I'm rejecting masculine stereotypes, I am doing it in a conscious, calculated way. I know they say gender is a performance, but I feel like I am completely artificial, day and night. That can't be natural, Teddy!

Sometimes I think I'm just a sad little kid looking for a daddy (not in a sexual way, but the fact that I need to say it isn't really says it all) But even that isn't original; I heard someone say it about James Dean. But what do these words even mean? Father, son? According to our culture, fathers aren't even supposed to love their sons, are they? They're supposed to inspire from afar, promising love but never really providing any evidence. Jesus was the one who put the idea in our heads to make a connection between Father and God. What a dangerous conflation.

Masculinity is utterly impossible, Teddy. It's a gas, I'm telling you. Why is it I am obsessed with it? Not that I'm the only one; I'm a product of a phallocentric society, a little smarty pants might say. Maybe that's all it means to be transgender. Obsessed with the wrong style of social performance. Not recommended, let me tell you. Well, I'm sure you already know. What does it feel like to not feel this way? How do normal people feel? Do they even feel? I want to stop feeling so fucking much!

At some point in their life, every tranny think it's funny to say, when someone mentions the opposite sex, "Well what, pray tell, would be the opposite of ME?" (I added the superfluous 'pray tell.') It isn't funny, and it isn't really even thought provoking, but do you think that we are opposites, Teddy? Or are we so close we're almost touching? Or are no two people even comparable in anyway? Are we all just disconnected, separate, isolated, (fill in your own synonym) nobodies, floating in the ether? Blah blah, and I repeat, blah!

My mind yearns for blacks and whites, for a place to hang my head and rest. (maybe that's why I appear a Smiths-era Morrissey clone: I'm easily brainwashed. But as my friend Viv likes to say, what's wrong with keeping the brain squeaky clean?) I tire of the chaos; gender bending is so blasé, so 90's. If you've found a peaceful place, please point me in that direction. I don't care if it's a lie; I just ask that it's an aesthetically pleasing lie. What else is religion? I understand that desire, not for the first time in my life.

I've got to do something; if I keep trying to be the best designer-man I can, I'll end up jumping off the Tappan Zee bridge, I just know it. Masculinity is a rule book full of contradictions and impossibilities, perfectly designed to baffle. Something like the Bible, mind you. I really ought to become a devout Catholic like my predecessors. There is something rather sexy about it. Or maybe I'm just deeply disturbed. No, more meaningless rules are the last thing I need. God, why can't we just throw all life's instructions away? What is the matter with me? I'd condemn myself to a monastery before I'd work at a grocery store. Do they even let transgender men work as vicars (in tutus)? Well, no bother then, get me to a nunnery! My my, how do you solve a problem like Dean? The same way you hold a moonbeam in your hand, I suppose. Indeed, the hills are alive--with celibate cries!

Am I making any sense or am I just a manic parrot? Tell me what it feels like to be Teddy, if you can, and I'll try to stop being an egomaniac for long enough to listen. Please write, and make haste. In the immortal words of Elvis Presley, I get so lonely I could die. Also, I'm sorry if you hate me and/or have forgotten me. Don't feel obligated to write back if this is the case.

Oh, also, if you want to be normal pen pals and not inappropriately honest about our neuroses, we can talk about the weather. It's raining here. Surprise.

Forever no ones,
St. Dean, Poet and Martyr

*

Dear Dean,

Yikes, kid! I don't think you're insane or annoying, but I do think you drink too much coffee. Did you really start quoting 'The Sound of Music' there? And somehow you managed to warp it to your own angst! My my, a man after my own heart. Be careful Dean, I may have to come and rescue you, poor dear. But be wary of rescuers; anyone who has the desire to help a snot nosed brat like you is bound to be the kind of person who tortured cats as a child. Rule of thumb, don't trust anyone who doesn't like felines, takes any interest in your wellbeing, or tries to suggest rules of thumb to you. That having been said, here are some more rules for your skinny little thumbs. Dwell over them to your liking.

Aesthetically Pleasing Lies for Dean:

1. Someone who is searching for their identity will never find it.
2. Someone who is searching for their identity shouldn't have lost it in the first place.
3. Try retracing your steps. Where did you see it last?
4. Well, if you hung it up on the hook like I suggested, this never would have happened.
5. You do not deserve an identity anyway. This is neither a compliment, an insult, nor a fact.
6. Identity crises are in style, so don't freak out. Questioning gender is especially hip. That's why American Apparel sells unisex jeans. Your pain is marketable, don't ever forget that.
7. Remember, a true intellectual has a post-identity crisis.
8. Everyone is make-believing, they just aren't having much fun. You say you feel like a method actor? Feel blessed, Marlon Brando. Most people have memorized the script.
9. It isn't just you. Everyone has to believe in some lie or other to keep from jumping off a bridge.
10. Prevailing lie of the transgendered? "I AM FASCINATING."
11. No one owns their body. At best we rent them like shabby lofts and pretend we are artists. At worst they are poorly built straw huts at the mercy of the elements. The number of tattoos, piercings, eating disorders or sex changes someone has is directly proportionate to how outraged they are by this fact.
12. The only subject more vulgar than gender identity is political identity. The most vulgar political identity, however, is moderate. Equally vulgar is calling yourself a radical. You cannot win- avoid politics at all costs. If someone corners you with picket signs, change the subject to your hair.
13. Regarding your decision to transition, good arguments can be made that you are sexist, selfish, insane, homophobic, narcissistic, even (somehow) transphobic. These assertions can be true and can be made with incredible style. Don't bother defending your position; you'll come off as pious.
14. Remember that you are not transitioning anyway; you are stylizing. Yes you are paying an absurd price to look transsexy (and I don't mean just in money, my little Faust.) But don't fret, sugar. Your sideburns are to die for.
15. Never read Theories late at night. In fact, never read at all if you're going to take academia seriously. A little television never hurt anybody, you know.
16. You don't owe anyone an explanation, especially not yourself. The world, however, owes you everything.

17. Devour as much Beauty as you can and then wallow in your own shit. No, you will never create something lovely or original, but at least that pile of shit will be yours. Pastiche without panache; that's the closest we get to freedom, baby. Start pooping.
18. Don't let people like me give you advice on how to be happier. If they try, plug your ears and scream "I can't hear you!" You weren't meant to be happy; brooding suits your facial structure.
19. Never, ever take yes for an answer.
20. And whenever possible, bury your head in the sand.

Hope that was life changing for you, sweetheart. I tend to be inspirational with little to no effort. And to answer your question, I have a suspicion we're not opposites. We could be spirit sisters, if you'd like. Something like blood brothers for the squeamish. You must tell me everything! What's your favorite color? Don't say black. Gray is permissible.

But enough about you. Send me cash, there's a good lad.

-Teddy

*

    I'm almost out of testosterone. As I explained earlier, my doctor said I needed to get my liver checked out before he'd mail me the new prescription. I phoned him and explained I don't have the money to come down to city. He suggested getting my blood drawn at a local lab and having my results mailed to him. Didn't realize that was an option. At twenty-two, I'm learning all about how the world works.

    Whatever, so I'm not a good listener. When certain words are used, I start tuning out the speaker. Any legal or medical jargon has this effect, which is no good seeing as transitioning depends on the law and doctors. But like I said, I can't help it. I was born that way. You cannot discriminate against me. I don't have Attention Deficit Disorder, the world is just full of bores.

    Alright, I'll go to a lab in Syracuse, and they can take my precious blood. Take everything I have why don't you? Want some breast tissue? The problem is, though I appear to be a boy, my name and sex on legal documents, including medical insurance, is that of a girl. This is all so tiresome. I've got better things to do than deal with all this real world hassle. Can't they invent some bodily organ that will just secrete testosterone for me? Way to drop the ball on that one, Jesus.

    But I suck it up and I go. I get my mom to drive me, and I seethe the whole way, as if she forced me. I try to flatten my hair to look more feminine but it's useless, given my sideburns. My heartbeat quickens. Not only do I hate publicly displaying my ambiguous gender, I also hate needles: more inevitabilities given my lifestyle. Yeah, I'm really not cut out for this whole transgender business. But you can't fire me, I quit.

Then, if I wasn't already immature enough, I start to cry. Not politely either. Loudly, blubbering. To my mommy.

"I can't do it, they're going to look at me weird, they won't know if I'm a boy or a girl, I'm so ashamed, I'm so hideous, I'm a freak, I hate Syracuse, Wah!"

Oh yes. It is all Syracuse's fault.

This is probably something of a panic attack. I can't breathe, and the car seems to be getting smaller. I feel like my body is bloated and disgusting. I want to cut my way out of it, like the real me is a tiny Jonah and my physicality is a giant fish that swallowed him whole. This is absurd, because a quick look at my twiggy limbs confirms that I am no whale. But such a mindset is as stubborn as the Old Testament character himself. There is no way I'm leaving the car.

My mom just sighs. She tries to rub my shoulder and I cringe at the slightest touch. I am apparently a toddler, or just evil like one. I can't turn off the waterworks, so she drives me home.

We park in the driveway. I get out of the car and see my dad is working in the yard. I try to creep by so he won't see my tear-stained face.

"Why are you back so soon?" he asks my mom.

"She's going to New York instead," my mom says, accidentally using the wrong pronoun. I cringe as I bolt for the door.

"Why?" my dad asks.

"She's more comfortable having her blood drawn down there."

My dad snorts. "More comfortable? Certainly don't mind spending my money."

"FINE" I yell from the porch, "FINE I'LL GO BACK TOMORROW. LEAVE ME ALONE."

I slam the door behind me. I imagine I'm the spitting image of Jim in *Rebel Without A Cause*, in that embarrassing scene where he yells, "YOU'RE TEARIN ME APART!"

I go up to my room and I scream into my pillow like a teenage girl on television. I go on a rampage in which I tear the sheets off of my bed, and then lunge at my book shelf, in search the most worthless piece of shit I can find that isn't myself. I go with my high school yearbook. I chuck it on the ground and spit on it. I break the spine and rip out all the pages of smiling seniors and their obnoxious hopes and dreams. Die, die, die! I rip up the almost empty page of signatures ("No! I will not have a good summer, Jamie Peters!") Then I remember my parents spent forty dollars so I could have that thing (even though I insisted I didn't want it). I'm overcome with guilt and I fall on the floor in a dramatic heap.

"I wonder if the fall from my bedroom window would kill me," I wonder absently, lying face down on the bedroom floor, "No, it probably wouldn't...what if I dropped one of those ten pound free weights on my head? No, no, too messy…"

There's a knock on the door. It's my mom.

"Don't come in!"

"I set up an appointment for you with a therapist," she says.

I'm too exhausted to argue with her.

I did go back to have my blood drawn the next morning. The nurse looked at me a little weird when she saw my name and gender on the paper, but she was went on preparing the syringe. Surprisingly, no one attacked me with pitchforks. Nothing exploded.

"You look nervous," she said.

"Yeah, I hate this."

"Aw, don't worry honey, it'll be over in a second."

It was. She bandaged up my arm and I was pleased. I thought it made me look more rough-and-tumble.

"By the way," she said as I walked out, "I just love your haircut. You look like Jimmy Dean."

I burst out laughing. "Why thank you! Have a nice day!"

I couldn't stop grinning all the way to the car, where my mother waited.

*

I feel guilty. I talk too much about myself, don't I? I should check in and see how you're doing every once in awhile. I'm not making you uncomfortable, am I? I sometimes worry I come off as a bit intimidating or out of touch. As it is my duty as a transgender writer to make you realize I am just like you, let me fill you in on some of my more ordinary current habits.

I wake up around eleven o'clock. I don't shower unless I smell. I roll out of bed (yes, I actually roll, it hurts when I hit the floor) and go downstairs. I eat oatmeal. This is my second favorite part of the day. Transgender people are known throughout the world for their love of oatmeal.

Then I will often go for a bike ride through my neighborhood. After all, transgender people have a rich history that includes many bicycle enthusiasts. Upon returning, I may eat some apple sauce. Don't get the wrong idea; transgender people are able to consume solid foods, it's just a custom that we often don't. Then, admittedly, I usually spend a lot of time shut up in my room, doing unhealthy things. Like what, you ask? Well, you'll never know. After that I sometimes nap with my Siamese cat, or feed the turtle I rescued from the seven year-old sociopath next door. Did you know transgender people can make great pet owners?

I take several more bike rides and walks. I watch sparrows and squirrels at the bird feeder. When I'm feeling outrageous, I'll mow the lawn. I eat more oatmeal and sometimes enjoy a soy hot dog or two. Fruit provides endless hours of entertainment. I also drink at least six cups of coffee and probably over a dozen mugs of herbal tea. See, we transgender people aren't so scary once you get to know us. We're well hydrated too.

Then it's nighttime. I'll make some more oatmeal and maybe eat some spoonfuls of hummus or hot sauce, and then its time for King of the Hill, the only television show I watch. For whatever reason, it works for me. It is, of course, a negative stereotype that transgender people only watch King of the Hill and nothing else. Oh, but I cannot lie. I laugh out loud and eat my oatmeal. What can I say, sometimes stereotypes exist for a reason. This is my absolute favorite part of my day. Life is swell.

Then I head up to my bedroom again and I start to get a little cranky. I can't help but think my parents were settling down and pursuing careers at my age. What's my excuse? I'm not even a stoner. Heck, life might be more interesting if I were. I ask myself, is it I am afraid to try? Or is it just I'm stuck in a rut and I've acquired too many bad habits? (How many times have I asked myself this? This book is annoying.)

And then I realize neither of those reasons explains why still live at home. The truth? Free cable and free oatmeal!

And now back to the show.

*

Dean spent the first few days of summer break catching up on sleep. When he was conscious, he sat in bed, reading occasionally, but mainly mulling over his situation with Colin. He decided to wait at least two weeks before contacting him. That would give him time to prepare, and would keep him from becoming too invested in their potential relationship. Each afternoon, he would stare into his large bedroom mirror for a good half hour, frowning. He wanted to ensure he appealed to Colin the next time they were together. He did crunches, lifted free weights, tried on different pairs of underwear, and perfected his hair. He would listen to music and imagine scenes, trying to desensitize himself, should the opportunity of intimacy arise. He wanted to be ready this time.

One evening he was doing just this when there was a soft knock on his door.

"Hang on," he spat, grabbing his jeans off the dresser and hastily dressing. "Come in," he said grudgingly after a moment, pausing his CD player.

It was his mother. She was a somewhat frail Irish-looking woman, about Dean's height, with wavy dark hair and librarian features. She wore a baggy brown sweater, and a gold cross hung around her neck. "A postcard for you," she said, "I didn't read it, don't worry."

Dean took it from her outstretched hand, curious. There was a picture of a donkey on the front. It said "Greetings from El Paso!"

"Huh," Dean said, "thanks."

"Are you going to come down stairs at all today?"
"Maybe in a bit."
She sighed and left him alone again. Frustrated she hadn't closed the door, Dean got up and did it himself. He then sat on his bed to read the back of the postcard. There was no stamp or return address, so he assumed it must have been placed in his mail box. It said:

Dean- You will be kidnapped this Friday, May 22nd. When you pack, prepare to be gone for a few months. Be waiting in the driveway at 1:00 AM, wearing all black. Most importantly, tell no one! (Except your parents, I suppose.) Destroy this postcard as soon as you read it, or if it pleases you, hang it on your wall.

There was no signature, but Dean recognized the handwriting as Vivian's. He smiled to himself and began to pack, excited for the road trip. It would be the first summer in years he would not spend alone and indoors.

*

Sheila's aunt's vacant house in Long Island was not a mansion like the Mahr's. It was a modest brick colonial, in a neighborhood not unlike the one Dean left behind. Still, something in the lack of patriotic or religious lawn decorations suggested it was a different world.

They pulled into the driveway around seven o'clock in the morning. Adrian was asleep and didn't wake when Dean nudged him.

"He's a ridiculously sound sleeper," Vivian explained, stepping out into the cool morning air. "A bomb could go off and he'd keep on snoring."

"Can you guys get my bag?" Dean asked. He undid Adrian's seatbelt and lifted the pipsqueak in his arms like a large cat. Vivian was right; Adrian didn't stir as Dean carried him up the path.

"That," said Vivian, "is adorable." She took a picture with her cell phone.

Dean rolled his eyes. "Hurry up and unlock the door, I'm not very strong."

Sheila fumbled with the keys and then held the door open. Dean carried Adrian inside, laying him down on the nearest couch. Wearing only a Nirvana tee shirt and baggy shorts, Adrian shivered in his sleep. Responding immediately, Dean unzipped his black jacket and draped it over him. Vivian watched him as she took a seat at the kitchen table, smiling softly.

Sheila yawned. "Well, I've been driving all night and I definitely need at least a few hours of sleep."

"I'm actually not that tired," Vivian said, avoiding her gaze. "I'm going to make some tea and stay awake for awhile, if that's alright."

"Oh sure," said Sheila, looking a little sad. "I'll be sleeping upstairs. I figured you and I could share the master bedroom and Adrian and Dean could fight over the other two. Come find me if you get sleepy." She yawned again and headed down the hall. "Help yourself to whatever's in the house," she added. "Make some tea, do whatever. There isn't much food, we'll have to go shopping later." She went upstairs.

When there was the sound of the door closing, Vivian turned to Dean. "So are you staying up as well?"

"Might as well," he said, untying his boots and setting them on a mat by the door.

Vivian went into the kitchen to boil some water. Dean sat down on a chair at the table, glancing around the room. It was simple and modern, lacking in the knick-knacks his mother loved and his father detested. All of the appliances looked fairly new.

"There's no way I'm getting any sleep," Vivian said, twirling her hair around her finger and facing the stove. "I'm too nervous. I didn't want to say so in front of Addie, but I'm still not sure running away was the best decision."

"Well you couldn't let your parents send him away to some Bible camp."

"No, but what does this really solve? Addie still has to go back home for school in the fall, and they're just going to be even more upset with him. I don't know, I really appreciate Sheila going through all this work, but maybe we should go home."

Dean sighed. "It's too bad we don't have enough money to get a place of our own, away from Syracuse, forever."

"You know, that's what Sheila was saying," Vivian said, leaning on the counter. "And honestly, both of us have a lot saved, but my parents would never allow it, and it'd most likely be illegal to keep him without their consent."

"Yeah. Well, it's lovely to see you at least, even if it's just for now. It's nice to be all together like a family." Dean felt a little stupid for saying this.

Vivian set down two large mugs on the table and poured them both some tea from the kettle. "Yeah, it is nice," she said. "I wouldn't have been able to visit you in Syracuse, and it would have been another dreadful summer. Dad was keeping us under constant surveillance. Not that it's much different than usual for Addie. I think Dad was half afraid you were going to come kidnap us. I'm sure that's what he will think happened, come to think of it." She sat down besides him, looking stressed. "Oh Dean, I'm really sorry."

Dean flicked his wrist and feigned a look of indifference. "What do I care? In a way, it's sort of flattering he thinks I'm such a bad boy."

Vivian frowned. "I suppose." She didn't approve of bad boys. "But really you have nothing to worry about. Sure he gets mad, but Dad wouldn't harm a fly."

Dean took a sip of his hot tea. He decided not to tell Vivian about her father's threats at the bus station.

"So," Vivian said, setting down her mug, "you must tell me everything. Start at eleventh grade onward."

Dean snorted. "There isn't much to tell. My life is pretty dull."

"That's such a lie and you know it!" Vivian said, shoving him gently. "You are one of the most fascinating people I've ever known."

"You must know some pretty boring people."

"Just tell me what happened!"

"Why don't you go first?"

Vivian sighed. "Because my life truly *is* boring."

Dean rolled his eyes. "Come on."

"Alright fine," Vivian said. "I went to Catholic school, found Jesus for awhile, then I got careless and lost him again. I almost had a boyfriend, felt guilty about you, realized I had to get away and went to college near the city, where I met Sheila and started dating her, the end." She sped through the story and concluded with a gasp for air.

"When did you realize you were a lesbian?" Dean asked.

"I didn't," she said. "I'm not. I'm not anything, I just happened to like Sheila. I could happen to like anybody intelligent." She took a snobby sip of her tea.

Dean smiled into his mug. "How did you meet Sheila?" he asked.

"A writing workshop at my college."

"Sheila writes?"

"Yes, she was the teaching assistant. Now come on Dean, tell me about you."

Dean sighed. "Well, alright. Senior year was stupid without you, not worth detailing. Then I went to an art school in Manhattan. It was a dreadful disappointment. No one liked my paintings and I was too shy, so I left." He blushed, picking at his fingernails. "The only good was starting on testosterone."

"Well that's good at least!" Vivian said. "You wanted that for so long."

"Yeah, I know. But anyway, I left, so I was stuck in Syracuse again, going to community college. I had no way of getting hormones because I was broke, and my parents sure as hell weren't going to help me at that point. So I just let that go, and fell into a dangerous depression or whatever. I didn't actually fall, stupid idiom, sorry." He took a sip of tea, his eyes darting towards the hall. "Anyway, I went to community college for about a year and a half and lived at home. It sounds like I'm making this up, but I really spent the entire time in my room. Well, when I wasn't taking general education requirements. I didn't make a single friend. Well, there was this once I almost did, but-" he shuddered, "let's not even talk about that. I felt like a freak. I had been on testosterone long enough that I didn't look like a woman anymore-"

"You never really did."

"-but without biweekly injections, I didn't look like a man either. People noticed and gave me awful looks. And one time, when I was waiting for the Centro bus, a teenager threatened me. He called me a faggot and said he'd curb-stomp me. Then there was that murder of that young trans woman nearby..."

"Teesha Green," Vivian said, "I remember. I thought of you."

"Yeah. So I was too afraid to go out after that. I had to beg my mom to drive me to classes. I never told her why." He frowned.

"Wow," Vivian said. "That's really awful, Dean. I'm so sorry."

He shrugged. "Well, I got through my classes and transferred. I came to Rye College in the spring semester of this year. It was really just a random choice. I wanted to be near the city so I could get back on hormones. I though that would solve everything. Luckily the doctors forgave me for disappearing and gave me the prescription. My body responded pretty quickly. So I'm manly again, as you can see." He laughed. "But anyway, I'm sorry if this is complicated, it doesn't really matter. January was when I met Colin and Maggie and well, the rest is history."

Vivian didn't respond at first. She took several sips of tea, her eyebrows furrowed. "I don't mean to be pushy," she said, setting down her mug, "but what are your plans, after you graduate?"

"That isn't really relevant."

"But how will you ensure you'll be able to stay on hormones?"

"I don't know. I don't think that far ahead."

"Can't you get your prescription filled in Syracuse?"

"Probably, I don't know. But it won't be free."

"How much is it?" Vivian asked.

"Like a hundred dollars a refill, every five months or so."

"Oh! Well you could easily handle that if you had a job."

"Yeah, but I don't want one."

"What? Why on earth not?"

"I don't know. I hate working. Why should I do something I hate for someone who doesn't even care about me, when life is so short?"

"Gee, I don't know," Vivian said. "To contribute to society?"

"I don't see it that way," Dean said. "I hate most businesses, so it seems dishonest and stupid to work for them. Besides, I tried once. I really did. But I'm too shy and lazy. Besides, I won't get hired because I have a girl's name and look like I do."

"You haven't changed your name yet?" Vivian said.

"No. It's a lot of paper work, and it's embarrassing to have to talk to the county clerk or whatever. I just keep putting it off."

"But Dean, what are you doing? You're setting yourself up for disaster."

He shrugged. "I guess I've just been buying time."

"You're gonna have to pay off your student loans eventually, you know, or the government comes after you. You need a job. I'm serious, Dean."

"Life is far too important a thing-"

"To ever be taken seriously, I know, I know. But you can't use little Wildean sayings to avoid responsibility forever."

"I don't know, it's worked so far."

"You're really worrying me," Vivian said, staring him down.

Dean stretched out in his chair, putting his legs up on the table and crossing his ankles. He put both hands behind his head and frowned, thinking. "Call me crazy, but I'm banking on becoming a writer. I'm not actually any good at it, but that's the only semblance of ambition I possess."

Vivian shook her head. She seemed less stressed and more amused. "Yes, I will call you crazy. All I can say is that I'm glad I found you when I did. You're definitely heading for a crash."

"Well, my name is Dean," he said, looking inappropriately pleased with himself. "Crashes tend to come with the title."

*

The next afternoon, Sheila took them shopping at the grocery store. On the way back to the house, they passed a big green sign on the highway and something clicked in Dean's brain.

"Hey! I just realized my friend Teddy lives here." He remembered it now from the address he wrote on the envelope.

"Teddy Foley?" Sheila asked.

"Yeah, do you know her?"

"Sure I do. Since high school. I knew her back when she was still...Teddy. Well, boy-Teddy. How do you know her?"

"Colin and I drove up here a few weeks ago to attend a support group," Dean said. "Teddy and I had somewhat of a connection. We became pen pals this summer." He noticed Vivian's reflection in the side mirror and wondered if he imagined it, or if she looked jealous.

"Pen pals?" Sheila said. "That's adorable. Yeah, Teddy was always a strange duck. She used to get teased a lot in high school. She was a few years older than my friends and me, but I remember we used to try to get her to come to our GSA meetings. She always declined, saying she didn't have a sexuality."

"Now who does that sound like?" Vivian said.

Dean smiled half-heartedly.

"Actually, I don't know if Viv told you this," Sheila said, "but I dated a trans woman back in college. Her name was Jen, and she was pretty close friends with Teddy. Teddy used to come up to St. Matthew's and we sometimes visited her in Long Island. So it's been a few years, but I still know her."

"Really? Wow. It is truly a small world," Dean said.

Adrian began to sing the annoying Disney song until Vivian gave him a look of death.

"Well, that's the queer community for you," Sheila said, "At least around these parts. A big, incestuous family. We're really close to Teddy's place right now, come to think of it. Would you want to stop by and say hello?"

"Oh, yes!" Dean said, "I would love that. You don't mind?"

"Nope." Sheila turned to Vivian. "Do you guys mind? It's not that far out of the way."

Vivian and Adrian shook their heads. The latter was starving to meet any transgender person.

"You should call first, though," Vivian said.

"Last I knew she didn't have a phone working," Sheila said. "Like I said, she's a bit of a strange duck. She's usually home, or at least she always used to be. She works from her computer and doesn't get out much. You're all going to love her place though. When her grandma died, she left it for her in her will. It's really cool."

They got off the highway and traveled down several city roads. Sheila turned and went up a hill called Telegraph Road. Dean recognized the name.

The houses on the street were all Victorian in style, and several were painted interesting colors. Many looked old and weatherworn but still remarkable. Dean couldn't imagine a more appealing neighborhood, nor one more different than the cookie-cutter development he left behind in Syracuse.

They pulled into the driveway of a light purple house with flaking paint. The lawn hadn't been weeded and was home to all breed of wildflowers. Dean's heart was pounding both with nerves and excitement. He worried Teddy wouldn't remember him, and then realized he was being stupid. Sheila turned off the ignition. The old fashioned car parked outside the old fashioned house brought Dean far too much pleasure.

The four of them made their way up the dirt path and onto the rickety porch. Sheila knocked the lion-head door knocker. No response. Dean and Adrian instinctively hid behind Vivian like shy children. Sheila tried ringing the doorbell. They waited several minutes. Still no response and no sounds of movement inside.

"That's so strange," Sheila said. "She was always here when Jen and

I would stop by without notice. She's the quintessential homebody. Well, who knows. Maybe she's out. "

"Does she drive?" Dean asked, but then he remembered she had been waiting for a ride at the support group. He was hit with an awful feeling. "Do you guys smell that?" His heart beat was so sharp now that it was hurting his chest. All his senses felt heightened.

"I don't smell anything," Sheila said, "What kind of smell is it?"

"I smell it," Vivian said almost at a whisper. "Dean, I know what you're thinking, and I don't think you should do anything rash. It could be a bird or a raccoon or something."

"What are you two talking about?" Sheila said. "I don't smell anything. Will someone answer me? Dean, where are you going?"

He was running around back. The other three stayed on the porch.

"Adrian, let's go back to the car," Vivian said.

"What's going on?" Adrian asked.

"I don't know, honey. Let's just go wait in the car."

Dean fumbled with the rusty latch on the gate and pried it open. The plant life in the backyard was even wilder than the front. He struggled through the tall grass, pausing for a moment to look at a sundial. At the base, there was a small statue of an angel, once white but gone to decay. One wing was missing, and moss was covering most its body. He turned away and kept trudging through the overgrowth, swatting away flies.

He took the back steps two at a time, and found himself on a second landing. He gripped the handle of back door. It was unlocked. He opened the heavy wood one with its chipping white paint, and then, fingers trembling, a second screen door. The stench now was unbearable. He was convinced his nostrils, his clothes, his hair, his entire being was absorbing it forever; he was certain it would never leave his body or memory. He heaved over and puked on the carpet several times. When he straightened up, there were tears in his eyes. He felt faint, but he plugged his nose and tried his best to gain composure.

He didn't want to step inside, but he had to know for certain. He removed one of his shoes for a doorstop. He was scared that if it shut behind him he would never be able to escape, as if his life was suddenly a horror movie. The lights were off and the blinds were drawn, but he could still see. Stepping inside, he felt the dampness of the carpet through his sock. He shuddered and almost turned around, but he didn't have to look far. In the kitchen by the furnace, hanging from the wooden rafters of the ceiling, was his worst fear materialized.

*

Sheila looked out the front window of her car. "What on earth?"

Dean trudged towards them, staring at his feet and carrying a mossy, broken angel statue in his hands. He didn't say anything as he opened the door and got inside, his face emotionless. Adrian eyed the statue in his lap with dread.

"Oh my god!" Vivian exclaimed, covering her mouth and nose with her hand. "Oh my god, the smell." She began to cry. "Dean," she managed to whimper, "Why would you go in? What if the killer was still in there?"

Dean didn't respond. Adrian covered the bottom half of his face as well and rolled down his window with his other hand.

"Oh my God," Sheila said, "Oh my fucking god. Dean, is she...is she dead?"

"Yes," Dean said, but it was not his voice.

They sat parked in the driveway for a few moments in silence, petrified.

"We need to call an ambulance," Vivian whispered, "or something. Just in case. You know? Oh god, oh god..." She was shaking all over.

An eerie smile was twitching in the corner of Dean's lips. He nodded, pulled out his cell phone, and dialed three numbers. He waited as the woman on the other line spoke, and then he said, "Yes, hello. Well, that's just the thing, I found a dead body." Pause. "I'd imagine a day or two. Yeah, I knew her, her name's Teddy. Yes, Teddy. Uh huh. Strangulation, I'd say...no, not hung, *hanged*...Jesus Christ, lady. Will you make sure you write that down right? It's *hanged.* Honestly. Uh huh. Telegraph...Telegraph Road...one minute, hang on." He covered the receiver with his hand and leaned away, giggling uncontrollably.

*

"I can't help but wonder," Dean said, stopping mid-sentence for a sip of wine, "if I had seemed more concerned with Teddy's wellbeing and less self-absorbed in my letter, if that would have made a difference." He had finished telling Colin the story, sitting outside on the veranda by the pond.

Colin shook his head. "You really can't blame yourself, Dean. You had no idea she was suicidal."

"Yeah, I knew you'd say that." He looked off at the evening sky, taking another sip of wine. A bat zigzagged by the Grecian column on his left. He sighed. "I just keep remembering how at the support group, she asked if it was okay to feel those ways. And TJ tried to tell her to go see a therapist, but I said it was normal, and implied that she didn't need help."

"Dean, stop it," Colin said. He leaned in to refill his wine glass then leaned back against the chair, crossing his legs. "You were nothing but nice to her that night. In fact, I was really impressed."

"Really?"

"Yes. You were responsive to her when no one else was. She's been at every meeting I've attended, and no one's ever done anything but dismiss her."

Dean groaned, feeling worse. "I wasn't responding out of pity. I thought what she said was honest and astute."

"I did too," Colin said. "I was just too shy to speak up. I really related to what she said."

Dean looked at him, overwhelmed with affection. "You did?"

"Well, not entirely. Don't get the wrong impression. But with the thing she said about not seeing herself in the mirror. Well, I'd be lying if I said there weren't ever days when I felt like that."

With this memory, Dean hid his face in his hands for several seconds. When he emerged, he was crying.

"Colin," he said, shaking, "I need you to understand that I am not going to be any fun for awhile. When I'm not feeling crazy, I feel empty and depressed. If you want me to go home, I won't take any offense. But if I'm going to stay, well, be prepared. It sounds stupid, but I'm in a fragile state."

Colin reached out and touched Dean's hand. "Hey. It's alright. I want you to stay. I- well, I want to help. I want to make you feel better. You're my best friend."

Dean looked up, stunned. "I am?"

"Well, of course." Colin pulled back his hand. "I mean, Craig too. But I feel like you and I have a different bond. I think we get each other. I know you haven't told me everything about yourself, but that's okay. Someday I hope I can earn your trust. I can just tell you've been through a lot, and now this happened. I'm so sorry. I think you just handle everything so well."

Dean didn't know what to say. "I...wow. Really? That's, well, that's so... sweet. I care about you too. I mean, I would hope that was obvious. You mean the world to me." He fidgeted.

"I think we should just go ahead and be roommates next year," Colin went on. "I mean, sure we got drunk and something happened. But I don't think we should let that stop us. I'd miss having you around. I mean, I can't tell you how many times I've gotten drunk and kissed my guy friends. It's not a big deal."

Dean bit his lip. "Oh. Okay then. Yes. I'd love to live with you." If Colin didn't want him, that was that. He'd just have to move on.

Colin smiled. "Great. Hey, do you want to have a bonfire tonight? It might cheer you up."

*

An hour later they were at the ocean, further down than before, isolated by the dunes. Colin built a fire and dragged over a large log for them to sit upon, but Dean was lying in the sand anyway, stargazing.

Colin began to play his acoustic guitar. Dean normally found this annoying, but Colin was different. He was fascinated by his abilities. It wasn't annoying kum ba yah hippie strumming; it was comparable only to his dream of the ocean and the lyre. It was soothing yet pulsing, melancholic and celebratory. It had a soul.

"Did you write that?" Dean asked, sitting up.

"Yeah," Colin said, "Do you like it?"

"It's extraordinary. Why don't you play music like that with your band?"

"I don't know. It's personal. I only write songs like that when I'm coping with things." He placed his guitar in its case so he could tend to the fire. "If people didn't like it, I'd take it pretty hard."

"Well, that's selfish," Dean said. "The world needs to hear it."

Colin laughed, poking the flames with a stick. "You're so dramatic. You're only flattering me."

"No, I'm not. When do I ever flatter people?"

"Good point. Well, thank you. But you aren't one to talk."

"What do you mean?"

Colin sat back on the log, looking down at Dean. His thin face glowed orange in the firelight. "Well, you're a writer, aren't you? When's the last time you let anyone read something you wrote?"

"Let's see," Dean said, rolling his eyes back. "Voluntarily? Never. Craig got a hold of some of it, unfortunately."

"He showed me," Colin said. "I read it."

Dean cringed and covered his ears instinctively. "Don't tell me what you thought!"

Colin reached over and, with some effort, pried his hands from his head. "Come on! Listen, will you? I really loved it. Really. I think you've got a serious gift, man."

"You have to say that," Dean said, leaning back on his elbows in the sand. "...man."

"No I don't," Colin said. "But I mean it. I've been thinking we should collaborate and write some songs. No pressure, it would just be between us. But I have a feeling it would help us both as artists. Since the first day we've met, we've connected over our love of music. I have a feeling this could be incredible."

Dean felt a rush of euphoria so strong it nearly sent him flying into the dunes. Could it be? This had been what he wanted all along; the reason why he crossed his fingers when a boy named Mahr showed up at his door in the first place, as well as the source of his initial disdain for Craig. Collaborate? At last his life would begin!

"I would love that, you have no idea," Dean said, blushing and climbing up next to Colin on the log. "How do we start? When? Now? Here?"

Colin laughed. "Sure, why not? But I guess we should start by playing a cover. Get comfortable with one another."

"You do know I don't play any instruments," Dean said. "I really have little to contribute."

"Yes, I know, and don't be ridiculous. I want you to sing."

Dean gulped.

"What's your favorite song?" Colin asked, "Something by Morrissey or the Smiths? I probably know it. We can warm up that way."

Dean looked down at the sand, his face still hot. "Well, no, actually. I mean, yes. I have a lot of favorite songs. But my absolute favorite?"

"Yeah. Just choose one."

Although more excited than he'd been in years, Dean still felt a pang of sadness when he realized the song he wanted.

"Candy Says," he said softly, "By the Velvet Underground. That's one of my top three."

Colin gave him a look that Dean told himself only appeared to be smoldering with love.

"That," Colin said, "I know how to play very well."

"Unfortunately I'll ruin it," Dean mumbled.

"Stop it. Just give it a try," Colin said, and he started to play the opening bar, waiting for him to come in. Dean took a deep breath. He couldn't believe he was actually doing this; he never sang in front of people. But something about Colin and his guitar was magic. He felt like a completely different person, as if he had been possessed by a confident spirit. It was fate, it was love, it was the atmosphere, it was the wine; perhaps a combination of all those factors. Who knows, who cares. He was singing at last.

Candy says,
"I've come to hate my body
And all that it requires in this world..."

Colin gave him a reassuring smile as he completed the rest of the song, and they harmonized the "doo doo wops" at the end. They got stupider sounding each time, and Colin eventually started laughing and stopped playing.

Dean was mortified. "Was I awful? I was awful, I'm sorry."

Colin straightened up. "No Dean! No, the end was awkward, but that was my fault. You were great. You have a unique quality to your voice. I love it, I really mean it. I'd be lying to say you sound professional, but you sing with emotion, and that's what counts. I really think we were meant to do this. You give me goose bumps, I'm telling you! Look." He rolled up his plaid sleeve and held out his arm, but it was impossible to see in the dim light whether he was telling the truth.

Regardless, Dean fell backward off the log, grinning. "Thank you Jesus!" he shouted to the heavens, crossing himself and then sticking out his tongue, throwing sand over his shoulder.

Colin laughed and plopped down beside him. "You are so, so strange," he said, shaking his head.

He edged close and rested his head on Dean's chest. Dean held his breath, for fear the slightest rise of his lungs could alter the balance of the space-time continuum and send Colin spiraling away from him. He wanted to commit this moment to memory, exactly as it was. Take note, he told himself, closing his eyes: this was what it felt like.

*

Colin's shed was the only place on his family's property that didn't resemble a Victorian estate and wasn't full of objects Dean was certain he would break. That was where they made music. It was large and spacious, the walls covered in flyers and posters. It was where Colin and Craig always held band practice in high school.

They had an evening routine. They would sit on Colin's bed, facing one another, as Colin would play a song repeatedly on his acoustic guitar and Dean would hum under his breath, trying out different melodies. Eventually Dean would disappear and go for a long walk by himself, often to the beach, while Colin prepared dinner. When Dean got back, they would eat on the veranda, have a few glasses of wine, and then head out to the shed. Colin would plug in his electric guitar and a microphone, and would play a louder, more virile version of his song. Dean would sing whatever he came up with in his head on his walk. Somehow it worked flawlessly. Colin never ceased to be awed by Dean's seemingly effortless contribution. It was almost eerie how well they blended.

Dean was astounded by his own nerve. Something about Colin put him at ease in a way he never felt before. It was as if he had been given a jolt of electricity, and the franken-star was born. His bizarre, manic-depressive antics had finally found a channel. He was performing, as he always was, but now he was melodic. Now he was amplified. Now someone was listening.

Colin watched Dean stumbling in his chest binder and that same pair of Levis, yelping words and rolling around on the dirty floor like a rabid Morrissey impersonator. He wasn't sure what he felt. A part of him thought "Thank God no one will ever see us doing this." At other times, he would think back to the technically skilled but stoic Craig, singing into the microphone and not using it to whip and or mimic strangling himself. He envisioned the typical indie bullshit his band inspired him to churn out, pictured Maggie's face in a crowd of hipster robots, all naïve to his pain. At those moments, Colin couldn't help but think "It's a crime for people not to see this." If nothing else, Dean was monstrously passionate. He didn't know if he desired or feared him.

Inspiration flowed almost too easily. When the song was done but still reverberated in their ears, they would stare at each other in awe, both sweating and panting in heat of the summer, wondering, "Could that have possibly sounded as wonderful as I think it did?" Possibly it didn't, but to them it was perfection. Such is great romance: sun shone out of their behinds.

PART TWO

Dean put on his headphones and crossed the traffic to the parallel sidewalk. The summer heat and bright light was blinding, but he knew this strip by heart. Baptist and Catholic churches faced one another on either side of Main Street, as if it were a standoff. The cemetery loomed on the hill, speckled with miniature American flags, left over from Memorial Day. He scowled at cheap wedding dresses and caged parakeets, on sale behind glass. The sunlight wasn't the only thing intolerable; he hated North Syracuse. To pass the time, he amused himself with a fantasy of a meteor shower.

He couldn't hear anything over his music, so when he turned at the stoplight to look over his shoulder, he wasn't expecting to see someone right behind him. He jumped.

The boy was straddling a bicycle. The bike seat was lowered, making him look something like a circus clown on a tricycle. He looked about Dean's age, dressed in baggy jean shorts that hung off his slim hips, so that from behind his plaid-boxer ass was visible. He was wearing a white ribbed undershirt, and around his neck was a gold cross on a chain. His dark hair was cropped close to his head, buzzed on the sides like Dean's, with thin side burns that trailed down his jaw line. His skin was dark, orangey; the hue of someone naturally olive skinned who still feels the need to go tanning. His eyes were shockingly light blue, like a husky dog. He grinned with wicked self-assurance as they made eye contact.

Dean removed his headphones and hung them around his neck. This boy was type who had harassed him in high school. Clothing and tan aside, he was physically perfect. Dean already hated him. "Can I help you?" he asked, anticipating the worst.

The boy held out his large, orange hand. "The name's Alessio." He stressed the second syllable with a raise of his eyebrows.

Dean kept his arms at his side. "So?" Why did that name sound familiar?

"I noticed you were getting ice cream with Viviana," Alessio said.

"So?" Dean said again. "Wait, how do you know her?"

"I'm a family friend," he said, again with his stupid grin.

Dean felt sick looking at him, so he focused on the church steeple in the distance as he spoke. "Listen, if someone sent you to watch us or something, just fuck off, alright? I'm not up to anything. We were just eating ice cream."

Alessio shrugged. "Yeah, I believe you. You look like you're into *dudes*." He laughed, eyeing Dean's white Keds.

"And you look like you're into spray tans," Dean said. "So who sent you, A*less*io? Was it her dad?"

"Don't get ahead of yourself," Alessio said, his forehead shining with sweat. "I didn't say anything about being sent. I just don't think you should hang out with Viviana anymore, if you wanna play it safe."

Dean snorted. "Wow, do you enjoy being a stereotype? Tell Vivian's dad if this keeps up, I'm going to call the cops."

Alessio held up his hands in mock defense. "Nah man, you got it all wrong. I'm on your side. I'm just telling you it aint safe. If you keep seeing her, something bad might happen."

"This is ridiculous," Dean said, laughing. "I really am going to call the cops if you don't stop following me. I mean it." He showed him his cell phone.

"Well, it's a free country," Alessio said, leaning back and accentuating his pectoral muscles through his undershirt, "But don't you think that would be sorta dumb, given that Vivian's dad is a sheriff?"

Although Alessio slipped in an out of proper grammar and a suspicious accent, he did have a point. Besides, Dean wanted nothing to do with the police, given the ordeal following Teddy's death. He wondered if Alessio knew what he was under his clothes. He couldn't help but find it ironic. "A free country." How typical. He scowled. "Is that all you want? To tell me that if I keep hanging around Vivian something bad will happen?"

"Yeah basically," Alessio said, "And I wanted to let you know that I'll be watching you from now on. You know, 'cause I want to look out for you. You're my buddy." He flashed his teeth. He had abnormally pointy canines.

Dean rolled his eyes. "Whatever. Just leave me alone, alright? As you can see, Viv went home."

"I will, I will. I just want to talk a little more first. What's your name?"

Dean put back on his headphones and continued walking. He didn't look over his shoulder as he entered the suburban developments, so he wasn't sure if Alessio was still following him. After about three minutes, he glanced and saw he was gone. He felt something like disappointment. He wiped the sweat from his forehead and crossed the road. The orange sun was starting to set, partially obscured by run down houses and telephone wires.

As he came around the bend of the cul-de-sac, Dean saw his parents' car was in the driveway, meaning they were finally home. He jogged up the driveway entered through the front door, kicking off his shoes. His mom was in the kitchen pouring herself some wine.

"Hey mom," he said.

"Hi...Dean." She finally used this name, though she never seemed enthusiastic. "How was the rest of your trip?"

While in Long Island, he talked to her once on the phone but hadn't mentioned Teddy. He considered telling her now, but something stopped him. He was once almost *too* close with his mother. But for the past few years there had been unresolved tensions. He also decided against mentioning his encounter with Alessio. It would only worry her. "Oh, it was fine," he said. "How are you?"

She said she was fine, frowning at his stubble.

He smiled politely, pretending he hadn't noticed. "That's nice. Where's dad?"

"Upstairs watching the baseball game," she said.

Dean nodded, not surprised. He had the feeling he wasn't the only one keeping secrets. "Well I'm going up to my room to do some reading," he said, heading towards the stairs. The distance between the three people in the house, literally and figuratively, was depressing, and he wanted to forget.

"Oh, that reminds me," his mom said. "I forgot to mention, a package came for you while you were away. I put it in the closet, let me go get it."

Curious, Dean waited at the foot of the stairs. His mom returned with a brown package covered in tape, about the size of a shoe box. She handed it to him. It was light. There was no return address.

"Huh. Thanks." He sprinted up the stairs.

Up in his room, not bothering to turn on a light, he took a pocket knife from his desk drawer and ripped through the tape. After a minute or so, he finally got the packaging off. He undid the twine and removed the lid of the box, his hands trembling, as they did when preparing syringes.

Inside he found a battered paperback book. It was white with a brown sketch of what he first thought was a tree, but then realized was two faces. He gently lifted it from its shoe box coffin. In black font it said: LIVE OR DIE. ANNE SEXTON.

He opened it and a piece of paper fell out. It said, in scrawled handwriting:

Dean,

It was a pleasure consorting with you, Angel.
I leave this in your possession. Take Heed.

Love Teddy

Dean couldn't believe it. He held the book tightly against his breast, his eyes shut. He stood for several minutes in the semi-darkness, breathing heavily through his nose. He decidedly did not cry.

Instead he went over to the window, book still in hand. With some effort, he plied it open it and climbed cat-like out onto the roof. The sun had set below the pine trees, but there was still enough light streaking the sky to allow for reading. A mosquito landed on his hand, but he didn't notice. Thunder rolled in the distance, prophesizing a storm.

He opened the book delicately. The passage on the first page was a quotation.

*"With one long breath, caught and held
in his chest, he fought his sadness over
his solitary life. Don't cry, you idiot!
Live or die, but don't poison everything..."*

-Saul Bellow

The last stanza had been underlined passionately several times with a dull tipped pencil.

*

On the Fourth of July, Dean sat out on his porch, sipping coffee despite the late hour and his elevated nerves. Vivian and Adrian had just picked up by Vivian's friend Kristen. They had spent the evening with him, telling their parents they were visiting a cousin for the holiday. Dean had sat on the couch, feeling like a therapist as he listened to Adrian work through whether he was *gender-queer*. Adrian said he thought it was more politically charged, and so did his internet friends. Dean could do nothing but nod and offer more tea and toast. It was Adrian's life to wreck his own way.

Now, as he sat in the half-light frowning, Dean was antsy for a different reason. He was expecting Alessio to show up and punish him for hanging out with Vivian. Was he foolish to believe he was actually watching him? He checked his cell phone, lonely and frustrated. It was nearly nine o'clock. He pushed two on his speed dial. After three rings, Vivian picked up.

"Hi," she whispered. "What's up? I can't talk very loud, Dad's down the hall watching television."

"I was just wondering," Dean said, "did you mention once that you knew a guy named Alessio?"

Vivian sighed loudly. "Yeah, you never listen to me, do you? I told you, he went to Bishop Ludden. I've known him since I was little, actually. Our dads are best friends. Why do you ask?"

"No reason," Dean said. Why was he so interested anyway? It occurred to him to tell Vivian what was going on. Maybe she could put a stop to it. But some stupid pride made him keep it between him and the other man. Another even stupider part of him was enjoying the thrill.

"I think I know him from somewhere," Dean said, trying to sound causal and failing. "Could you by any chance tell me more about him?"

*

Dean waited outside on the porch until ten o'clock, downing several glasses of wine. He could hear fireworks in the distance. He was thinking of heading inside to evade the mosquitoes when he heard, then saw, a junky white pickup. It sped around the cul-de-sac and screeched to a halt by his mailbox. Out stepped Alessio. Dean stifled a smile as he made his way up the driveway. "Good evening."

"Yo," Alessio said, "What's good?" His breath smelled like beer.

"Why, what *isn't* good on such a beautiful summer evening?" Dean said.

Alessio stared at him, using one hand to hold up his jeans. "You're retarded."

"Ah yes, this coming from a guy who can't figure out his pants size," Dean said with a smirk.

Alessio pulled a cigarette out of his pocket and lit it.

"Nice touch," Dean said as he watched him take a drag.

"Whatever. Listen, I know that Viviana was here today, and her little sister too. I gave you fair warning."

"Why do you insist on calling Vivian by her full name?" Dean asked, sounding dreamy and curious, not hostile, "It's interesting. You've known her a long time, huh? She told me a great deal about you today."

Alessio's orange face turned red. "What? You told her? Big mistake, man."

"No, no, I wouldn't do that. I, uh, *aint* a tattletale, unlike some people" Dean said, wafting the cigarette smoke away from his nostrils. "But you did come up in conversation. It's interesting. You used to be a lot different, I heard. Very religious and studious. In fact you almost dated Vivian, I heard."

"So?" he said, accidentally dropping his cigarette and bending down to pick it up. "What of it?"

"Well, why didn't you?"

"What do you mean?" The accent was gone now.

"Why didn't you date her? She said you guys were really close back in the day. Don't you think she's hot?"

"You better watch it, I'm going to tell Uncle Joe everything you say," Alessio said, trying to keep the upper hand but clearly losing his cool. "He's super protective of his daughters. He doesn't care if you're a fag or not."

"Was it because of what she found on your laptop?" Dean asked. "Is that why you stopped talking to her and dropped out of school?"

"You better shut up you, you fucking cock-sucker," Alessio said, his eyes bulging and making him momentarily ugly.

"Well, you set yourself up for it. Ahem. It uh, takes one to know one, isn't that how the saying goes? Something about a pot calling a kettle black? You get my drift I'm sure."

"I'll kill you, you know," Alessio said quietly.

"No you won't," Dean said, examining his nails and secretly not so confident.

"So now *you're* threatening *me*?" Alessio said.

"Possibly," Dean said, getting to his feet. "Let me be clear. If you should tell *Uncle Joe* about what happened today, Vivian is going to tell your dad about your old internet habits."

Alessio took a step closer in a last attempt at intimidation. "Yeah?" He smelled like cheap cologne, beer and the faintest whiff of body odor.

"Yeah," Dean said. "But that's irrelevant, isn't it? Because if you want to know the truth, I don't think her dad sent you at all."

From his strained expression, it appeared Alessio was doing some quick thinking. Dean looked him up and down, feeling warm. "Could I have a cigarette?" he asked.

Alessio's expression remained the same. "Sure," he mumbled at last, fumbling in his pocket. Fingers trembling, he handed Dean a menthol cigarette and turned to leave. Dean stood on the step, examining it with disappointment. Alessio paused when he reached the truck, scratching his head and looking distressed.

"Forgetting something?" Dean asked with feigned innocence, tucking the unlit cigarette behind his ear. Similar to the night when he sang for Colin, he felt possessed by a spirit of confidence. He was not himself; that much was clear.

Alessio took another drag of his cigarette, regaining a shadow of his cocky composure. He pulled a flask out of his enormous pocket and took a swig, gripping the rearview mirror to steady himself. "Come on," he said, wiping his mouth. "I won't offer again."

*

"Has it ever occurred to you that you might have an anxiety disorder?" my newest shrink asked me the other day.

Like I said, I was too tired to argue with my mother, so I ended up going to therapy. This guy works out of his apartment. Apparently he let his license expire, my mom said. That inspires confidence. She assured me she told him I'm transgender, and he didn't have an issue with it. He told her he wouldn't try to change my mind. How magnanimous!

To answer his question, of course an anxiety disorder has occurred to me. I've pondered every disorder on my hypochondriac search to figure out what is wrong with me. He was asking because my mom told him I freaked out over blood work.

"It sounds to me like you had a panic attack," he said. Honestly, the guy had a name, but it escapes me. He was chubby and old and had a beard. He kind of looked like Ernest Hemingway. Let's call him Ernest.

"Could be," I said, my eyes lingering on a frightening troll statue he had by the window.

"Do you experience those often?" Ernest asked.

I thought for a minute. "Only when under a considerable amount of stress," I said.

"And when do you feel stress?"

"When I have to deal with doctors. Or checkout clerks. Or teachers, or cops, or people's parents. Or when I'm meeting new people. Or seeing old friends, or often current friends. Or family members. Or neighbors. Or when I'm with romantic partners."

A cluster of fragments, but I never claimed to be eloquent. I especially regretted my unfortunate phrasing on the last one. I'd never had a "romantic partner." Of course, that was what Ernest chose to zero in on. A discussion about check-out clerks would prove more illuminating, if you ask me.

"Romantic partners cause you anxiety?" he asked. "So would you say you have a fear of intimacy?"

"Doesn't everyone?"

"No," Ernest said.

"Huh," I said. "Well, that's silly of everyone."

Ernest wrote something down on his steno pad. "When was the last time you had sex?" he asked.

I hardly felt this was his business, but said, "Define sex." This would prove a predictable mistake.

"When was the last time someone touched your vagina?" he said.

I actually sputtered.

"Never mind then," Ernest said. "When was the last time *you* touched a woman sexually?"

I felt very awkward, but tried to cooperate. "Well, let's see. It must have been nearly seven or eight years ago. I'm not very experienced when it comes to women. Or men. Or others."

Ernest raised his bushy eyebrows. "You've had sexual intercourse with men?"

"Not intercourse," I said quickly. "I was, uh, intimate with a boy once, in his car. Last summer." Images filled my head of Alessio and a smooth leather passenger seat.

"So you gave him head?" Ernest asked.

I blushed. Granted I'm prude, but this still seemed awfully blunt. Was he supposed to be talking to me this way? "In a manner of speaking."

"And did he know you were a transgender?" There was something accusatory in Ernest's tone that I didn't appreciate.

"No," I said. "I expect that's why I was able to do it." We were also trashed, but I decided against mentioning that.

"So he was a homosexual. How would he have reacted if he discovered your breasts or your vagina?" Ernest asked, looking right at me.

I blushed and fidgeted. I felt like he could see through my clothing. "Uh... negatively?"

It wasn't as if the thought hadn't occurred to me. Who knows, maybe it would have comforted him to know I was somewhat female. Most likely not. You hear about this sort of thing happening with transgender women, but never transgender men, so I'm not sure how it would have gone over. At the time I fully expected a violent reaction if discovered, and that was most of the fun. I guess I do get a sick thrill from tricking people. Go figure.

"Do you experience more sexual pleasure from men or from women?" Ernest asked.

"I really couldn't say."

"Can you feel arousal? In your vagina?"

That wasn't even proper *anatomically*. The room felt hot, or rather, I did. I don't remember how I answered the rest of the questions. I imagine I must have stammered awkward responses, but I was in a nervous daze and they were coming at me too fast.

"At what age did you discover your genitalia? Are you upset that you'll never have a penis? When you masturbate, do you imagine you ejaculate?"

"I have to go," I said. I handed him the two undeserved twenty dollar bills my mom told me to give him and rushed for the door.

I hurried down the dimly lit hall and caught the elevator. I pressed the button for the first floor and leaned against the wall, burying my face in my hands and breathing heavily. That panic attack theory seemed more valid by the second. This solidified my decision- I'd just have to keep swallowing my problems, no matter how poisonous. There was no way in hell I'd go back to a psychiatrist. Talk about a nosey Nancy.

*

Vivian's friend Kristen parked in the lot outside of Dean's dorm building. Since Dean had several bags and boxes, the two girls offered to help him before they headed next door to St. Matthews. They took a load up the elevator while Dean retrieved his key from the RA.

A few minutes later he met them in the hall outside of his room.

"Glad to be back?" Vivian asked, struggling with a box.

"You have no idea," Dean said. Since the night with Alessio, he had been counting the days, desperate for academic distractions. He unlocked the door and took the box from Vivian, holding the door open with his back, while the other two carried in the first round of luggage. From the contents of the room, it appeared Colin had been there awhile.

"Oh, sorry guys," he heard Kristen say.

"No, no it's alright," Colin said.

Confused, Dean let the door close behind Kristen and stepped inside and around the corner. Colin and Maggie were on the left side of the room, lying in bed, their limbs entwined. His fingertips prickled with invisible needles of shock, as if he had almost fallen off a ledge.

"Hey Dean!" Maggie said, buttoning up her blouse. She was tan and covered in freckles.

Colin was shirtless. He smiled too, as if there were no reason in the world why he shouldn't. "Hey pal."

Dean painfully forced the muscles in his face to look friendly. "Hey you guys. How was your summer Maggie?"

She sat up, smiling even wider. "Oh, it was great! I worked at a summer camp for little kids. I was the art teacher. It was so cute and fun."

Dean wondered if he was imagining it, or if Maggie seemed bubblier. "Oh, that's cool. How about you, Colin? What did you do the rest of the summer?" He turned to him with sad eyes, wondering if he noticed at all.

"Well, after you left I spent some time alone in Long Island," Colin said, stretching his arms. "Then I had to drive down to the city in early August to run some errands. After that I ended up going to Maggie's and staying with her family in Connecticut."

"He helped out at the camp," Maggie said, rubbing Colin's back. "He's really got a way with kids. He's going to make a great father."

Dean felt a little sick and considered ducking into the bathroom. He steadied himself on his desk. "Ah. That's nice."

"Dean?" Vivian said. "Want us to get the other bags?"

Dean turned, startled. For a moment he forgot she and Kristen were there. "Oh, yes, right," Dean said. "Should be just one more load, be right back."

"It was nice meeting you both," Kristen said waving.

As soon as the door was shut, Dean's face fell and he kicked at the wall in frustration. It hardly made a sound, but Vivian still noticed.

She stepped over and rubbed his shoulder. "Don't worry about it, Dean," she whispered as Kristen walked ahead. "Remember, I'm not far away if you need anything, ever. And we're seeing each other every weekend. I'll make sure of it."

Dean cringed, brushing off her hand. "Yeah, thanks, but I'm fine."

*

Alone again, Dean decided to go for a walk. All over campus there were signs of move-in day. Parents lugged boxes up the steps, and eager freshmen were everywhere. Watching them, Dean wondered if he would feel attached to the school, had he gone there from the start.

He walked through a pile of leaves, purposefully scattering them on the pavement. He was angry. Colin had apparently gotten back with Maggie, without so much as giving him warning. He half expected this would happen; he just hoped he would be wrong. How many more times this year would he have to walk in on those two? He'd never be able to escape it.

"Hey, Jimmy!"

Dean heard someone shouting over his music and ignored it.

"Yo! James Dean!"

This time he turned. It was the kid from the support group in Long Island, with the shaved head and tattoos.

"Oh," Dean said, stopping and pausing his CD player. "You."

"Hey," the kid said, doubling over to catch his breath. "I thought I saw you and I ran over. I could see your hair from way over there." He pointed across the quad.

TJ, that was his name. Dean was relieved.

"Yes, my hair works something like flag," he mumbled. "You go here now?"

"Yeah, it was a last minute decision," TJ said. "I hadn't planned to go to college, but the job I had planned fell through. But no biggy, I'm really excited to be here. There is such a thriving queer community on this campus."

"Oh," said Dean, sniffing the air, "is there?"

TJ laughed. "You're so funny Dean. Man, I've really wanted to talk to you all summer! I messaged Colin and let him know I was coming, but I couldn't find you anywhere on Facebook."

"Oh, I don't have one of those," Dean said.

"Really? How do you communicate with people?"

"I generally don't," Dean said. He yawned.

"Are you the kind of guy who uses snail mail?"

"Well, not literal snails. But yes, sometimes." He thought of Teddy and wished he still had a reason.

"Well, you should get a Facebook!" TJ said. "I'm having parties this year, and you wouldn't want to miss an invite. No one wants to miss out on free booze."

"Hm," Dean said, unable to hold off his sneer any longer. "Where are you living then?" he asked to distract himself, not actually interested.

"An apartment in Benson."

"Ah," Dean said, not sure where that was. He barely even remembered where Maggie's apartment was, which was sad given how small the campus was.

"It's a good place," TJ continued. "I wanted to see if you and Colin wanted to live there, but he said you guys were all set. But yeah, it's a gender neutral apartment and it's pretty sweet. You should really come over sometime. Two of my room mates are freshmen trans guys, I'm sure they'd love to meet you."

Dean nodded politely and managed an almost convincing, "Cool."

TJ adjusted his baseball cap, nodding as well. "Word. Anyway, I gotta meet some people for dinner at the dining hall. You should come!"

"That's okay, I already ate," Dean lied, turning his back. "See you." He put back on his headphones and headed towards the woods, his stomach aching with hunger.

*

Colin was sitting up in bed, playing his unplugged guitar and watching the television on mute. He heard the sound of the key in the door, and gazed over as Dean entered. "Hey," he said, smiling. "About time! Where were you all evening?"

Dean sat down on his old bed, still lacking sheets. "Oh, you know." He had walked for hours in the forest, and then sat behind the dorm building, waiting to see Maggie leave.

"So how are you?" Colin asked. "How was the rest of the summer?"

"Boring," Dean said. "So you got back with Maggie." It wasn't a question.

"Ah. Yeah. I went to visit her near the end of August," Colin said. "We ended up working it out. I don't know. It's good. I missed her."

Dean avoided his eyes. "*Right*." He picked at a hole in the mattress, wrapping a thread around the tip of his finger.

Colin's lip curled. "Are you annoyed with me or something?"

"No," Dean lied. "Just surprised is all. I mean, you seemed pretty positive you wouldn't get back together." He wished he could just shut himself up. His tone was irritating.

"Well, I was upset she kissed you back then," Colin said. "But we talked about it a lot. Turns out she really didn't have feelings for you. She was just drunk."

"I could have told you that," Dean muttered.

"Yeah, I know... But hey, you and I kissed over the summer, right?" Colin lowered his voice. "So it's even. No big deal, it's all in the past. Just some random, drunken kisses between friends." Again with his stupid smile.

Dean scoffed. "Well, the difference is, I didn't *want* to kiss Maggie. She just planted one on me. And I'd say you and I did a little more than just kiss."

Colin blushed, his smile faltering. "Did we? I don't remember."

Dean rolled his eyes and laughed. "You don't remember that we made out? You don't remember touching one another? For hours? In your bed?"

Colin looked panicked, like he wanted to make Dean lower his voice.

"To be honest, I really don't," he said, almost whispering. "I was pretty drunk, if you recall."

"Convenient," Dean mumbled.

"What's that supposed to mean?" Colin said.

"Nothing," Dean said, "Just, that I was drunk, but I still remember."

Colin rolled his eyes. "So you think I'm lying? I honestly don't remember."

"Right. So you've forgotten how you practically begged-"

"If you were so hung up on it," Colin said loudly, "why didn't you say something before? Why did you act like everything was fine when you came to stay with me?"

"It *was* fine," Dean said. "We were making music. It was great, it was all I wanted." He realized Colin had a point. "I mean, yeah. It's still fine. I'm not saying you shouldn't date Maggie. I'm just surprised is all."

"Well, it's my business," Colin said. "You don't have any right to be upset. It's not like you and I were together or anything." He smirked rudely.

"I didn't think we were," Dean said, submitting. "I'm sorry."

"I'm not gay, Dean," Colin said.

"I'm not either," Dean said, but it sounded stupid to him now. He felt like he might cry, which would only serve to embarrass him further. "I'm going for another walk," he said, and he hurried out the door without looking up, aware how ridiculous he must seem.

Colin sighed. He stared out the window, thinking. After a few minutes he shook his head and went back to playing his guitar.

*

"You look thinner," Vivian said.

Dean shrugged. "Maybe I am." He stared out the café window, in his own world. Outside it was pouring rain. It was mid-afternoon, but dark. The campus was beginning to flood.

Vivian frowned, taking a sip of her chai. Something wasn't right with Dean. Granted he was never right, but in the past he'd been willing to vent. Lately, he seemed like he only wanted to sleep. She hated to admit it, but he wasn't much fun to be around. It seemed he'd lost his sense of perspective. Or worse, humor.

"Can I buy you something?" she asked. She had a habit of offering money and gifts when she felt helpless.

Dean shook his head. "No. I'm fine." He continued to stare off into space. Vivian noticed his clothes were wrinkled and his hair unkempt. Something had to be wrong if he wasn't keeping up his appearance.

"Dean, I'm sorry, but are you alright? You seem to be taking this really hard. I mean, I know you really liked him, but it will be okay. You do know it will be okay, don't you?"

Dean shrugged. "Yeah. Of course I know that." He clenched his jaw, looking at his reflection in the window. His eyes and cheek bones looked sunken in and it pleased him. "I think," he said, startling Vivian, "that I was using my feelings for Colin as a distraction."

Vivian was relieved. "Yeah? A distraction from what?"

"Reality," he said, waving his hand listlessly. "The truth is I'm meant to be alone." He went back to staring at his reflection.

Vivian raised an eyebrow. "Dean, I adore you, but sometimes you're a tad dramatic."

He scowled. "Eh, I was half kidding. Fuck off."

"Excuse me?"

"Oh, so *you're* offended now?" he said, crossing his arms. "When you were the one who called me dramatic?"

"I was just kidding," Vivian said. "Well, no, I wasn't. You're being dreadful, snap out of it. It's been over a month. I mean, it's fine if you're sad, but will you at least talk to me about it?"

"No," Dean said. "You'll just call me dramatic. I don't even want to see you. I don't want to see anyone."

Vivian made an upset-laughter noise. "Well fine. It's not like I don't have other things to do than watch you mope."

Dean sighed. "You know what, forget it. No one understands what I'm going through. You didn't find Teddy's body. You don't have to think about these things all the time. Nothing bad has ever happened to you." He automatically wished he hadn't said that.

She shook her head. "Right. Nothing bad ever happened to me. Bah, I don't even know who you are anymore."

"No, you don't," he said quietly. "No one does."

She laughed. "Are you serious right now? Listen to yourself, Dean. How old are you again?"

He glared at her. Though unrelated, the words slipped out. "Yeah? Well, remember how I asked you about that kid Alessio? You know why? Because over the summer, we fucked."

Vivian blinked several times, her face flushed. Her expression suggested that she was quickly assessing whether this was even possible. Then, in the middle of the crowded café, she slapped Dean hard across the face.

*

Outside, Dean's face was stinging as he apologized over and over to Vivian.

"Leave me alone," she said, storming ahead of him under her umbrella, not caring that he was getting soaked in the down pour.

"Viv, please. I'm really sorry. I was being awful, I don't know what got into me."

"How did you even meet him?" she demanded, turning to face him as they reached the bus stop. "How?"

Dean looked at the ground. "Well. I didn't want to tell you before. He lives near me. He followed me on his bike that one day after we got ice cream and threatened me. And then after that he was always riding by my house, watching."

Vivian looked shocked. "He threatened you?"

"Yeah. He said something bad would happen if I hung out with you again."

"And you didn't tell me about this because...? "

Dean shrugged. "I'm not really sure."

"Right, why would you? And how on earth did this turn sexual?"

Dean blushed. "Well, that's really a good question. I had been drinking. Things got carried away..."

Vivian bit her lower lip, looking stressed. "So he threatened you, and you thought it would be smart to go off and have sex with him. Do you realize how risky that was? I mean, he's not as tough as he acts, but still. I would think you'd know better, given who you are."

"He didn't know I was transgender, if that's what you're implying," Dean mumbled.

"That's even worse then! What if he found out? Oh god, I just remembered his father has guns!"

"Well it wasn't like I planned it," Dean said. "Like anybody, I can get caught in the heat of the moment. I'm only human."

"You never did stuff like this before. You were always rational when it came to these matters."

"Well that's because no one ever wanted me!" Dean blushed.

Vivian raised her eyebrows. "So you'll have sex with any jerk who will take you? Is that what you're saying?"

Dean sighed. "No. I don't know. I was drunk, I was curious."

"Well great," Vivian said, "Next time you feel the urge to experiment, please don't do it with a guy who broke my heart, alright?" She turned away and stared at the stone wall behind the bus stop.

Dean sighed. "I'm really sorry Viv. I never intended to tell you."

"That's worse!" Vivian said, starting to cry. "You're practically my best friend. I tell you everything, and you were going to hide this huge secret from me? "

"I'm sorry..."

The bus was pulling up, the headlights cutting through the rain.

Dean panicked. "Viv, please stay longer. I'll make it up to you. I'm really sorry."

Vivian wiped away her tears with the back of her hand. "No. I don't want you in my life anymore."

She got on the bus, leaving Dean standing alone. After a few moments, he walked back to his dorm, the rain soaking his clothing and plastering his hair to his forehead.

Dean found Maggie and Colin cuddling in the dark, watching a movie. He suppressed a groan and headed straight for the bathroom, without saying hello.

He locked the door, turned on the shower, and stripped naked. He stared at his torso in the mirror while the hot water ran and steamed up the room. Vivian was right: he was rapidly losing weight. His stomach concaved slightly, emphasizing the muscles that, ironically, he only knew to be called *penis lines*. His hipbones and ribs protruded, and yet, no matter how much fat he might burn, nothing could be done about his chest. Squinting his eyes, he could almost tell what he would look like, had he not endured female puberty. He looked down at the dark hair trailing from his pubic area to his stomach and spreading over the two raised lumps of his chest. He figured the unfortunate combination of male and female secondary sex characteristics could be nothing but repulsive, to anyone of any orientation.

He stepped into the shower and closed his eyes, letting the water rush over his face and slick back his hair. He felt sick with himself, inside and out. He wished someone would slap him again.

Ten minutes later, he stepped out into the dorm room, wearing boxers and a black tee shirt, his chest already tightly bound beneath. He tossed his dirty clothes in the hamper and crawled into his bed, although it was still afternoon. Lying on his side, he was relieved to see Maggie was gone. Colin was lying on his stomach, reading a schoolbook.

"Hey," Dean said, his voice croaking.

Colin looked up. "Hey. How was Vivian?"

"Bad. We go in a fight," Dean said, still lying on his side. His eyes burned. He told himself it was shampoo.

Colin clucked his tongue. "That's too bad. I'm sure it won't last though." He paused. "Are you in a bad mood then? Can I talk to you about something?"

"Oh, no, go ahead," Dean said. His hair was soaking the pillow.

"Okay," Colin said. "Well, hypothetically, if someone offered you a big opportunity- like, a chance to be famous over night, would you trust them? And would you take the offer?"

Dean stuck his tongue out the corner of his mouth, thinking. "No, I wouldn't trust them," he said. "But yes, I'd take the offer. I mean, it's that or prison."

"Huh?"

"Never mind. But yeah, I'd definitely take the offer. Why do you ask?"

Colin hesitated. "Well...because I've sort of been given that chance."

Dean raised his eyebrows. "Really? How so? You mean with your band?"

"Yes," Colin said.

"Seriously? What happened?"

"Remember that manager I told you about? Well, I knew it was a big deal that he wanted to help us. But I hadn't realized *how* big of a deal, until I met with him in August. I mean, he thinks Owl Eyes could be really popular."

Dean looked up. "Really?"

"Yeah. But there are two decisions I need to make. One, do I want to sign to a record company. We've got offers. I mean, the one I'm thinking of going with is like a *huge* deal. It's got like, Jenny Lewis, Antony and the Johnsons and Belle and Sebastian all signed to it. It's in London, so it's kind of irrational, but-"

"Wait a minute, wait a minute," Dean said. "Are you talking about Rough Trade Records?"

"Yeah, you've heard of it?"

Dean fell backwards on his bed laughing. "Of course I've heard of it! Are you messing with me?"

Colin laughed. "No, of course not! Why would I? I know, it's a huge deal right?"

Dean laughed and laughed. He hadn't realized how much he missed it. He looked a little crazy, kicking his legs in the air. Colin rubbed his arm, waiting for him to stop.

Dean wiped tears from his eyes. "Wow. You have to say yes."

"Well, I'm really taking my time and thinking it over," Colin said. "I promised Cooper I'd have a decision by November. But I've still got to talk to the other guys."

"You mean you haven't even told Craig?"

"No," Colin said. "I guess that's sort of awful."

Dean didn't say anything.

"But the reason I've been so secretive," Colin said, "is because Cooper recommended something else to me. Something really personal. I can't for the life of me decide whether or not it's a good idea."

"Yeah? What?" Dean propped up his head on his hands and lay on his stomach, his ankles crossed above him.

"Well, he thinks it would help to be more upfront about being transgender. He says it's *in*." Colin made quotation marks with his fingers. "He said it could make all the difference between being just another guitarist and being important. And I just don't know how I feel about that. First of all, I can't help but wonder if he's full of shit. Since when is transgender *in*? And like I've said to you before, I want to be known for my artistic merits, not my identity. But maybe that isn't enough these days. And Cooper seems to think I could do a lot of good for the community."

"What community?" Dean said.

"The transgender one."

"Does that exist then? I thought we were all isolated maniacs."

Colin frowned. Sometimes Dean made him uncomfortable. "Well, regardless. He thinks it would do good."

"Eh, bullshit," Dean said. "He thinks it could make him money. I'm not saying don't do it. But don't kid yourself with the crap about becoming a transgender ambassador. Pop music isn't going to destroy the gender binary, or whatever it is we're supposed to want. Of course it probably has a better shot than most things."

Colin wanted to say it wasn't pop music it was *indie* music, but he anticipated Dean making a snotty remark and he wasn't in the mood. "So what would you do?" he repeated. He knew Dean had little knowledge of the music industry, but he craved his opinions.

"Me?" Dean said. "I mean, if I had the success you already have- heck, if I had *one* gig in the city, well… I'd probably die of shyness, first off. You know better than me, clearly. Trust your instincts. My only advice would be, if you do play up the transgender thing, do it with originality. No rainbows or tacky badges, if only for my sake. I don't want them thinking we're *all* philanthropists. I've got a reputation to uphold." He smirked.

Colin frowned. "Are you okay?"

"What? Me?"

"Yeah," Colin said, "I feel bad. I was mean to you."

"What are you talking about? When?"

"The first day back, in September…when you found out I was back with Maggie. I was pretty mean, and I never apologized."

Dean shrugged. "Oh, that. Well, I'm over it now."

They both knew this wasn't close to the truth.

"Well, I just wanted to say sorry," Colin said. "And I mean, I've been thinking. And it's not that I'm *not* gay. I mean, I'm not. Well, like you've said to Maggie, trans men aren't really accepted in the gay-guy community…"

Dean wondered on what plane all these communities existed.

Colin misunderstood his frown. "Or maybe they are, I dunno. But my point is, hanging out with you has opened me up to things. I'd be lying to say I'm not a little curious about men, occasionally. And I didn't mean to make it seem like I was judging you for being gay-" Dean opened his mouth to protest but Colin kept going, "-or whatever it is you are. Bisexual, asexual, I don't know."

"Just sexual," Dean said. "Once in a blue moon."

Colin smiled. "Right, blue moons, I'll remember that. God Dean, you're so weird." It was, as in the past, a term of endearment.

Dean bit his lip, his eyes smiling. "Not as weird as you'd think," he said. "I'm pretty run of the mill, underneath my outlandishly flamboyant exterior."

"Of course," Colin said. "But are you sure you're alright?"

"Yeah, I'm feeling much better," Dean said, and it was true. This was the first time he felt close to Colin since July. "I mean, I hope you're okay too," he said. "Don't stress the music stuff. No matter what you decide, you're doing what you love, right? And best of all, you won't have a normal job when you grow up. That's what matters."

Colin smiled. "True. But hey, since we're both a little under the weather, you want to watch a movie?"

"Sure, why not?" Dean said. "Got anything in mind?"

"Well," Colin said, "this is probably really gay. But when I was a kid, whenever I was sad or stressed, I liked to watch *The Sound of Music*."

"Oh my god!" Dean said. "I'm not even kidding, I did the same thing. We had identical childhoods. Essentialism wins!" He gave a deadpan stare. "Unless musicals *made* us this way."

"Uh, sure," Colin said. "But anyway, would you want to watch it?"

"Of course I want to watch it!" Dean crouched on all fours and leapt in the air, doing a little twirl. He nearly bounced off the bed when he landed.

Colin laughed. "Fuckin' basket case... But yeah, you should come lay in my bed, because you'll have trouble seeing the television from over there."

Dean was sure he could see the television fine, but he wasn't about to argue. He crossed over to the other side of the room and crawled in the bed while Colin put in the DVD.

"Mind if I take the inside?" Colin said, returning. Dean got up and let him in, trembling a little.

"Thanks," Colin mumbled, "I like leaning against the wall."

They lay on top of the comforter, their bodies almost touching. Dean hardly breathed as he reveled in the tension.

The beginning of the movie was the long Overture but neither of them complained.

"You know," Dean said softly, "Teddy liked this movie too. She said so, in a letter. We joked about it. I really want to start a stereotype that all transgender people have a weird attachment to this movie, just for kicks."

Colin laughed, but then said, seriously, "How are you holding up with all that?"

"Well, I don't know," Dean said. "It's hard. I mean, it doesn't directly affect me. She wasn't family, and it's not like I even knew her that well. But it's still hard for some reason."

"Well, yeah," Colin said. "What you went through was really traumatic. Don't downplay that."

Dean sighed, uncomfortable. "Well, let's just watch the movie. The Vontrapp family can fix everything. Even if in real life Maria was awful and basically forced the kids to sing. It's a dreadful story, actually, let's not talk about it. Art is always preferable to life, don't you find?"

"Sure," Colin said. He wrapped his arm around Dean and, despite that he was smaller, became a proverbial big spoon. Shocked, Dean tried not to seize up from nerves. He didn't want to send the message that this rare contact was unwanted. He took a deep breath and relaxed his muscles. Slowly, the experience became more pleasurable.

"I missed you," Colin whispered, snuggling his face in Dean's hair.

Dean smiled at the television. "Really?"

Colin kissed the back of his neck in response and pulled him closer. Dean made a whimpering noise, and Colin laughed gently, reaching under his shirt and feeling the muscles his stomach. His breathing grew labored as his hands traveled over Dean's ribcage and back down the band of his boxers. They were locking mouths by the time Maria started to sing about the infamous hills and their consuming music.

*

The morning of Halloween, Dean once again accompanied Colin and Maggie to the dining hall. They were eating breakfast with TJ and the transgender freshmen before heading to their Friday classes. Dean was less than pleased with this daily routine, but it was clear Colin wanted to buddy up with the new guys. He hoped his good behavior would eventually pay off. Since their movie night, Colin hadn't made eye contact with him, let alone finished what he started.

Dean glared at who he supposed were his new friends, taking dainty spoonfuls of vanilla yogurt. The chubbier, blonde boy was named Mitch. He had a round, jowly face and unflattering square glasses. He always wore checkered shirts and an orange *Hooters* baseball cap, explaining it was ironic. Dean didn't really see how, but didn't comment. The other boy, Jaydyn, had a dark, floppy mohawk that he usually failed to gel. Unlike his friends, he wasn't on testosterone, but like Dean, always seemed angry. He wore a black jacket with patches and safety pins, no matter how warm the weather. Mitch's hat and Jay's jacket were their distinguishing features.

"You're coming to our party tonight, right?" TJ asked Dean, a piece of syrupy sausage on his fork. He had been on hormones a few months, and his voice sounded pubescent and hoarse. Dean glared and spoke to the meat, not TJ's increasingly pimpled face. "Maybe."

"No maybes," Maggie said, rolling her eyes. "You have to go. It's Halloween, Dean." The rhyme rang unpleasantly.

"I said maybe," Dean repeated, as if this were generous. He was in a mood. Colin stayed over at Maggie's place the previous, leaving him to sit at home imagining unpleasant scenes. He was beginning to resent her.

"Noncommittal as usual," Mitch said, shaking his head.

Dean scowled. They weren't good enough friends for Mitch to insult him so freely. "Well, sorry if a night of beer pong and listening to Beyonce on repeat doesn't appeal to me," he said. This was what he endured the one time he went to their apartment, where he was ordered repeatedly by strangers to "put his hands up" and informed that if he "liked" a vague, unnamed "it" then he should have "put a ring" on the aforementioned mystery object.

"Oh come on, you love it," TJ said.

"I do?"

"Yes!"

"Hm. Does love always feel this nauseating?"

"Dean," Colin said in a low voice. "Come on, man."

Dean blushed. "I'm sorry. Sometimes my humor is in poor taste. Thank you for inviting me."

TJ shrugged.

"No ones making you go," Jay grumbled.

Dean stared at his oatmeal, embarrassed. He missed Vivian. How did he get on without her all those years? She had to be the only person on the planet who didn't take offense to his abrasive attempts at conversation. On the contrary, she made him feel eloquent, like they were characters in an Oscar Wilde play.

(*Lady Vivian: I simply do not understand! How can these philistines continually overlook your cleverness?*

Lord Dean: My dear Lady Vivian, it's as I always say- to disagree with queer college students is the first requisite of sanity!)

In reality, he was not at all clever, just whiney and rude and-

"-pessimistic, for the most part." Maggie said. Dean missed the first half of her sentence. "I've been trying to work on it," she said. "The past summer really helped. And Colin, of course, since he's the best boyfriend in the world." She beamed and touched his hand.

Colin smiled briefly without showing his teeth. Dean stuffed his mouth with oatmeal, not trusting himself.

"Now Dean, you strike me as a classic pessimist," Mitch said.

Really, what was it with this kid? Dean sniffed the air haughtily. He caught an unpleasant whiff of TJ's sausage. "No I'm not. To be a pessimist, I'd have to care enough to even have a world view."

"No, it just means you're emo all the time," Mitch said. "Like, what would you say if I showed you this glass?" He held up his somewhat see through red plastic cup of milk. "Is it half empty or half full?"

"That doesn't dignify a response."

"Just play along!"

"Never."

"Oh, come on, just pick one!" Mitch whined. "Which would you say?"

"I would say who cares about glasses. We're all going to die." Dean struggled to keep a straight face. No one else seemed to have difficulty.

"Sounds pessimistic to me," Jay said. "Let's talk about something else already."

"You didn't let me finish," Dean said. "What I was going to say is, who cares about glasses. We're all going to die- so let us immediately seize the day!"

No one laughed. Vivian would have, Dean thought as he stared at his hands. She always managed a genuine smile for even his worst quips.

Dean listened to the rest of the breakfast conversation, holding back his urge to appear impressive and simultaneously alienate others. Mitch went back to the kitchen for more food. TJ and Colin discussed some lesbian television show that had offended the (purported) transgender community. Maggie talked to Jaydyn about her experiences as a *sofa*. She apparently now identified as furniture, Dean thought with a smirk. It was truly a slippery slope. He fiddled with the gold brooch on his sweater, silently mocking everyone but Colin in his head.

*

Hours later, Dean stood against the wall of the cramped apartment, watching strangers dance. On such a night, he had to be the only sober individual within a five mile radius, and it showed. He folded his arms, aware he must appear a stereotype. Or at least he assumed he would, if anyone noticed him at all. The room was dark and hazy with smoke, blurring everyone's identity. Watching two boys dance, Dean wondered if Craig had arrived on campus. Maybe he'd want to sneak off and listen to more Patti Smith. Anything was better that this scene.

Colin and Maggie burst into the room, arms around one another. Dean scowled and focused his eyes elsewhere as they grooved to the hip-hop beat. He considered sitting on the couch, but two girls beat him to it. To pass time, he made lists in his head of things in the room that disgusted him.

"PBR can, vomit stain, dead cockroach, strobe light, Madonna poster, couples kissing, boy in fashion scarf..." He narrowed his pale eyes at no one in particular.

"Hey Dean!" It was zombie TJ, shouting to be heard over the music. He had a girl with him. She was wearing a low cut dress and her hair was styled in a faux-hawk. She was wearing Halloween make-up as well, but only enough to appear a sexy-zombie. She was hanging off TJ's arm, drunk and apparently pleased about something.

"So are there perks of being a wallflower?" TJ asked, leaning against the wall and imitating Dean's pose.

Dean glared, and the girl giggled.

"I like that you're dressed as James Dean for the party," she said, touching his upper arm. "It's perfect for you."

Dean looked down at his clothes. He was wearing a black tee-shirt tucked into Levis: an accidental costume. "Thanks," he said, looking away. Out of the corner of his eye, he saw the undead drunks still hovering. "Can I help you with something?" he asked.

"I was just telling Lyra about you," TJ said.

"Who is Lyra?" Dean asked.

"I am," the girl said.

"Oh," Dean said, "Why?"

"Why am I Lyra?"

"Well, sure, if you'd like. But more importantly, what was said about me?"

She said, without any hesitation or shame, "I think you're hot."

Dean blushed. "Oh. Um, thank you."

"Come dance with me," Lyra said. It wasn't a request, but more of a demand. "Loosen up."

Dean was about to decline when he noticed Colin looking over his way. Maggie was dancing in an embarrassingly suggestive manner in front of him. Dean looked down at Lyra, attempting a smile. "Okay. Lead the way."

Grinning, she took his hand and led him into the dizzying strobe lights.

The song playing was something about sweaty male genitalia and bitches. Dean had trouble tuning out even those lyrics. He shuffled back and forth with his hands at his side and his head down, miserable.

"Here," Lyra said, "Have some of this." She handed him a water bottle full of a dark brown substance.

"What is it?" Dean asked, his eyes still on Colin.

"It's candy," Lyra said.

A few sips and Dean was willing to bet it was actually rum mixed with warm soda. Just as sickeningly sweet as candy. He winced. "Thanks." His mind immediately felt clouded and his chest glowed with chemical warmth. Lyra was dancing closer and closer, her hips swiveling and her face nearing his own. He kept his chin down so she couldn't get any ideas. Frustrated, she placed his hands on her hips. Dean winced and recoiled.

"You know, TJ is giving away PBRs," Lyra said loudly over the music. "You should chug a few."

Dean nodded, and ran for the kitchen. Why was he caving? Did he really think he could get somewhere with this girl? He had no interest in her whatsoever, so why was he playing along? It would only lead to eventual embarrassment.

As he chugged his third beer by the sink, holding back vomit, he felt a hand on his waist. He turned, wiping the foam from his mouth, and faced Colin. He too was without a costume. The armpits of his dark tee shirt were drenched in sweat.

"Hey," Colin said, "I saw...Teej tryin' a set you up wi' tha' girl... mussa fel' awkward... tol' 'er yer gay, so she woulna get the wron' idea."

Dean blinked. "What?"

"I tol' her yer gay. The girl."

"I know what you said. But why would you do that?"

"Jus' tryin'a help, bro," Colin said, giggling. "Just tryina be yer wingman."

"No," Dean said, slamming down his beer. "You were trying to sabotage me. Why?"

"Like you woulda made a move," Colin said, smiling, "C'mon Dean. Yer so gay. C'mon." He reached out to ruffle his hair but Dean pushed his hand away.

"No! Fuck you, asshole!" Although he was genuinely upset, and his voice sounded high-pitched and flirtatious.

"You wouldn'ta have," Colin said, still smiling. He stepped closer. Dean went to push him back, but he closed his hand around his wrist. "You know it's true," Colin whispered, tightening his grip. "You know."

Dean held still for several seconds, his fists and teeth clenched. "You have Maggie, so why don't you just leave me alone?" he whispered, giving Colin a cold stare and breaking free. He turned to get another beer from the refrigerator.

"I don' wan' Maggie," Colin said, watching Dean as he bent over.

Dean hesitated, closing his eyes. "Well then what the *do* you want?" he asked. "Illuminate me, Colin. I'd really love to know what the fuck it is you think you're entitled to here."

Colin didn't answer. Dean stood up and leaned against the counter, beer in his hand, biting his lip. They both stood in silence, the pounding bass and chattering party goers in the background. Dean shifted his weight, looking at grimy floor. "If it's what I think, well..." He traced the rim of the beer can with his finger. "Well, maybe tonight would be different," he said, looking up. He smirked, but his eyes were smiling.

Colin's eyes were dulled by the alcohol, but Dean momentarily saw a light that hadn't been there since summer. Since the music. Colin raised his head, as if to nod, when they were interrupted.

"Yo!" TJ had joined them.

"Hey," Colin said, smoothing back his sweaty hair. It formed an impromptu pompadour before falling flat again.

Dean took the opportunity to open and chug his beer. This was followed by an awful coughing attack. No one got him any water, so he hurried to the tap and cupped some in his hands. He splashed his face, sputtering.

"So, sorry about Lyra, dude," TJ said when Dean recovered. "I hadn't realized you were a fan of the cock. I always assume, 'cause all my other trans bros...you know, dig chicks and all."

Dean stared at him for several seconds, his mouth agape. He crunched the beer can in his fist.

"He's pretty drunk," Colin mumbled, not sure whose behavior he was excusing to whom.

"What did you just say to me?" Dean asked TJ.

TJ shrugged. He pulled out and lit a brown cigar-like object. Dean guessed it was full of marijuana. TJ took a drag, held in the smoke, then exhaled in their faces. "I dunno, I think the whole trans-fag thing is cool. I mean, it's confusing to cisgender people, but what isn't, right?" He laughed and slapped Dean hard on the back. "I think it's really radical of you, dude."

Dean's face was red now, but with anger not embarrassment. He was drunk, and more than that, he had lost his will for verbal retaliation. TJ was standing too close, so he shoved him.

"What the fuck man?" TJ said, knocking into the refrigerator. "What the fuck is your problem?"

Dean was already leaving. "Get out of my face!" he shouted, slamming the apartment door. Colin, TJ, Maggie and a small crowd of nosey partygoers in costumes followed.

The yellow moon, nearly full, was visible through the sparse trees. Brown leaves covered the pavement, wet and clinging to Dean's boots. He made the mistake of stopping to light a cigarette on the path, allowing the crowd to catch up to him. He cursed, taking a drag and nearly tripping over his shoelace. He again stopped to tie it, and noticed Craig coming from the other direction. His face was painted like a skull and he looked confused. Dean nodded hello.

"Why is everyone outside?" Craig asked, looking down at him tying his shoe. Dean had a cigarette in his mouth and couldn't respond. The noisy crowd was advancing.

"Why the fuck did you shove TJ?" Jay asked Dean's back.

"He called me names," Dean mumbled, blacking out for a second as he stood up. The beers' effects were quickly gaining on him. His boot was still untied.

"I didn't call you names," TJ whined. "Trans-fag is what it's called. How was I supposed to know you wouldn't like that? I was just saying that's what people call it."

A few people started laughing.

"That's not the point!" Dean shouted, feeling delirious. "All that about...about..." He couldn't bring himself to say the words and instead turned to the crowd. "Why are you all staring at me? Go away!"

Colin stepped forward. "Dean, relax. No one was insulting you. TJ was just saying that's what some people call it. He was actually saying he thinks you're cool."

"Go away," Dean repeated, and he turned to leave.

Jay grabbed his shoulder. "What's your problem?" he shouted, "Why are you so rude all the time?"

"Because I hate this place," Dean said, shrugging off his hand. "Please, just leave me alone. I want to go home."

"What's wrong with this place?" Jay said. "You're so fucking ungrateful. I saved all through high school to go here. Fuck, where I come from people have *real* problems, and all you can do is freak out when someone calls you the wrong name? How are we supposed to know when you never told us? Can't you see we're just trying to be your friend? You wait til you're in the real world and your mommy and daddy aren't paying for you anymore. You just fucking wait. People won't deal with your shit. They'll call you much worse things out there."

"Leave me alone," Dean repeated, this time in a whimper. "Please, just leave me alone." He felt dizzy, like he might puke at any moment.

"You're just a whiney little bitch," Jay said, shoving him. Dean fell backwards onto the pavement, skinning his hands.

Jay spat on the ground next to him. "Pussy."

"Knock it off!" Craig yelled. He moved towards Jay but Colin restrained him.

Dean giggled from the ground. "Be cool, Craig." He got to his feet, wiping his hands on his jeans. "I'm not going to fight you," he said to Jay.

Jay spat again. Dean smirked, and then his face went slack. He started to keel over, and Maggie rushed to steady him. He shook his head, coming back to life.

"Guys, let up," Maggie said, standing beside him. "Dean had a tough summer. He's not himself."

"We all had tough summers," Jay said. "Try living where I live. Try living with my dad. I'll show you a tough summer." He laughed bitterly.

"Shut up Jay." It was Colin's authority everyone seemed to respect. "Maggie is right," he said, stepping forward. "I told you guys to cut him some slack." He turned to TJ and Mitch. "I told you how difficult he is. I warned you, didn't I?"

Dean gripped his hair, feeling tears in his eyes. Colin thought he was difficult?

"Oh right, because of Teddy," TJ said. "But it's no excuse, man. He barely even knew her. Besides, he's never been polite, not even once. I don't know why you put up with it."

Dean was fading in and out of consciousness. Maggie helped him stay standing, supporting him under his arms.

"Who the fuck is Teddy?" Jay shouted.

Dean started to cry silently, his head drooping as he leaned back against Maggie. "I want to go home," he said again.

"Shh, baby, you're drunk," Maggie said, staring intently at Jay and TJ.

"Do remember in high school, when you stayed with me for awhile?" TJ said. "Remember how we went to that support group?"

"Yeah," Jay said, "So?"

"So she was the weird trans chick. The one who always talked nonstop. Anyway, she killed herself this May."

Jay looked skeptical. "I don't remember her. I don't remember there ever being a trans woman at that thing."

"Really?" TJ said. "Well, maybe you assumed she was a guy with long hair." He laughed sheepishly. "Someone actually told me she wasn't really trans, but like, a dude with a fetish. She didn't pass at *all*."

Though still dizzy, Dean broke free of Maggie and lunged at TJ. He didn't actually hit him but instead punched the air with frustration. He never fought anyone in his life, but he never felt such anger either. He flailed his arms, never making contact.

"What the fuck!" TJ shouted, shoving Dean, "This kid's a psycho!"

"Hypocrites!" Dean shouted, struggling to stay standing, "Don't you dare talk about her! How would you-"

He was cut off as Jay punched him in the stomach and threw him to the ground. Dean curled up in a ball, covering his head as Jay repeatedly pummeled him all over his body.

The crowd was laughing and chanting something.

"Fierce trannies!" someone yelled with a fake lisp, "Real tuna, real tuna!"

"Stop!" Colin yelled. "Stop it, or I'll get the police!"

With effort, he and Craig pulled Jay off. Dean lay motionless in the muddy grass, curled up like a fetus. He was muttering something, or perhaps singing.

Craig glared at Jay. "Big mistake, man."

"Everyone go back inside," Colin said. "You too, Craig."

"Not a chance."

Colin sighed. "Fine. Everyone else, scram. For real, or I'm calling the cops. Show's over."

The crowd, including Jay, reluctantly retreated. Soon it was only Colin, Craig and Maggie. They helped Dean to his feet and after a few moments, he steadied himself and was able to stand on his own. His nose and lip were bleeding, and he looked stupefied. His clothes were smeared with mud.

"Are you okay?" Maggie asked. "Colin, should we take him to the hospital? Are you sober enough to drive?"

"I'm fine," Dean muttered, clutching his ribs. "Just achy. I want to go lie down."

Colin sighed. "Do you need one of us to walk you home or can we go back to the party?" He sounded annoyed.

"I'm okay," Dean said, his eyes tearing up again with shame. "I can make it back."

"Well, then I'm heading in," Maggie said, "Good night Dean."

She and Colin walked away, holding hands. Colin kissed the top of her head. "It'll be alright. Let's try to forget about it."

"I knew something like this would happen," Maggie whispered.

"People will forget all about it," Colin said. "Let's go drink someone more, baby. It's Halloween."

Craig stayed where he was. He looked at their backs with disgust. For the first time in awhile, he spoke. "Are you serious right now?"

"What?" Colin said, turning around.

"Nothing," Craig said, shaking his head. "Nothing, Colin. Go drink. Come on Dean, let me take you home." He put his arm around Dean's shoulder. The two of them walked down the path away from the apartments, traveling the mile across campus by the light of the moon.

*

Dean sat by the windows in the dining hall, sipping his third cup of tea and watching the flakes falling outside in the dark. It was the first snow of the season, and a draft crept under the windowpane, making him shiver. He buttoned up his cardigan. He was thinking of heading to the library when he heard familiar voices coming from over his shoulder.

He turned and saw Colin, Maggie, and a large group of their friends were standing a few yards away, looking for a place to sit and eat dinner. Colin met his eyes. Dean looked away, not wanting to appear expectant. He checked again after a few seconds, and was relieved but hurt to see they chose a table as far from him as possible. Figuring he drank enough tea, he decided to take leave.

Outside the air was frigid. The wind whipped snow around the quad and stung Dean's cheeks, turning them a rosy red he despised. His ears and fingers ached, so he hurried across the lawn back to his dorm room. Once inside, he kicked the snow off his shoes before removing them. As he crossed the room and flopped down on his bed, he was hit by free-floating shame. He realized he was again embarrassed by his behavior on Halloween. He didn't blame Colin for avoiding him these past weeks. He felt like an idiot.

He looked at his wildlife calendar tacked on the wall. It was December, and the scene depicted two polar bears, clearly Photoshopped onto icy tundra. Dean sighed. In two weeks he'd be back in Syracuse, without even Vivian for company. Productive as usual, she was interning over break at the New York Public Library. He rolled onto his stomach and pressed his blushing face against the cool pillow. It seemed he just moved from one bedroom to another, with no purpose. He shut his eyes tight and tried to nap.

A half-hour later, the key turned in the door and Colin came rushing in, not bothering to remove his winter clothes or boots. He grabbed some items from his dresser drawer, rousing Dean in the process.

"Hey," Dean said, stretching.

"Hey," Colin said. "No time to talk. I'll be back on Monday."

"Oh," Dean said, disappointed. "Where are you going?"

"SoHo. I've got a show."

"Are you driving?" Dean said, aware he was slowing Colin down with his questions.

"Not in this weather," Colin said, heading for the door. "We're taking a train."

"I'd love to watch," Dean said. "I've only seen you play once, after all. Mind if I tag along?"

Colin bit his lip. "I guess so."

"If you don't want to me to that's fine," Dean said, looking down.

"No, no, you can come," Colin said, grabbing his ipod from his bed. "But you'll have to find your own way home. I'm staying a few nights. Also, we have to leave now. I have to catch the next shuttle bus to the train station."

"No problem," Dean said. He leapt to his feet. "Let's go," he said, grabbing his jacket and not bothering to tie his boots.

*

Maggie, TJ, Jay and Mitch were waiting at the bus stop. The reason for Colin's hesitation was now apparent.

"Dean!" Maggie said. "I hadn't realized you were coming." She looked straight out of the sixties, dressed like a Mod in belted white coat and a matching cap. Dean wondered why an attractive couple like Maggie and Colin endured the company of the others. Perhaps sensing his snobbery, Jay glared at Dean from under his mohawk, cracking his knuckles.

"Hello," Dean said to Maggie, ignoring the other three. "You look stunning."

Maggie smiled. "Oh stop it, you do! Look at that fantastic pea coat you're sporting. Of course you always look great," she said with a wink.

Dean smiled, adjusting his scarf. Colin cleared his throat loudly. It was then Dean remembered Maggie's kiss, and realized he should probably tone down the flattery. It seemed absurd that Colin felt threatened. What a bizarre triangle he'd found himself in.

"Stop it," Maggie said, this time to Colin, pulling him to her side. "You look handsome as well and you know it." She kissed his cheek, receiving no reaction. It would make an interesting picture, Dean thought, the three of them standing in the swirling snow, beneath the awning. As far as the other three, well- that was the benefit of Photoshop.

The bus ride to the train station took all of ten minutes. Maggie and Colin sat together, and so did Jay and TJ, which left Dean and Mitch to awkwardly pair off. Neither one attempted small talk and instead stared straight ahead at the seats. Dean eyed Maggie and Colin the entire time, his expression difficult to read.

After arriving at the White Plains train station, they hurried up the stairs to catch the next train. Everyone purchased tickets at the machines, and then stepped outside on the platform despite the cold, smoking cigarettes. The train arrived in minutes.

It was rush hour and they were lucky to find six seats all together. The three trans-bros sat across from Colin, Maggie and Dean. Jay and Dean's knees were uncomfortably close. It would be hard to say which of their scowls were more pronounced. Everyone was on edge, so they all listened to their ipods. Dean was an exception, as he forgot his CD player in his haste. Luckily he had the window seat, and the train was an express. He watched as they zoomed past several towns in the dark, eventually reaching the city.

When they stopped at Harlem and 125th Street, Colin removed his headphones and tapped Dean's leg. "So I've been meaning to tell you. I signed with a record company after all."

Dean raised his eyebrows. "Did you now? Which one?"

Colin told him the name of a famous independent label, located in New York.

"Wow!" Dean said, "Well, that's really something. Congratulations."

"Yeah, I've been in the city a ton this week, working shit out," Colin said. "That's why you haven't seen much of me."

It had been more than a week, but Dean didn't say anything. "When will you guys put out a record then?"

"Well, it depends on some things," Colin said. "I've been saving material for this. I mean, the CDs I produced were fine for selling at our shows, but I always hoped for a real release, you know? I'm working with a producer this time around. And I was thinking I'd take your advice and use some of the songs I showed you over the summer. They really are my best work, and I think I'm finally ready."

Dean's throat tightened. He knew he had no right, but he felt those were *their* songs. It never occurred to him that Colin would use them for other purposes.

"So then you'd take the songs and add Craig's lyrics?" Dean asked, trying to hide the hurt in his voice.

"Well, that's the thing, isn't it?" Colin said. "Even Craig admits his lyrics suck. And I was thinking if you didn't mind, maybe we could just use the songs as they are."

"You mean with my lyrics?"

"Yeah, I mean, maybe tweak them a bit. I could credit you, of course, if it's a big deal. And reimburse you, naturally."

"Well, I don't know," Dean mumbled. "It's not about money. Those songs were personal."

"So you'd mind then?" Colin said. "I wasn't sure. I mean, I thought maybe you'd be thrilled. I know you always wanted to be a famous writer, and well, it would certainly be a way of getting your voice out there."

Dean considered this for a minute. It wasn't what he'd always had in mind, but maybe it was better than nothing. But was it really his voice? "Are you sure Craig doesn't mind?" he asked.

"Well, I haven't honestly asked him yet. It's still a long ways off. It's just an idea I have in my head. We definitely wouldn't start working on the new album at least until after I graduate in the spring. I still think it's important I finish up my degree, just in case."

"Right," Dean said.

"I mean, think it over. You've still got a lot of time. I just thought of it because of what my manager told me, you know? I figured your lyrics would go well with our new image, if I'm going to be open about the transgender thing."

"So you've decided?" Dean said.

Colin nodded. "I think so."

The train was pulling into Grand Central Station, cutting their conversation short. The other four removed their headphones and conversations started as they walked with the crowd up to the main concourse. Dean was still thinking about Colin's offer. A daydream was forming in the back of his mind, almost as wonderful as it was unlikely to come true. Still, he couldn't help but lose himself in imagination all the way downtown, and therefore had no idea which subways he would need to take home. The snow was now falling in heavy clumps, obscuring their vision. As usual, hurrying down the streets to the warmth of the venue, Dean had no idea where he was.

*

There were no seats inside, so Dean found a place to stand by the wall. The venue was a run down old warehouse with bits of hay on the floor, packed with self-important looking people. Dean was both anxious and bored, and wondered if he should have stayed home.

Maggie and the guys went to find alcohol at a convenience store, hoping to smuggle it in. Dean wasn't interested; he was back to obsessing over his calorie intake. Of course, denying himself sweets only made him think of them constantly, so as he watched the second band perform, his mind kept wandering to the vegan cupcakes on sale in the corner.

He found the band boring. It was mostly synthesizer based, a throw back to an era best forgotten. The lead singer was an Asian woman in a faux-fur coat, with large rings on her fingers. Dean admitted she had some talent, but the musicians were putting him to sleep. It puzzled him why stuff like this was popular, as he listened to the anorexic looking boys next to him dispassionately discuss the band's merits. Did anyone really like anything or was it all for show? Was it crazy of him to expect a live performance to be an experience?

Looking around, Dean observed that skinny, pale, cardigan-clad gentlemen seemed to make up the majority- something unheard of, where he was from. This only annoyed him more. If behaving awkward, starving yourself and dressing like your grandma was fashion-forward, why did he still feel like a leper? Shouldn't these hipsters build him a monument already? Dean felt sick to his stomach. If there was one thing worse than feeling like the freak in the room, it was feeling like you didn't stand out at all. He was glad, at the very least, he wasn't wearing tight pants. His saggy-assed jeans were his wild act of rebellion.

At last Owl Eyes took the stage. Dean clapped daintily, slipping deeper into the shadowed corner.

"Hey everyone," Craig said into the microphone, "Thanks for coming out tonight in the weather." He nodded, then they started to play, all three musicians firmly rooted in place. Colin swayed his head from side to side, at a half-hearted attempt to seem less catatonic.

"That's it?" Dean thought, "Where is the hatred, the lust, the Dionysian abandon?" He realized it was probably for the best he wasn't up there. He would have insulted the crowd somehow in his desire to win their love. Still, someone had to do something to save the night- no, no, more than that: someone had to save music! What was the point of coming all this way to hear polite stage (would-be) banter and boring songs? In his manic state, Dean believed it symbolic of his over all disappointment with his life; always boring and polite, boring and polite, nothing else!

But why was this causing him so much distress? Did he really think he could do better? He could envision the hipsters discussing his imaginary band.

"Yeah, and then this Morrissey drag king came on stage and started insulting us for dressing like him/her. It got pretty weird when he/she started throwing the vegan cupcakes at the crowd and screaming about Greek mythology..."

He smirked to himself. Owl Eyes wasn't great, but was at least tolerable. It beat sitting home alone. He tried to meet Colin's eyes, but he never did.

After the set was finished, Colin and Craig joined the crowd. People were starting to head out. Several fans chatted with them while Dean stood off to the side. He noticed a tall black man in a casual suit, eyeing him. He quickly looked at his watch, making Dean wonder if he'd imagined it. The man was older and more conservatively dressed than the rest of the crowd. Dean began to blush uncontrollably as he approached.

"Hey Cooper," Colin said, smiling and shaking the man's hand. "So glad you could make it in the weather."

Dean exhaled with relief, toying anxiously with his cell phone.

"Of course," Cooper said, smiling. "I wanted to congratulate you in person on your record deal."

"Record deal?" Craig said. "You mean offer, right? We're still unsigned."

Cooper looked at Colin. "You haven't told him?"

Craig turned as well. "You signed us to a label? Without telling the rest of the band?"

"Oh," Colin said. "Well, I told the other guys. I could have sworn I told you. My bad. Well, I assumed you wouldn't mind."

Craig looked stunned. "Colin, can I talk to you outside please? Excuse us," he said to Cooper and Dean. The two of them pushed through the crowd.

Cooper shook his head. "This could get messy."

Dean smiled weakly, pocketing his phone.

"I'm Cooper by the way," Cooper said. "their manager."

"Oh yes, I figured," Dean said, cringing slightly as he shook his hand. "Dean."

"Nice to meet you Dean," Cooper said. "I love your hair."

Dean scratched his head. "Oh, well, thank you." He noticed Cooper gave him a quick up and down with his dark eyes. It was a scan Dean knew all too well, and he now assumed Cooper was trying to determine his gender. He rounded his shoulders and buttoned up his pea coat as he noticed Craig returning.

"Sorry about that," Craig mumbled, his eyes red. "Colin left though, so there's no use waiting around."

"Oh, alright," Cooper said. "Well, I guess I'll be going as well. It was nice meeting you Dean," he said, nodding. "Good night Craig."

When Cooper was out of earshot, Dean turned to Craig. "Are you alright?"

Craig shrugged. "I don't know. I just can't believe Colin did that. He *knew* how I felt about the whole thing. I always let him have the control because I knew he liked that sort of stuff. I never expected him to break my trust. I mean, it's not just *his* band. It never would have existed if not for me."

"I'm sorry," Dean said.

"How could he have forgotten to tell me? That just doesn't make sense. Something doesn't add up."

Dean didn't say anything.

Craig looked on the verge of tears. "It's like I don't even know him

146

anymore."

"I'm sorry," Dean said again. He didn't want to change the subject, but he was getting a little stressed. "So Colin left already?"

"Yeah, he's staying somewhere with TJ and those kids. There's some stupid party in Brooklyn. He left in a huff. I mean, heaven forbid he ask me to travel with them."

"Um," Dean said, "this probably sounds pathetic, but I followed Colin here and I really have no clue where I am or how to get home."

"Oh that's right, you're not a city person, are you?" Craig said.

"I'm not an anywhere person," Dean said.

"Well, it's easy, just- " Craig started spouting off letters and numbers and Dean's brain froze.

"I'm going to be honest," Dean said, "just because I don't want to end up sleeping in a snow heap. I have no idea what any of that means."

"They're subway directions," Craig said. "Want me to write it down for you? Actually, come to think of it, I have the weekend off. You want to just come back and sleep at my place?"

"Oh," Dean said. "Yeah, that would be great. Are you sure you don't mind?"

"Not at all," Craig said, "I'd love the company. I have to come back to your way tomorrow anyway."

They headed outside, bundling up. Craig wore a black jacket on over his hooded sweatshirt and a hunter's cap lined with what Dean hoped was fake fur. Snow clung to his glasses and the new blonde beard he was sporting. He seemed to be experimenting with a woodsman look. He at least appeared warm.

He led Dean down the stairs into the subway, where they waited several minutes for the train. Never one to wise up, Dean still ignored where they were going and blindly followed Craig's lead, his mind on other topics.

The train finally arrived, and their car was empty. They sat in orange plastic seats on either side of the aisle. Dean was lost in thought.

The idea of living in the city after graduation seemed laughable, unless he isolated himself to one neighborhood and only left when accompanied by a chaperone. Maybe over time he'd grow accustomed, but somehow he doubted it. Never did he feel more suburban than when navigating the subways. He reminded himself, watching his reflection in the dark window, that James Dean came from Indiana and still managed to master Manhattan life. Of course, James Dean probably wasn't spatially retarded. Growing up, James Dean could probably find his local grocery store.

"So," Craig said, interrupting Dean's thoughts, "I haven't seen you since Halloween. How have you been?"

"Oh, I've been fine," Dean said. "That reminds me. I wanted to thank you. For walking me home."

Craig shook his head. "You were clearly hurt and about to pass out. It was really shitty of Colin and Maggie to abandon you." He removed his hat and scratched his blonde hair, scowling.

"Hm," Dean said. "I guess. They were drunk though."

"That's no excuse," Craig said, "Colin has used up his quota when it comes to that. Honestly, the two of them have a serious problem when it comes to drinking. Don't get dragged down."

"I won't," Dean said, though he had. "Thanks for the warning." Was it wrong to be talking about his friends behind their backs?

Craig coughed into his sleeve. "I hope you don't mind me complaining to you," he said. "I know they are your friends. I'm just so upset right now. And honestly, from what I can tell, they don't treat you like they should."

Dean was surprised to hear this. Admittedly, he didn't have many friendships with which to compare, but he figured he was the rotten one. "How so?" he asked.

"Well like I said, I can't believe they'd just abandon you when you were hurt. But beyond that, I'm surprised they'd even *want* to hang around those kids after that."

"Really?" Dean said. "I figured everyone thought I was out of line."

Craig shook his head. "No way. I don't know exactly what TJ said to you, but I'm sure it warranted your reaction. That kid is beyond irritating. Colin has put up with him for years, and I haven't a clue why. Honestly, if he'd called me a fag, I would have shoved him too. I don't know where he thinks he gets off doing that."

"Really?" Dean said.

"I hate being labeled," Craig mumbled. "I mean, that sounds stupid, I'm sure. Only people who love being labeled say that. I basically put up with being called gay. It's true, I am only really attracted to men, but it's still just stupid." He glared at his reflection in the window. "I've never been one to get excited about queer shit. All this *reclaiming* and *pride* seems so juvenile. I wish everyone would just get over themselves and grow up."

Dean nodded. "Yeah. I guess the tranny-fag comment put me over the edge. I was having an awful night. I mean, it is just words, I know I overreacted. But it was more the way he said it. As if he knew precisely who I was. As if he'd...pinpointed me."

"Well, he just came out as transgender, didn't he?" Craig said. "So he's still in the phase where he's trying out his new vocabulary. The phase where he's excited."

"I was never excited," Dean said.

"Nor was I," Craig said, "About being gay, I mean. Well, that's a lie. I was a little at first, until I wised up." He snorted, but looked sad.

"Well, anyway," Dean said. "I'm glad you understand where I was coming from."

"Clearly," Craig said. "That Jay kid is nuts. He was just looking for an excuse to pummel someone. This is awful to say, but sometimes trans men are the worst when it comes to macho shit like that. It's as if they've got to prove something."

"Hm," Dean said. "Yes."

"I'm sorry, that was out of line."

"No, no," Dean said, "It's okay. It's true. I hate transgender men."

"Well, can't say I blame you," Craig said. "I hate gay men."

"We should join a rightwing crusade," Dean said, "against the queer agenda."

Craig smiled. "That sounds healthy."

"Hm," Dean said. "Actually, why don't we destroy all men while we're at it? The straight ones don't do much for me either."

"Now that's some SCUM Manifesto shit," Craig said.

Dean laughed darkly. "Indeed."

"Of course we'll have to die as well."

"It's for the best," Dean assured, as the train came to a stop. "I've always just adored the idea of joint suicide. Call me crazy."

They walked up the steps out into the streets. The storm had calmed, and the sounds of the city were muffled by the accumulation. Dean was content as they walked to Craig's apartment. There were Christmas lights in one of the windows, making him smile slightly. "What are your plans for Christmas?" he asked.

"I'm Jewish," Craig said, sounding a little peeved.

"Oh I'm sorry," Dean said, blushing. It was stupid of him to assume.

"But I don't have any plans for the holidays," Craig said. "My family is getting together I'm sure. But I'm unwelcome at this point."

"What happened anyway?"

"My parents don't like that I'm gay. They particularly hated my last boyfriend. Well, that was actually warranted. But even after we broke up, they still complain constantly about my uh, *lifestyle*. Absurd, I know. This is the twenty-first century, after all."

"No, it's not that absurd," Dean said. "My friend Vivian's parents are the same way."

"Yeah, but you're from Upstate," Craig said.

"Ah right, and we're all inbred and backwards," Dean said, hands on his hips.

Craig shrugged. "Alright, alright, sorry. We're even now."

"Nah, it's okay, I hate living there," Dean said.

Craig laughed. "And I hate Judaism."

"Well, we are just bundles of joy, aren't we?" Dean said, shaking his head. "A regular pair of disaffected youth."

"This is my apartment, by the way," Craig said.

They stepped inside the warm building, shaking the snow off their clothes. It was a narrow entrance way, with a harsh wood staircase that appeared recently constructed. There was a dim light bulb hanging from the ceiling, bare in its socket.

"Be careful on the stairs," Craig warned, "The carpenters made some mistakes, that's why I got a discount on the place."

"After you," Dean said. He followed Craig up to the second landing, almost slipping on saw dust, clinging tightly to the railing.

*

"I'm going to pour myself a glass of wine," Craig said as they entered his apartment. "Care for some?"

"Sure, thank you," Dean said, looking around. The room was small but tidy. There was a kitchen and several bedrooms attached.

"I'm warning you, it's cheap stuff," Craig said.

"That's fine. Good wine is boring." Dean examined the shelf. "Are these books yours?"

"Yeah, most of them," Craig said from the kitchen, "I've got more in my room. My roommates don't read much, so I took the liberty. Looks like they're all out tonight, by the way," he said, eyeing the bedrooms. "My roommates I mean."

Dean examined the books. Several familiar titles jumped out at him. *A Taste of Honey*, *Billy Liar*, *The Picture of Dorian Gray*, *James Dean Is Not Dean*, *Manchester And Its Regions*...

"The record player is mine as well," Craig said, still in the other room. "You can put some music on if you want."

Dean saw the old player in the corner, and examined the records. Among many others he observed *Horses* by Patti Smith, *Lipstick Killers* by the New York Dolls, *Cosmic Dancer*, By T-Rex, *Viva Hate*, by Morrissey, along with every major Smiths record and a several singles. He even found a few dusty Sandy Shaw and Nancy Sinatra records.

Craig returned with the wine.

"You're a Smiths fan," Dean said. "You never told me."

Craig shrugged. "Oh yeah, I've got all their records. Put on something happier though, if you don't mind."

"It's more than the records," Dean said, with a sly grin. "It's everything you own. You've done your research. You are a diehard fan."

Craig blushed, and Dean's suspicions were confirmed.

"Well, I used to be obsessed with Moz as a teen," he mumbled, "I mean, back when I was depressed and in the closet and well...you know, whatever." He was blushing more and mumbling. "But you know, it's so irritating, right? Everyone does that. I mean, I hate people who are like, *Oh, so and so band saved my life, oh these lyrics sum up how I feel*. It's extremely juvenile. I mean, all bands are out to make money. Even mine, apparently. The Smiths are something people grow out of."

"Methinks thou dost protest too much," Dean said, taking a sip of his wine.

Craig looked bothered. "I mean, sure there was a time when I listened to those records and thought it was something special. But I was young."

"People are better when they're young," Dean said.

Craig snorted, "I beg to differ."

"Well aren't you the clever swine," Dean said.

"I hope you're aware how creepy you sound."

"I'm too aware."

"So I take it you're still obsessed with The Smiths then," Craig said. "Actually, I could have guessed from your appearance. Yeah, they're definitely one of those cult bands that can consume people."

Dean shrugged. "I love being consumed."

"Yeah, well, I don't. I had to grow up. The songs lose their charm when you actually have to get a job and work for a living."

"Well, you didn't *have* to," Dean said, and he knew immediately this was a mistake.

"Yeah?" Craig said, "So when my parents practically kicked me out, I didn't have to start working, is that what you're saying? I could have survived on old records and hairspray, I take it? That would have put me through college? I'm sorry if I want to do something with my life. I'm sorry I don't want to be another lazy, self-indulgent faggot living off other people."

"Whoa, whoa," Dean said, holding up his hands in defense. "I'm sorry I said that. I suppose you did have to start working."

"You suppose?"

"No. You're right, you had to. I'm being an ass."

Craig sighed. "I'll say."

"You can beat me up if you'd like."

Craig laughed bitterly. "Not tonight. Who would walk you home?"

They stood for a few minutes in silence. Dean put on a Leonard Cohen record.

Craig snorted. "Are you allergic to happiness or something?"

"No... I suppose I just have a bizarre definition of it."

They sat down on the couch, sipping their wine, listening to the song Dean selected. It was "Take This Longing From My Tongue."

"Why are you looking at me?" Craig asked, eyeing Dean. "Are you already drunk?"

"No," Dean said, though he was a little. "Sorry, I was just thinking."

"Thinking what?"

"That you *are* quite rough around the edges."

"Who said that?" Craig asked.

"No one. Never mind."

"Well, gee, thanks," Craig said, scowling into his wine.

"I like it," Dean said.

Craig rolled his eyes. "Of course you do. Can we change this song? I feel like your trying to seduce me or something."

Dean laughed, blushing. "I'm not," he said, unsure if this was the truth. "Do you really want me to change it?"

"No," Craig said, "it's fine. Relax." He went and got his bottle of wine and several of liquor. They sat quietly for a half hour, downing glasses and listening to the record in silence. Dean felt jolly watching the snow outside the window. When he turned for more wine, he was surprised find Craig staring at him.

"What?" Dean said.

"How drunk are you?"

"Quite."

"Alright, me too. I'll just say it." Craig grinned. "I've wanted to mess around with you for a while now. You're a really attractive guy. I don't think you realize that."

Dean giggled.

Craig sighed. "Well, way to ruin it," he said.

Dean blushed. "Sorry. Really?"

"No, I still want you."

They both sat in silence for a few moments, listening to the end of the song. Then Craig crossed the room and switched the record. A much more aggressive, all too familiar song began to play. The transition was laughably abrupt.

"Okay," Craig said, crossing his arms, standing over Dean and looking down. "You win. I love The Smiths. Happy?"

Dean avoided eye contact, instead staring at Craig's belt buckle.

"Let me get my hands
on your mammary glands," said Morrissey.

"Don't get any ideas," Dean warned, wagging his finger.

*

As a twenty-third birthday present to myself, I decided to take a bus to the county clerk's office and finally change my name. I filed the paper work, but it will be several months until it's official. Still, little gestures like this are important. For many transgender people, it's a milestone worth celebrating with football or whale-shaped ice cream cakes and cheering friends. For me, it's a reminder that I'm in this for the long run.

I suspected many people in line were young brides taking on their husband's last names. Though we were the same age, the same sex and filling out the same paper work, we couldn't be more different. Or maybe not. Though I will never marry (the idea of being *civil* let alone forming a *union* with another is laughable) I am making a lifelong commitment to a man, for better or for worse, in sickness and in health. The man just happens to be myself.

Of course with matrimony comes responsibility; someone's got to support this Dean character and I suppose it should be me. Once the name change goes through, it should be easier to find work, as long as no one looks into my legal sex. If that letter "f" offends their delicate sensibilities, they don't have to hire me or they can fire me at any time. It's a little nerve-wracking, wouldn't you say?

I remember when I was still in college, TJ was rallying students around this bill called ENDA or GENDA or something like that. The goal was to push the New York government to outlaw discrimination in the work place based on gender identity or expression. This terrifies politicians, because a man could come to work in a dress. Once that happens all hell will break loose. Cities will burn, civilizations will crumble. But I'm getting political, and that's something I try to avoid. My point is, maybe I should have helped instead of turning up my nose.

"We must fight the stereotype that transgender people are unemployable!" said the activists.

"But that's one of my top five favorite stereotypes!" I said. Oh well. My contribution wouldn't have changed anything.

So until I get the notice by mail that says I am legally Dean, I am going to take advantage of still more time alone in my bedroom. Doing what, you ask? Well wouldn't you like to know? The possibilities are endless. But once that little slip comes, I'm going to have to make some serious decisions. I find myself leafing through the Anne Sexton book as of late and thinking of Teddy. As you age into numbness, suicide seems less about ending agony and more like a rational option you can't help but consider. A valid conclusion in a world that hardly recognizes your existence and does what it can to cover you up. A final attempt at romanticism for an imitator of art. A tempting back up plan, you have to admit. Not because living is excruciating (though it is) but if I'm honest, it's because I'm incredibly lazy and don't see that the world is worth my effort.

"Oh Dean, why?" legions of weeping fans will say, as they make their grand exodus to my sepulcher by the sounding sea. "Oh beautiful, tragic Dean, why, why, why?" Though I will take my secrets with me to the grave, a hint to my sufferings will be forevermore engraved on the wall of my lipstick-kiss covered whitewashed tomb:

"If only someone
cared enough
to buy him
an ice cream cake."

*

Dean swatted at the ringing smoke detector with his hands, attempting to waft away the smoke to no effect. He was back in suburbia for the holidays, dressed in a floral apron and making gingerbread cookies. His parents were away.

He shut off the oven, grabbed a magazine from the counter, and began waving that around instead. Finally the clanging ceased. No sooner was the house silent when the doorbell rang.

He froze. He never answered the door. He rarely answered anything. But that afternoon, he was compelled to. It may have been he was half expecting Alesio; for whatever reason his curiosity trumped his anxiety.

He opened the first wood door, and was surprised to see it was Adrian, bundled in a black down coat, at least three sizes to large. "Adrian! What are you doing all the way out here?"

"I need to talk to you," he mumbled, looking miserable as he brushed off snow from his body and removed his boots.

Dean led him inside. Adrian was dressed all in black. Even his spiky hair, naturally black, looked dyed even blacker.

Dean pulled him up a kitchen chair. "So what's on your mind, sport?" he asked, sticking out his tongue.

Adrian looked confused by the gesture; a natural reaction. "Why are you wearing an apron?" he asked, narrowing his eyes.

Dean looked down. "Oh, I was making cookies. Want one?"

Adrian hesitated then said slowly, "Sure."

Dean retrieved a three-legged gingerbread man from the oven and handed it to Adrian without a plate. It was hot, so Adrian placed in on a napkin and waited. The head was burnt and the middle looked undercooked.

"How did you get here anyway?" Dean asked.

"I walked," Adrian said.

"From Cicero?"

Adrian sighed. "Yeah. My dad just flipped out on me and I don't have anyone to talk to. Vivian is still in New York City."

"Yeah, I know," Dean said, flinching slightly. He tried to forget her. "Why did your dad flip out?"

"My Social Studies teacher called him," Adrian said. "She told him about what happened at school."

"What happened?" Dean asked.

"Well, don't think I'm stupid," Adrian said. "But a week or so before break, I decided to ask my teachers and classmates to start calling me by male pronouns. My online friends said I should stand up for myself. So I approached my teachers before class."

Dean raised his eyebrows. "Wow. That is…ballsy." Unfortunate phrasing, he realized. "How did they react?"

"Most of them looked at me like I sprouted a second head," Adrian said. "None of them listened. I left a note on my math teacher's desk, because by the end of the day I was too scared to speak anymore. When he did roll-call, he said my name as *Miss* Adrienne. And he said *not Mister*. The whole class laughed and a boy threw a pencil at me."

"Teachers are idiots," Dean muttered. "So someone called your dad?"

"Yeah. She wanted to know if my parents knew what I was doing, and whether she was obligated to actually call me by male pronouns. I guess she figured if my parents didn't approve, she didn't have to."

"That is very awkward," Dean said.

"And so of course Dad freaked out. He started screaming at me and blaming you."

"From what I can tell those are his passions in life."

"But what should I do?" Adrian said. "Now everyone thinks I'm even weirder. I don't mean to be high maintenance, I just hate being called *she*. And my online friends said that it's okay to voice that. They said younger people are coming out as transgender and that high schools have to accommodate us."

Dean ran his fingers through his hair. This was beyond his scope. "Well," he said, "unless you want to wage war, our high school isn't going to accommodate you. You have to keep in mind, most people don't even know we exist, or if they do, they think it's on some separate, isolated, Jerry Springer planet. They don't even speak our language. To them, a transgender man is a dude who wants to cut off his penis. And as far as transgender females, well, they don't even consider that we could exist."

Adrian sighed. "I don't want to battle anything. Never mind I guess. I don't know why I can't stop feeling this way. I try but I can't. The more I read the worse it gets. You were right. If gender shouldn't matter then I should be fine as a girl. I shouldn't mind being a *she*."

Dean shrugged. "But you're not fine. You do mind. What can you do?"

"I could try harder."

"You could," Dean said, taking a bite of a gingerbread man, "but that sounds miserable. Well, really it's miserable either way."

Adrian frowned. "So you have no advice to give me?"

"Sorry, no," Dean said. "I've heard oatmeal releases endorphins. Try oatmeal." He didn't know why he was so short with Adrian. If he were kind, he would take him under his wing and show him the ropes of trannyhood. He just couldn't bring himself to pretend he had any expertise.

"I guess I should head out then," Adrian said, looking glum, "before Dad comes looking for me and kills the both of us."

Dean felt bad. "But you came all this way. Is there anything I can do to cheer you up? Want to watch television or something? Go for a walk?" His tone was similar to how one would address a puppy. He wished he could offer to drive him, but he didn't have a license or a car.

"No, that's alright," Adrian said, "I'll just call Vivian later. No offense, but she's a lot more comforting than you are."

"None taken," Dean said, "I wholeheartedly agree. I'm the worst."

Adrian headed for the door, leaving his untouched cookie on the table. Standing in his apron, Dean felt helpless. Did he really have nothing to offer?

"Wait, Adrian, before you go...I'll be right back."

He ran up the stairs to his room. He pulled four CDs off of his bookshelf. It was painful to part with them, but he had the tracks saved to his computer. If he'd prepared ahead, he could have burned Adrian some copies, but really, this was more quaint.

He came down the stairs and met Adrian in the entranceway. "I don't know what kind of music you're into," he said, "but you're entering prime emo years and you should at least go about it correctly." He handed him the four albums. *The Smiths, Meat is Murder, The Queen is Dead,* and *Strangeways, Here We Come*

"Listen to them in that order," Dean said. "I don't know that you'll like it, but give it a try. Really, this could be the worst thing for you. Keep in mind, the funny British man says things that are purposefully over the top." He'd never forgive himself if tracks like "Nowhere Fast" prompted the fifteen year old to lie in the middle of the street or if "This Charming Man" gave the impression it was wise to accept rides from strangers who flatter you.

Adrian smiled. "Thanks Dean. I've never heard of this band before, but I'm always looking for new music. Can I keep these CDs then?"

Dean snickered. "Oh hell no. I need those. Make sure to get them back to me by New Year's. In perfect condition, mind you, or you'll be hearing from my lawyers." He opened the door and nodded his head. "Now shoo, I have baking to do."

*

I copied and pasted this from the webpage Maggie emailed to me a few days before New Year's. The article was also published in print, with pictures.

Female-to-Mahr

Colin Mahr is the guitarist and songwriter of OWL EYES, one of our "Top Ten Bands to watch in 2010." (see pg. 7) Only twenty-one years old, he has already collaborated with many stars. In the following year, and will be working with award-winning producer Jeremy Davidson on the upcoming Owl Eyes album. Though only an undergraduate in college, Mahr's diverse body of work has garnered some flattering comparisons. His guitar-heavy songs have been described as "early Neil Young meets Radiohead." But Colin's most obvious doppelganger (due to his surname as well as his catchy riffs) is Johnny Marr of The Smiths. We sat down at a café in Chelsea to discuss his recent record deal, his plans for the future, and his commitment to the rarely mentioned "T" of the LGBT community. (Click here for more...)

Comments: (905)

Drunkkidcatholic wrote:
I heard rumors that this guy used to be a chick but I thought it was made up. like when people were saying Ciara was a dude. Wow. That is messed up. Gotta admit, he's talented though.

Hangthedj wrote:
Johnny Marr he aint. Sorry. Never a big a fan of Owl Eyes, but I'm glad that he's willing to finally come out publicly about this. Very brave. Drunkkidcatholic, check your privilege.

Antondm89 wrote:
That's sick. I'm fine with gay people and all but this is taking it too far.

Goodbyecomet wrote:
Agreed, too far. These are feminist ideas turned inwardly upon themselves, to the point of contradiction. There is nothing to be learned from this self-impressed discourse.

Bella7896 wrote:
Agreed. FTM Transgenders are just self-hating lesbians if you ask me. It's really unfortunate she felt pressured to do this to her body. Hangthedj, you really think "Colin" Mahr is brave? What would actually be brave is if she stayed a woman. You can bet that the music press wouldn't give a shit about her as a lesbian though. It's sad that young girls who want to be guitarists are going to read this garbage. Shame on Owl Eyes.

Jayd789 wrote:
I don't give a shit about it either way. Just another idiot looking for attention. Guy, girl, transgender- it's just another whiney emo kid with an ego. Enjoy your 15 minutes of fame. Early Neil Young my ass. Where do

they come up with this crap?

Indieemu65 wrote:
I saw Owl Eyes at the Sidewalk Cafe a few months ago. You can tell "he" is a transgender from looking at "him." It's obvious. "He" is really small in person and pear shaped if you look close. Shouldn't wear such tight jeans!! I didn't know this was news. Can we please focus on the music and not people's sexual orientation for once??

owlol90 wrote:
I think Colin is very brave. Most these comments are insensitive and just show the difficulties queer musicians have to face. Being ftm isn't easy, you know. And he's not a self-hating lesbian, that's just ignorance talking. By the way, to the person who commented before me, you definitely can't tell he's transgender. He's really hot, just look at those pictures!

Ppjone99 wrote:
I agree he IS really hot; that's what makes it so disturbing.

Yuuyuu8974 wrote:
Gross gross gross. I never even heard of ftms, and I wish I hadn't. If I was dating some guy and I found out he was lying and really an ftm, I'd freak. This band sucks anyway. fuckin hipster trash.

Joe67 wrote:
so he'ss got a vaj or wut? Ii dont get it. wuts that got 2 do with music neway?? so fraekyyy......

(...more)

*

It was 11:45 on New Year's Eve. Dean was home by himself, lying in bed, listening to music. He considered making resolutions, but it seemed pointless. Maybe he'd make a TV dinner instead. He was about to go downstairs and raid the freezer for vegetarian options when his cell phone vibrated on his desk. Curious, he went over and looked at it. The screen said it was Colin. He answered it, surprised. "Hello?"

"Hey Dean," Colin said, difficult to hear. "Having a happy New Year?"

"Oh, it's fine," Dean said. He realized he'd never talked to Colin on the phone before. "How are you?" he asked, his voice quavering. "Back in Long Island? Have a good Christmas?" He didn't give Colin time to respond before moving on to the next question.

"Nah," Colin said. "I'm in Brooklyn. They're having a party." His voice sounded strange, listless.

"Who are you referring to? Are you drunk?" Dean asked.

"Yeah," Colin muttered, "I am. And *they*, well, *they* is TJ I guess. And whoever. Whatever, they

Dean heard the static of wind. "Are you outside?" he asked.

"Yeah," Colin said, "On the roof. In Brooklyn. I can see those water tower thingies and all the lights."

"Aren't you freezing?"

"Nah, too drunk to feel it," Colin said.

"Well, you're still going to freeze," Dean said, "and it's icy, I'm sure. Make sure to stay away from the ledge."

Colin didn't say anything.

"Are you still there?" Dean asked.

"Yeah," he said, "Yeah, barely. Dean, I'm sad."

"I can tell," Dean said. "What's going on?"

"I'm a sell-out," Colin said. "I'm so gross. Everything about me is fake. Everything. I'm always faking and I don't know why anymore."

Dean bit his lip. "It's okay. Just start trying to be real then, if you want."

"Can't," Colin said, "Can't, can't, can't. Ugh, Dean, you have to believe me."

"I believe you, calm down," Dean said. "You aren't a sell out. Are you referring to your interview in that magazine?"

Colin drew in a shaky breath. "Yeah, that's part of it. It was a mistake. A huge mistake. Did you read it? I sound like an idiot. And all those comments on the internet. People hate me. They think I'm fake. They want me *dead*."

"No," Dean said. "You didn't sound stupid- the journalists and the people who commented sounded stupid. You aren't fake. Really. No one wants you dead."

"Yes they do. Someone called my parents," Colin said. "Someone called them saying they were going to rape and kill me."

"Seriously?"

"And someone got my phone number too. I keep getting texts calling me a freak and shit."

"Oh my god. Did you tell the police?"

"Of course not," Colin said. "What can they do? What can they ever do for anybody?"

"Well, trace the number for starters. You have to tell, you could be in danger." But as Dean said this, he knew he personally wouldn't have gone to the cops.

"I don't want this anymore," Colin said, and Dean realized he was crying. "Being famous just made it worse. I thought'd make it better, but nothing can. I hate myself. I seriously, seriously hate myself. I try to cover it up but I'm so fucking worthless. I just the hurt people who care about me and fake everything. I hate myself, inside and out. I'm awful." He began to sob.

"Colin, no. You're a beautiful person," Dean said. He realized this sounded stupid, but it was all he could think to say on the spot. "You're beautiful. You're wonderful."

"No," Colin said. "No, no, no. I wish I could be like you. You don't fake it."

"I do too," Dean said. "Are you kidding? I'm always faking."

"But you're honest with yourself."

"Bah, I don't know. Colin, you aren't near a ledge or anything, right?"

"Why?"

"You're just making me worry."

There was silence.

"Colin?"

Still more silence, except the wind. Dean was about to hang up and call Maggie when Colin spoke at last. "I need to tell you something. If I don't now, I never will."

"Don't talk that way," Dean said. He was crying now as well. "Please."

"I just mean, if I don't say it now I'll lose my nerve," Colin said. "So I have to tell you. I think I'm in love with you."

Dean started crying harder. He covered his mouth to stifle it, tilting the phone away.

"I don't love Maggie," Colin said. "I thought I did, before I met you. But now that I know, it can never be the same. Every time I look at you, every time you speak, I just...I can't even explain. It's like I can't get rid of you, even when I'm alone."

"You don't have to explain," Dean said after uncovering his mouth. "I love you too, Colin. Really I do. More than life."

Colin stopped crying. Now he groaned. "What am I going to do?"

"It'll be okay," Dean went on. "It will be hard, but we can be together, I know it. It's meant to be." Words were coming out he didn't know were in his brain. "You just have to tell Maggie the truth. It's fate- I always knew it was fate that I'd meet you." He wiped his tears, starting to get carried away. "We understand each other like no one else can. We're both messed up, that's why it's perfect. We can be happy: you just can't hurt yourself tonight. You're only drunk, you don't really want to die. You have to believe me. Through everything, I'll always be here. I love you."

There was a moment's pause.

"No," Colin said, "No, I believe you. You're right. I don't want to die."

Dean sighed. "Thank God. Will you please go inside? To put me at ease?"

"I will," Colin said, "It's just so beautiful out. I wish you were here, Dean. Fuck, I always wish you were here."

"I wish I were too," Dean said. He looked at the clock on the wall. It was exactly midnight. "Hey Colin?"

"Yeah?"

"Happy New Year, pumpkin."

Colin laughed. "Happy New Year, Dean. It really is going to be a new year. Things are going to change. I'm going to start being honest with myself."

Dean closed his eyes and smiled. "I really hope so. I meant everything I said."

"I know," Colin said. "But I have to go now. Don't worry, okay?"

And with that, he hung up the phone, leaving Dean to his dark, silent house, wide awake and hoping. A second later his phone vibrated, startling him. It was a text from Colin.

Tonight was a blue moon ;)

Dean closed his phone. He looked over at the calendar on his wall, now obsolete, checking the lunar phase in the corner next to the date. Well, well. So it was.

*

A DREAM: SCENE ONE

I am sitting in a large room with ivory colored walls and plush white furniture. I am dressed in a green velvet suit and smoking a gold-tipped clove cigarette. I am apparently on a set, because I can see the audience in my peripheral vision.

Adrian comes into the scene, dressed in his usual garb.

DEAN

Adrian, so good to see you! Do be careful of the drapes; I just bought them and you look rather...sharp. *(He eyes Adrian's spiky wrist bands and hair with disdain.)*

ADRIAN

I haven't the time or energy for your insults, Dean. I've come to discuss the albums you lent me.

DEAN
Ah yes, splendid! I take it you want to thank me in person?

ADRIAN
No. Quite the contrary. I've had them destroyed.

DEAN
Destroyed? But why?

ADRIAN
They are dangerous. They encourage negative and narcissistic attitudes, particularly in confused young boys like me.

DEAN
Well that's the whole point!

ADRIAN
No Dean, enough! *(His face is red)* I understand you have given up on authenticity entirely. But why must you inflict your shallow views and dangerous keepsakes upon innocent people?

DEAN
There are no innocent people. Haven't you heard the story about the garden?

ADRIAN
Ugh, shut up. You aren't Oscar Wilde. Though you deserve to be sentenced for what you've done to me.

DEAN
True. "I could have been Wilde and I could have been free, but Nature played this trick on me." *(He gestures inward towards his body)*
What could I have possibly done to you? I can count the amount of times we've spoken on one hand. *(He wiggles his white silk gloved fingers)*

ADRIAN
That's just it. I came to you on several occasions and you always turned me away. Often literally, sometimes by doing that thing you do.

DEAN
What are you referring to? Be more specific; I have an abundance of

alienating traits.

ADRIAN
I'm referring to your essential, garish flaw that you overlook, even when people try to point it out. That's the problem with men who value wit above all things: they never listen, because they are too busy planning their clever comeback. And then they turn around and wonder why they are alone.

DEAN
I don't mind being alone. Really I prefer it. I'm a writer; if I get lonely, I can always invent some friends. Real people just aren't literary enough, I find.

ADRIAN
You say these things but I know you don't really mean them.

DEAN
That's the beauty of Dean.

ADRIAN
That's the tragedy of Dean.

DEAN
They are one in the same.

ADRIAN
Ugh! Will you listen to yourself?

DEAN
Well I never listen to anyone else.

ADRIAN
(Raises his hand and smacks Dean across the face. Dean is reminded of Vivian. The sting is strangely pleasurable.)
Snap out of it! Stop using people as props, stop playing off our faults to accentuate your delusions of grandeur! You selfish over-grown baby!

DEAN
(Angry now. To be called selfish is one thing, but over-grown?) I don't. I am not malevolent. I only act out when people like you insist on cornering me. I just want to be left alone.

ADRIAN
And so you will, Dean. The days when I admired you are over. You

use your halfhearted sex change as your excuse; you make broad, sweeping statements about our community but you do not speak for us. Being transgender is not what holds you back, there is something else: you are horribly ill. I don't yet know the right way to be a man, but you have shown me the absolute wrong way.

DEAN
(Composed again, he bows)
Adrian, it was really nothing.

ADRIAN
(Ignoring him)
You know, I destroyed those albums you gave me, but I will say this: there was one song I loved. Do you know which?

DEAN
"Girlfriend in a Coma?"

ADRIAN
No. "I Know It's Over." Do you know why? Because it was authentic. Consider it, Dean. "If you're so funny, then why *are* you on your own tonight?"

DEAN
Your words are a silver dagger, my boy.

ADRIAN
Ah, yes, right. "It's so easy to laugh and so easy to hate," isn't it Dean? Becomes highly addictive habit. And much like the cigarettes you smoke, it will surely kill you. You aren't as complex as you think. You need to be loved, perhaps *more* than most. Your quick tongue is not rebellion, but conformity- a symptom of your pathetic need to please. But of course Scrooge, I'll leave you alone. Expect the second ghost when the bell tolls.

DEAN
Ghost? But you aren't even dead! Are you?

ADRIAN
You were my role model, what do you expect? A happy ending? I'm surprised you're upset by the news. Suicide is *literary*, right? And isn't that all that matters?
(Adrian evaporates.)

SCENE TWO

I am sitting alone, now in a purple bathrobe. A white kitten is rolling around on the white carpet. I watch it intently, lost in thought, when I remember the audience is watching me. My posing becomes affected as I cross the room and gaze at myself in a large, gold-framed mirror encrusted with emeralds and rubies. I am startled when I see Teddy standing behind me. She is dressed all in white, opposite of when she was living.

TEDDY
Hello Dean. Recognize me?

DEAN
(turning)
Of course I recognize you. But I thought you were dead. I saw your body. I smelled the decay.

TEDDY
Yet here I am before you. I suppose this must prove we are more than bodies, wouldn't you say?

DEAN
Or it proves fairies sprinkled absinthe in my seltzer again.

TEDDY
Always the skeptic. Why are you so afraid?

DEAN
What makes you think I'm afraid?

TEDDY
Because you are always trying to be clever. Are you afraid of your body, is that it?

DEAN
What, this old thing?
(He has no clever comeback and therefore feels afraid.)

TEDDY
Is it because you know you will grow old and die?

DEAN

You have no evidence that will occur.
TEDDY
Dean, I fear for you. I know what it is like to be afraid of your body, of aging, of sex, of other people, of your very existence. I know where that fear leads. It is we who are most afraid of death who take our own lives.

DEAN
(Puffing on his cigarette)
So? I might as well take my life. No one going to *give* it to me.

TEDDY
Give it to yourself. I have been you, Dean. I understand more than you know. Think of what happens when you become your own god, your own lover, your only friend, a stand up comedian with you as the audience. You put so much weight upon your shoulders when every night is a performance. Think of Wilde, Dean. "All men destroy the thing they love…"

DEAN
(Pensive for a moment)
"The greatest lie that men will ever tell: you will find true love when you learn to love yourself."

TEDDY
Who said that?

DEAN
I did. I sang it, actually. For Colin. Ah, Colin…Loving other people is the true challenge, wouldn't you say Teddy?

TEDDY
Yes. But don't be quick to dismiss that old truism. You say you love yourself, but I think that this is your biggest pretend.

DEAN
Bigger than my convoluted gender?

TEDDY
Yes. If Narcissus really loved himself, he could step away from the pool. It his doubt, and not his conceit, that keeps him rooted.

DEAN
(Sighs)
I want to be natural, Teddy, but I've truly forgotten how. Higher education does that to you. I never knew how to be a woman, but I don't

know how to be a man either. All I know is this. This Dean. This condescending beast with a pompadour: this perpetual snobby three year old that calls itself God. I've tried everything. I don't know what to be. Somebody wrote, "I'm not man trapped in a woman's body; I'm just trapped." And that's what I am. Horribly, horribly trapped. See, I can't even speak from the heart without quoting.

TEDDY
Be yourself.

DEAN
Be serious.

TEDDY
I am. The dead don't joke.

DEAN
Well that is truly disappointing; I was banking on an eternity of gallows humor. In that case, I refuse to die.
Teddy shakes her head and she too starts to evaporate. Dean panics.

DEAN
No! Please, come back! Don't leave me, we were just starting to have a conversation! I'm sorry! I'll be natural! I'll be authentic, just don't leave me! No!

(The curtain falls)
*

I awoke with a start, sweat pouring from my pores. My heart was racing, so to speak. It was five AM. I crossed the room and turned on the fan, feeling sick to my stomach. Maybe it's this awful August heat wave, but I feel the gates of Hell have opened. I find myself believing in mysticism once more; that dream was a sign, I tell-you-what. Some awful disaster is soon to descend- a devastating event, the likes of which I've never known. A catastrophe that will force me to take a stand- something wicked this way comes, I can sense it. But what would be infinitely more terrifying is if I am wrong.

Oh Lord, hear my prayer, the same as every Sunday: Come Armageddon come!
*

After ten hours of travel, Dean returned to Rye College to find his dorm uninhabited. He was anxious to see Colin. He was terrified, but knew it was worth it. He practiced his lines under his breath as he unpacked. "Why not give it a shot?" he whispered to an empty room. "It wouldn't be so bad, would it? Might be fun, really. We could help each other through it."

After his bags were emptied, he tried reading, but couldn't focus. As he could think of nothing better to do, he decided to give himself his injection. It was a little ahead of schedule, but he was antsy.

Having injected testosterone every two weeks for the past year, Dean felt he should be more at ease with the procedure. His fingers still quivered as he drew the thick fluid from the vial into the syringe, and as he screwed on the twenty-two gauge needle, he always felt a lurch in his stomach.

He placed the syringe on his dresser and stripped down to his underwear. He sat on his bed, his legs stretched out before him. He wiped the corner of his left thigh with an alcohol swab and relaxed his muscles. Adrenaline took over, and holding the syringe like dart, he slowly lowered the needle, breaking the skin and penetrating the muscle. He slowly pushed the stopper down, releasing the fluid. Then he withdrew, drained but happy.

It never ceased to disgust and thrill, this solitary act. Craving power, he enjoyed the idea of taking control of his masculinity. It was a flawed but pleasurable concept. Dean never took Chemistry or Health in high school and he was glad for it; he preferred his physical transformation to seem magical. Nature never made a man of him, but this sacred ritual just might yet.

He lay back on his bed, still in his briefs, crossing his arms behind his head. He felt content with his flaws tonight. It was a trick of covering up and diverting attention; years of practice left him a master. His chest binder and briefs worked as chastity belts, keeping his maidenhood under lock and key. It was for the best. No male body could live up to his obsessive imaginary. Well, except maybe one.

He conceded in his thought that this was probably the definition of a trans-faggot, or whatever it was TJ called him.

But he was sick to death of courting himself. He had high hopes for the future, high hopes for him and Colin. The pure Plato shit would suffice, but he also entertained a fantasy in which their similar, discarded bodies would fit together perfectly.

Feeling pleasantly warm, he rolled onto his side, responsibly leaving a used syringe on his bed stand. He fell asleep imagining a life with Colin by the ocean. They would go for walks, talking until their throats were hoarse, and then tackle one another in the sand, battling and laughing uncontrollably. They would watch old movies in a huge bed with a dozen colorful pillows, and splash in the shower, unashamed of their bodies. Dean would read snobby novels in a bathrobe by the fire and Colin would tease him for being so uptight, stealing his book and running all over the house, howling like a gibbon. They would live like movie stars, behave like animals, and never grow old. In time, they would learn to love themselves through their love for one another. Their house would be full of music and flowers, with open windows and absolutely no mirrors. For the first time Dean could remember, the future didn't terrify him.

*

Colin was still absent in the morning and the day after. When he wasn't there on Monday, Dean started to worry. Coming back that night after his class, he was relieved to see Colin's suitcases and electronic devices. This confirmed he was back on campus, if not yet crashing into Dean's arms.

It wasn't until Tuesday evening Colin returned. Dean was lying in bed reading. He shoved his book under a pillow when he heard the sound of the key in the door. Colin came in with a notebook under his arm. When he removed his jacket and winter hat, he revealed a different person. He was wearing new navy corduroys with a white button shirt, but more importantly, he had cut his hair. It was cropped close on the sides and longer on top, where it flared out in front. It was a hipper version of Dean's quif.

"You cut your hair!" Dean said, stating the obvious.

"Well, a hairdresser did," Colin mumbled, setting his notebook on his desk and taking a seat at his computer.

"It looks wonderful!" Dean said. "It really compliments your facial structure."

Colin didn't respond. He was checking his email.

"I really like your clothes too," Dean added. "Can I borrow those pants someday?" A large, shared wardrobe was another part of his fantasy.

"Uh, maybe," Colin said, focusing on his email.

Dean frowned. "Where have you been anyway?"

"Oh I just got back late," Colin said.

"Oh, right. Well, I'm glad you're here now. How have you been?" There was concern in his tone and Colin caught the implication.

"Oh, I was really fine on New Year's. I had too much to drink. Disregard whatever I told you." He bit his lip, still staring at the screen.

"Oh," Dean said, caught off guard, "Well, not everything, right?" He laughed.

"What do you mean?" Colin still stared at the computer screen.

"I mean, you meant some of the things you said, didn't you?"

Colin shrugged. "I don't remember."

Dean hesitated, with a sense of foreboding. "Colin. Please don't tell me you're staying with Maggie."

Colin didn't say anything.

Dean scoffed. "Are you kidding me? After all you said?"

"I'm really sorry," Colin said, turning at last. "I was under a lot of stress and I was really drunk. I was speaking without thinking."

"Then maybe you were speaking from the heart! I don't understand, why do you always do this?"

"It wouldn't work," Colin mumbled. "I mean, of course I have feelings for you. Complex ones. But I think in a way it's just vanity. I see myself in you, you know? We're too similar. I need someone who can balance me out."

"We aren't similar at all!" Dean said. "Just because we're both transgender?"

"Well partially," Colin said, "But it's more than that. When I'm around you, it's strange. I don't know exactly how to explain it. It's like I see a part of myself in you- a part I don't like. You just…consume me. I lose my sense of things. And honestly, it brings me down."

Dean swore under his breath and tears welled in his eyes. He'd heard this before. "I have two sides," he said. "I'm not always this negative beast. I didn't used to be, I swear. If you loved me, I'm certain I'd change: into a happy prince! I wouldn't mope about and criticize everything constantly, I promise. I swear I can be downright sweet. Ask anyone who really knows me."

Unfortunately there was no one to ask and Colin wasn't convinced. He shook his head. "I wouldn't want you to change for me. Your attitude works for you. It just wouldn't suit a relationship."

"Well thanks," Dean muttered. "Thanks a lot."

"I meant a relationship with me. I didn't mean in general."

"I know what you meant," Dean said, "and that's fine, you're probably right. But you're the one who sought me out. I was fine by myself before. So in the future, just leave me the hell alone. Call someone else when you feel the urge be a drunk asshole."

"Dean, please don't be mad. I still consider you my best friend."

"Leave me alone," Dean said, putting on his coat. "We're not friends."

He slammed the door and headed out into the dark snowstorm, unsure where he was going.

*

Spring came early Downstate, and by mid March the trees were budding. Rain showers brought a plethora of perennials, tulips trimmed the brick buildings, and alliteration was accidental and awful. One Saturday afternoon, Dean sat out on the bleachers in his usual spot, watching the sparrows and enjoying the sun. He couldn't help but soften. His moods were easily influenced by the weather, and he was sick of feeling nothing but hate. He was also enjoying his lecture class on The Bible. That Friday, they had finally reached the Gospels.

"Just try it, for one week," the professor had said. He looked like a wizard-hippy, with his grey pony tail and granny glasses, standing before the class, grinning about god-knows-what. "Try to love your neighbor unconditionally. You'll see how hard it really is." It was the only time Dean bothered to write down a homework assignment in his notebook. He usually hated hippies, but he was strangely fond of this old man.

His first move would be to seek out Colin. They hadn't talked all semester- he'd practically been living at Maggie's, only stopping by the room a handful of times. But when Dean got back to his dorm, he found Colin's belongings had vanished, most likely for spring break. He cursed. The fact Colin was not available to forgive made him ever angrier. He could have called, but he decided to wait. Looking out the window, he thought it a good day to read on the quad. He was getting together his books when there was a knock on the door. He froze. He crept over as quietly as possible and peered through the peep hole. It was Craig.

It was incredible how Dean suppressed all thoughts of him since the incident in December. He felt overwhelmingly embarrassed, and was going to pretend he wasn't home when he remembered his teacher's challenge. A loving person wouldn't shut out a friend. After all, Craig was probably embarrassed as well. He took a deep breath and opened the door.

"Hey," Craig said. He sounded bored as usual, but a slight blush gave him away. He was wearing a maroon cardigan over his white tee shirt with blue jeans. He wore new, rectangular glasses, and had shaved his beard.

"Hey," Dean said. "What's going on?"

Craig folded his arms, slouching. "Well, I wanted to take you somewhere, if you aren't busy. I have a surprise."

"For me? What is it?"

"If I tell you, it won't be a surprise," Craig said in a flat voice, purposefully emphasizing the cliché.

"Should have anticipated that," Dean said. "Well okay, lead the way, grumpy." Secretly he was excited.

"Your phone isn't turned on, by the way," Craig said as they walked down the stairs.

Dean didn't really care and left it that way.

Outside, Craig led him to an old white car parked in the lot. Dean recognized it immediately.

"I borrowed Sheila's car," Craig explained. "I would have taken the train, but I need a car to get to our destination."

"No complaints here," Dean said, getting in the passenger seat. "I love car rides, especially in this one. Where exactly are we going?"

Craig gave him an exasperated look.

"Oh," Dean said. "It's a surprise. Right."

They rode for awhile, listening to the Neko Case album Sheila left in the car. Dean rolled the window down and enjoyed the breeze, watching the scenery. They rode in silence until the album ended. After a few moments of staring at the pine air freshener, Dean addressed what was on both of their minds. "Listen: I'm sorry about that night. I should have stayed..."

"It's okay," Craig said. "You didn't want to, and that's fine. Really, I was upset at first, but I realized it wasn't personal."

"No," Dean said. "It wasn't, at all. I'm sorry. I've been too embarrassed to contact you, after how I behaved."

"It's alright," Craig said. "If I was mad, I wouldn't be doing this."

Dean nodded. He leaned back in his seat, watching the roadside scenery. Craig put on a CD of a female artist he didn't recognize. It was calming, and he accidentally dozed off. He didn't dream.

*

Dean woke to Craig nudging him on the shoulder. They were parked.

"Hey," Craig said. "We're here. Don't look yet." He formed blinders with his large hands on either side of Dean's face, and leaned in close. "I want to explain something first."

Dean's eyes darted back and forth between Craig's palms. "Uh, okay."

Craig's face was the only thing he could see. For a millisecond, he thought they might kiss.

"Alright," Craig said. "Understand that this isn't a happy surprise, exactly. It's not a puppy or anything- just something I hoped would help. But anyway, that's my disclaimer. I guess you can look now." He lowered his hands and sat back.

Dean looked out over the dashboard. They were parked in a large cemetery. He smirked and undid his seatbelt. Was this what people thought he was into? "Why did you drive all this way?" he said. We've got a cemetery by the campus, you know. Where are we anyway?"

Craig looked nervous as he stepped out of the car. "Well, we're in Long Island." He went over and popped the trunk, reaching inside.

"Why?" Dean asked, "Did you want me to meet your dead relatives?"

"Here, maybe this will explain." Craig slammed down the trunk with his elbow and handed Dean the object he had retrieved. It was wrapped in a muddy plastic bag.

Dean frowned. "Please tell me it isn't a human head." He peered inside, removing the bag as he did. It was the mossy one-winged angel statue from Teddy's yard. His arms and neck prickled with goose-bumps. "How?" he asked, looking up.

Craig avoided his gaze, looking uneasy. "You left it at Sheila's aunt's house this summer," he said. "Sheila told me the story. And I thought maybe you might want to bring it here. For closure." He rubbed his arm again, and Dean saw he was sweating. "In retrospect, it was stupid to make it a surprise. This is probably upsetting for you. I just know how it is to lose someone that you, like, connected with. And well, little symbolic things can mean a lot. And I just wanted it to be…special. Or something. I really should have asked first. I'm sorry, I'm an asshole."

Dean's expression was impossible to read as he stared down at the statue for several seconds. Then, he did something unexpected. He stepped forward and pulled Craig into a one-armed hug.

"Oh thank God you aren't angry," Craig said, his body relaxing.

"No," Dean said, still clinging. "That is the most thoughtful thing ever. Thank you." Overwhelmed with emotion, he tried to kiss Craig on the cheek but landed awkwardly on his ear lobe.

As they pulled away, Craig waved away the praise, blushing. "It was nothing, really. I mean, it was also just an excuse to hang out. I've missed you."

"Really?" Dean said.

"No, I'm lying." Craig rolled his eyes. He looked around the cemetery, squinting his in the sun. "The grave is that way," he said, pointing down a path to the left. "By the trees. It's gray, with a cross, you can't miss it."

Dean wasn't sure if he was being sarcastic, seeing as most the graves fit this description. He wondered how Craig already knew the location. Had he been taking trips home? He decided against asking. "Why don't you just show me?" he said.

"Oh, I don't want to intrude," Craig said, opening the car door.

"Don't be stupid," Dean said, taking him by the arm. "I want you to come."

Craig closed the door, smiling softly. "Okay. I'd love to."

They walked along the paths, observing the graves. They were engraved with mostly Irish names, as it was a Catholic cemetery. Dean wondered whether he and Teddy shared a similar heritage. Some of the markers were old, dating back as far as the 1800's. They read the names in silence, deep in their thoughts, arms still linked. Dean bent down a few times to rearrange flowers or to wipe away dirt from the headstones. Finally, they reached the trees.

"This is it," Craig said, motioning towards a tombstone in the shade.

It was indeed gray, with the luster and cheap, marble-like appearance most new graves possessed. There were fake pink tulips in a terra cotta pot, but no other adornments. A faint stone cross was overlain with the inscription of a banner. It read:

THEODORE PATRICK FOLEY

The dates confirmed Teddy had been twenty-seven years old.

Dean stood in silence. A crow cawed in the distance.

"I should have warned you about the name," Craig said.

"No," Dean said. "No, I expected as much. Well, if anything it's incentive for me to change mine, heaven forbid." He made the sign of the cross and stuck out his tongue. "Ah but what does it matter? What's in a name, right?"

Everything, he well knew. As silly as it was, a life could be spent fighting for a name- the word that meant *you*. To declare others could not decide that word, to insist it have a meaning many would condemn- that admittedly took courage. There *was* something in a name, at least for people like him and Teddy. He felt tears in his eyes and bowed his head.

Craig squeezed Dean's hand, startled by how small it was. "It's alright," he said, looking down at the top of his hair, "Just think, it's Dorothy backwards."

"I know. For all I know she liked it fine. It's just that to me, she was Teddy. One word." Just as he felt he was only Dean- he avoided his surname when possible. Their ties to their fathers were severed, their lineage muddled; they were a people apart. Letting go of Craig's hand, he kneeled at the grave. He placed the angel on the footer beside the silk plant. He realized it would seem a typical talisman to passersby, just as Theodore Patrick Foley would seem a typical man. The gesture felt powerful none the less. He curled up over the grave, hugging his knees. He put his lips to the dirt between the grass and closed his eyes. After a few moments, he whispered into the ground, a variation of something he'd accidentally memorized by heart

"And alien tears will fill for her
Pity's long broken urn.
For her mourners will be outcast men
And outcasts always mourn."

*

Dean was back in Syracuse in time for St. Patrick's Day. His parents were throwing their usual party with extended family and the dreaded neighbors. Dean hid in his bedroom all night, and his mother knew better than to protest. He entertained the idea of sneaking down for beers, but decided against it. He'd lost his short-lived interest in drinking.

He was listening to his CD player when his cell phone vibrated in his pocket. He didn't recognize the number- it looked like it came from a pay phone. Once again, his curiosity beat his anxiety. He paused the music and answered it. "Hello?" He flopped down on his bed, looking at his reflection out of habit.

"Hey Dean!" It was Maggie. "You're Irish, right? Happy St. Patrick's day, baby!" She was yelling. It sounded like she was at a bar. He wondered if she was drunk dialing everyone she knew. The new, optimistic Maggie was sugary and off-putting. He missed the days when she was a quiet knitter who talked about Southern Gothic.

"Thanks," he said. "Yeah, I'm Irish." He was American really, but he liked identifying with his ancestors. Admittedly, deceased potato farmers knew as much about his life as the bunch downstairs. "Hey, um, sorry I haven't talked to you in awhile," he said. "I've been pretty busy these past months."

"Oh it's okay, Colin told me what was going on. You're upset with us and I understand. Because well, you know, I understand. It's hard to get over people."

This annoyed Dean greatly. He felt sick, imagining what Colin must have told her. "I'm actually over it," he said, his voice cold.

"Oh, good! Then you'll be our friend again?"

"Sure." What else could he say?

"Awesome, sweetie! Oh my god Dean, we're at a gay bar in Chelsea. The drag queens are fierce. You would so love it."

Dean winced. "Would I?"

"Yes!" Maggie yelled. "I'll try to find you a cute boy even though you aren't here."

"Uh, that's really alright," Dean said. "I wouldn't know what to do with one of those."

Maggie misunderstood him. "Oh, that's right, you're taken! What's going on with you and Craig anyway, hm?"

Dean sighed, making a gravelly noise in the phone. "We're just friends. Good friends and nothing more."

"*Sure*," Maggie said. "Friends with benefits! Oh, Colin is back, I'll put him on! Baby, come talk on the phone!"

Dean tried to protest but it was too late.

"Hello?" It was Colin. "Who is this?"

"Hey," Dean said.

"Oh, it's you," Colin muttered.

"Yeah," Dean said. "It's me. Still with Maggie then, eh?"

"Yeah," Colin said. "Of course. I love her."

"Great," Dean said, and then he remembered his old professor's challenge. He swallowed. "Listen Colin. We're graduating in a few months, and there's no reason we can't be on good terms."

"I couldn't agree more," Colin said. "I've really missed you, you know. But I get it. I mean, I was a jerk, and I feel awful. I really should watch what I say when I'm drunk."

Dean wasn't going to argue with him there. Instead he changed the subject. "How are things going with the band?" he asked.

"Great!" Colin said, relieved to talk about something else. "I've still been getting threats, but what can you do? I've also gotten some really nice letters, saying how inspiring my story is. I'll show you when we're back at school."

"I'd like that," Dean said. He'd missed the sound of Colin's voice, especially when he was excited.

"But the shows have been excellent lately," Colin said. "Very different- things are changing for certain. They're livelier. I'm a little tipsy, so I'm having trouble articulating."

Dean noticed Colin lapsed into a more typically feminine speaking pattern when he was drunk and happy. It was hard to explain what changed; the emphasis on syllables was different: less monotone, not peppered with *mans* or *dudes*. He sounded more musical, more Irish even, though that could be the holiday speaking. He loved it, and it reminded him of something. He crossed to his bookshelf and started leafing through his copy of *A Portrait of The Artist as a Young Man*, searching for a specific passage. He then remembered he was still on the phone. "Oh, uh, that's great," he said, "I'm really happy for you."

"That reminds me!" Colin said. "I haven't told you. We're going to be on television!"

Dean felt a sharp pang. "Oh really?" he said. "When? What show?" He hated how little it took to make his body respond to distress. He rubbed his breastbone, wincing.

"Well, they've already started circulating a music video. It plays on late night indie countdown things on MTV2 and Fuse. Cooper says if we play our cards right, the single for the next album could go on the regular daytime circuit."

"Wow," Dean said.

"And in addition to that, they're interviewing us! They have a short talk show in between the videos, it's a program called *The Dish*. I don't know if you've ever watched it."

"Wow," Dean said again. "Yeah, I've seen it before. What night is that going to air?"

"The 25th, at eleven thirty. We're recording it that morning."

"Wow," Dean said for the third time. "Well, I'll make sure to watch." Colin was becoming a celebrity. He felt even more like a loser.

"Thanks!" Colin said. "Well, I'd best be going. I'll talk to you soon. Should I put Maggie back on?"

"No," Dean said. He felt bitter. "Say, Colin?"

"Yeah?"

"Whose idea was it to go to a gay bar on St. Patrick's Day?"

"Oh. It was mine."

Dean snorted. "That's what I figured. Night."

"Night," Colin said, sounding defeated.

*

On the 25th, Dean's parents were once again out of town, leaving him the house. He came down to the family room at eleven thirty, and turned the television to channel 173. A music video was playing by a band he didn't know, which he figured was the point of an indie rock program. It was awful in his opinion, but he knew it was what his generation loved. An emaciated lead singer with huge sunglasses, neon colors, meaningless metaphors, an ironic accordion solo; an infallible recipe for success these days.

The video ended and the metrosexual television host returned in all his hair gel glory, announcing he would be talking to the *boys* (he emphasized this word with an oh-so clever raise of his plucked eyebrows) from Owl Eyes right after a commercial break.

Impatient, Dean went into the kitchen and made instant oatmeal. The microwave beeped just as the show came back on. With a jolt, he realized it was Colin and Craig sitting on the couch besides the host. He hurried back into the room, forsaking brown sugar for his steaming cereal.

"And we're back," said the host. "Tonight's guests are from the critically acclaimed indie rock quintet, Owl Eyes. On my left I have Craig Roth, the vocalist and lyricist, and Colin Mahr, the guitarist and songwriter."

Dean stared into Colin's dark eyes as he waved at the camera. His smile was charmingly confident as usual, but there was something different; something slightly sinister. He was hypnotically attractive, dressed in a button shirt and tight grey slacks, revealing his skinny ankles when he crossed his legs. His hair was brushed back, looking even more like Dean's. Craig scratched the back of his head, looking shy and uncomfortable in a brown sweater. He hadn't shaved, and his face looked pasty.

"So guys," the host said, "How did you come up with the name Owl Eyes?"

Colin nodded his head to the left, "Craig here came up with it. I wanted to be called The Velvet Underground, but he said it was too much of a mouthful."

Dean nearly choked on his oatmeal. He took a gulp of water. The host didn't share Dean's enthusiasm. He chose to move on. "Colin, a lot of people have been talking about your recent interview in *Line Out* Magazine, where you claim you are a *transgender.*" He emphasized this again with a raise of his eyebrows. "Can you explain to viewers what this means?"

"No," Colin said with a flippant wave of his hand. "That's the beauty of the term. It can mean whatever you want it to mean."

"But if you don't mind me asking," the host persisted, "could you please explain what exactly you…are?"

Colin sighed. "Well Travis, what exactly are you?"

The host laughed. "Well, I'm a man, obviously."

Colin cocked his head, feigning interest. "Really? Could you explain how you know?"

Travis squirmed in his seat. "Well, I just know! How does anyone know?"

"Beats me," Colin said.

"I guess the doctors told my parents who told me," Travis said, with a laugh.

"Hm," Colin said, wagging his finger, "You are awfully trusting."

"Well there's some other evidence as well, if you know what I mean," Travis said, nudging Craig with his elbow.

Colin shrugged his shoulders with theatrical flair. "If you say so, Travis."

"Well," Travis said loudly. "Once again, that was Colin Mahr and Craig Roth of Owl Eyes. Thanks for coming on the show, guys."

"It was our pleasure," Colin said, winking at the camera. "Good night America."

"And now, the top ten viewers' picks of the week!" Travis said, and it was back to bad music videos.

Dean sat back, setting his empty bowl on the sofa. The new and improved Colin was breathtaking. How would he feel if he hadn't attended college and simply saw this on television? Saved, perhaps. In love, for certain. He'd probably have a picture of Colin on his bedroom wall. He wasn't sure if he felt excited or heartsick. He opened his phone and texted his friend one word: "Bravo!"

He cracked his knuckles, practically vibrating with energy. Colin Mahr was the first transsexual in the media to fill him with pride. Colin Mahr had stature and force of Napoleon: he just might change people's perceptions. Colin Mahr would bring destruction, one douche-bag interviewer at a time. Colin Mahr would eventually make transsexuality cool even to middle-schoolers. Through Owl Eyes, Colin Mahr would unite and take over. No more would female-boys be barred their little proms; they would be the homecoming kings! No more would they be harassed in gym class; they'd be rock stars, football heroes! They'd move up the food chain at last, and Dean would have his vengeance on all who had ever doubted him. The imposing rules would no longer apply to his kind; they would only burden...well...

As quickly as it skyrocketed, Dean's mood crashed. He watched a bare-chested man on the screen, face covered in suds, dragging a razor along his chiseled jaw-line. The commercial promised the closest shave yet. They always promised that. Dean muted the television. He didn't know what he felt.

He stared blankly out the window. It was too dark to see much of anything, other than the lights from the neighbors' houses. Turning back to the television, he saw a vaguely familiar actress was lifting her shirt with one hand to reveal her perfectly toned stomach. In her other hand, she held a container of yogurt. It was followed by the scene of a wedding, full of smiling guests.

Just what was it he wanted destroyed anyway?

Unable to stomach it any longer, he turned on the DVD player with the remote and pressed play, knowing the film would pick up where he left it.

"*Moon river, wider than a mile*
I'll be crossing you in style someday," sang Audrey Hepburn.
"*Dream maker, you heart breaker*
Wherever you're going, I'm going your way
Two drifters off to see the world
There's such a lot of world to see..."

Dean watched in a trance. "*We're after the same rainbow's end,*" he quietly sang along, rolling his eyes. He suddenly wished, more than anything, it was his and Colin's music the world would hear. He chucked his cell phone onto the other couch. "Fuck you!" he shouted to an empty house. He cradled himself in his own arms, his body shaking. He cried himself to sleep, a muted boxing match on the television.

*

The weather in April was miserable. After spring break, rainstorms lasted for nearly two weeks, confining Dean and Colin to their room. Maggie would hang around as well, lying in Colin's bed, watching old movies while Dean read by flashlight. Sometimes, when Dean couldn't stand seeing them any longer, he'd go in the hall for solitude.

One Friday night he was doing just this, when Maggie came out into the hall and noticed him on the ground. She gave him a look. "Why are you sitting out here?" she asked.

"Oh," he said, adjusting his glasses, "the movie was a little loud, I didn't want to say anything."

Maggie shook her head. "It wouldn't have bothered us to turn it down. Well, anyway, I'd best be off. Colin's gone to bed. He's got to get up early to catch his flight."

"Flight?" Dean said.

"Oh, he didn't tell you? He's headed to Boston."

Dean closed his book. "Boston? What for?"

"He has an appointment with his surgeon," Maggie said.

"But he's already had surgery, hasn't he?" Dean didn't know why he asked this. He knew the answer.

"Chest surgery, yes," Maggie said. "He's having genital reconstruction."

Dean raised his eyebrows. "Oh wow." He didn't know what to say.

"Yeah," Maggie said, "it's scheduled for October. I'm sure he'll tell you all about it if you ask. He has information on the doctor if you're interested or anything. She's supposed to do great work."

Dean shook his head. "No thanks."

Maggie shrugged. "Well, I have to be getting some sleep as well. Call me if you want to hang out, I don't have work on Sunday."

"Okay," Dean said, not really hearing her. "So is Colin going to be able to change his gender legally then? I know they don't let you do that unless you've got a letter saying you've had an official sex change operation."

Maggie nodded. "Yes, that is the added bonus. I mean, of course he's doing it to feel better in his body, but on top of that, it means we'll be able to get married in New York."

Dean couldn't help smirking. He thought it was stupid when young couples believed would be together forever.

"Why are you smirking?" Maggie asked.

"Oh, am I? I'm sorry, I didn't realize," Dean mumbled. "My face just does that."

"He didn't tell you we're getting married, did he?"

Dean frowned. "What are you talking about?"

"Colin and I are engaged. We're getting married next spring, after everything winds down."

Dean scratched the back of his neck. "He proposed to you?"

"Yes," Maggie said. "Yes he did."

"You have a ring and everything?"

Maggie held up her hand, displaying the rock.

"But we're only kids," Dean said.

"No, we're really not anymore," Maggie said. She was frustrated Colin lied to her. He said he would tell Dean as soon as they got back to school. Well... Colin had a lot on his mind, she couldn't blame him. "Anyway, good night Dean," she said, and she headed towards the stairwell.

Dean bit his lip, lost. "Maggie?"

She turned. "What?" At first she looked angry, then wounded. Then, as if catching herself, she smiled unconvincingly. "What is it Dean?" she said, softer this time.

Dean stared into her eyes. He knew there was nothing he could say. "Never mind. Good night."

Maggie smiled again. "Good night," she said, and she left.

Dean sat in the corner clutching his book, paralyzed by the news. He had gone through too many ups and downs with Colin to feel anything now but steady sorrow. What was the point of getting angry only to forgive once more? He felt weak. He wanted to sleep, and he wasn't too keen on waking.

He opened the door and stepped into the dark room, keeping his watery eyes off his sleeping roommate. He stripped down to his underwear and tee shirt as he climbed into an empty bed.

*

Dean spent Saturday resting, leaving a few times to retrieve snacks from the café. With his windows open, he watched the rainfall, his head resting on his pillow, listening to opera on Colin's radio. His thoughts were looped, it seemed. He didn't want to do anything but lie very still.

On Sunday, the weather cleared and he went for several long walks. It was the first day of May, and all his schoolwork was done, except a few in-class finals. He would be going home for good in a week. As he walked by the academic buildings, he knew he had no interest in attending graduation. It wouldn't be special for him like it would for others; his attendance at this college was a stab at practicality, a temporary escape, but nothing to which he felt any allegiance. A weird anglophile from the get-go, he once sworn to his elementary schoolmates, with a Lincoln log in his mouth, that he would attend Oxford and smoke a pipe by the fireside. Anything less didn't seem worth celebrating.

Colin came back on Tuesday evening but didn't mention the surgeon or the engagement. Dean didn't bother approaching him; with less than a week to go, it was better to keep the peace. They coexisted in strained civility. The subject didn't come up until their second to last day on campus when they were packing. Colin was fitting his television into a large cardboard box when he addressed Dean across the room. "So last time I asked, you didn't have any plans for after graduation. Is that still true?"

Dean was shoving socks and underwear into his pillow case. "Yeah. No plans."

"Are you stressed?"

Dean shrugged. "Whatever." He noticed an embarrassing item was fully visible now in his sock drawer, and though Colin wasn't looking, he covered it with an undershirt, blushing. "What are your plans?" he asked.

"I have a lot on my plate actually," Colin said. "The band isn't doing any shows for awhile at least, but I've got to start writing and planning the new album. I'll be having rehearsal-type things with Craig and the others all summer, probably at my parent's place for convenience. Everyone but Craig lives in Long Island. I'll have to come to the city for promotional things- working with Cooper, interviews, another television slot hopefully. But come fall, I'm planning to move into an apartment with Maggie in Brooklyn, which will make everything easier. That's also when we're going to start recording the album and working with the producer. So yeah."

Dean nodded and turned to fold his shirts. "Maggie mentioned you have plans for surgery," he said. "Is that true?"

"Oh, yes, I almost forgot," Colin said, scratching his hair. "Yeah, I had that scheduled for October." He hadn't forgotten. He wasn't sure why he was ashamed to tell Dean.

"Are you nervous?" Dean asked.

"Quite," Colin admitted. "I mean, there's only so much that can be done, given medical technology. I always figured I'd wait it out, see if options improved. But I'm getting impatient, and it causes me a lot of distress, so I figure, well, you know, you're only young once. Small is better than nothing."

Dean looked up, acknowledging he heard him. There was no reason to agree with or contest his statement.

"You know, I have some information on chest surgeons," Colin said. "My dad actually knows a guy, and I could probably get you somewhat of a discount. Mine only ended up costing seven thousand or so."

Dean smirked at his shirts. Only seven thousand dollars. He'd never held on to more than a hundred at a time. "Thank you," he said, "But no."

"Because of the cost?" Colin asked. "It's really not bad. If you buckled down and worked a lot, I bet you could raise the money in no time. Definitely by next year."

"Yeah," Dean said.

Colin piled his books into a suitcase. "You know, maybe if I get some free time, I could come up north and visit you this summer. We have to keep in touch. I'm really going to miss you."

Dean nodded, looking at his feet. Nothing Colin said could affect him anymore. Even if his sentiments were true, it was meaningless in the grand scheme. "Feel free," he said.

"Where are you planning on spending the summer then?" Colin asked, putting his prized Les Paul in its hard shell case.

"Syracuse," Dean muttered, with a superfluous shrug of his shoulders and a short laugh. "Where else?"

*

We've reached the summer when our tale began and will end. I was hoping to gain insight by recording all this, and I guess, in a sense, I can now see the past two years for what they were: melodrama.

You always hear horror stories about the suburban girls who are home schooled, ultra religious, leading sheltered, flower-like lives. They head off to college and are overwhelmed with stimuli, devolving into some unholy conglomeration of a girls-gone-wild and heroin addicts. My experience was as devastatingly predictable. What can I say? Colin Mahr was the answer to years of stifled daydreams; a fellow gender deviant, a musical genius, a lover and best friend who finally "got me". It was almost too awful to be true, and sometimes, I'm convinced it wasn't. Colin seems to me another idle daydream I made to pass the time, an imaginary friend to keep me company when I wasn't listening to Morrissey albums. Our connections were intense but short lived, overpowered by miscommunication- the inevitable folly of most relationships. Now, in the silence of this suburban refuge, I have to face facts. We are of different worlds.

For too long I have placed the blame for my melancholy on outside forces. I believe I am growing up. Words, concepts, society- none of these are at fault. One by one, my ancient tormentors line up before me: Woman, Man, Nature, Body, Self, Truth. By demonizing these words, I gave them their power. And none more than the ringleader: Love.

So I brought the pills up to my bedroom, and they loomed over me all the while I wrote. I matured this summer, but maturing was something I never wanted to happen to me. The child in me was dead. I was nothing but a hack, a grumpy old man in a cardigan. My night terrors made me realize, even worse, I had the capacity to hurt others- a kid like Adrian, for example...Vivian. Maggie. Even writing this now, I loathe myself. *Live or die, but don't poison everything!* Let me blunt:

I couldn't keep those pills floating around; it was time for me to make a stand. Having found Teddy hanging, I knew the pain my decision could inflict. There was no denying the terrible, terrible selfishness of what I was considering. At the very least, I wanted to spare those who knew me from the sight, the smell, the haunting, disgusting reality of our bodies. That is something from which no one can recover. That was why I left my bedroom.

I woke up early, around four in the morning. I drank a cup of coffee and ate oatmeal as usual at my kitchen table. Outside it was still dark, and I didn't bother turning on the lights. To observe my childhood home in detail would have been too painful; my heart already felt like it might soon explode from that heavy, physical ache that had persisted for weeks.

When I was young I read a book about a wolf dog whose heart exploded, right before the finish line of his sled race. It was called *Stonefox*. I was young and naïve, so ending came as a shock. The rest of the novel was enjoyable; everything seemed to be going so well up until that point. How could the author do that to me? It was the *Three Little Pigs* all over again, and I was outraged in the way that only a seven year old with a lisp can be. I even wrote a humorous sequel where the dog somehow rises from the dead, and vowed to have it published one day, as my revenge. Little Lord Yahweh decreed: Everything must be funny, always!

I used to see absurd comedy in a world that turned its back on me. But nothing is funny when you realize it's actually you who turned your back on the world. And so I ate my oatmeal with a straight face, alone in the dark of the kitchen, the handful of pills barely perceptible in my jeans' pocket. The oats were my body and the coffee my blood. It was my last supper after all, even if I had no disciples with whom to share. It was better that way. Words, I fully believed, had the power to save. Just not my words.

*

I pedaled my Schwinn bicycle, the morning air cool on my face. The weatherman predicted the heat wave would break, and it seemed he was right. Nature treated me with civility, and I appreciated it. Had I controlled the weather, I couldn't have created a more perfect morning. And so it was an easy coast down Main Street, past the closed library and pet store. There were no cars on the road, so I abandoned the sidewalk and tore full speed down the left side of the yellow lines. It was a final, unobserved act of useless defiance. As I passed the stoplight, I couldn't help but think of Alessio. He had joined the Marines. I saw it on the local news.

I was restless all night, imagining him in fatigues, wandering some Middle Eastern desert. I never thought I could relate to the enemy: the wretched, enviable *ordinary* boy. And yet, I can't help but feel empathy for this soon to be killing-machine. We're all looking for honor, aren't we? And nine times out of ten, we are misguided. Like me, that paradoxical rulebook of masculinity failed Alessio. Or maybe it was he who failed. Either way, it seemed we were both going down together in our futile attempts to please the invisible Father.

The sky was starting to illuminate. The contrast of the world was lessening, as if the Almighty was messing with brightness controls on the holy computer screen. I would have to hurry if I wanted to reach my destination before sunrise. I pedaled harder.

I was soon at the cemetery gates. I left my bike, not bothering to lock it. I strolled among the graves, concentrating thousands of memories into one potent sting of nostalgia. This was my favorite haunt as an adolescent. It was here I took refuge when fifteen years old, with the same mission in mind. It was here Vivian and the others found me. But well, that's another story.

I retired under the trees, the fresh dew on the grass soaking the seat of my Levis. I leaned back, surrounded by graves on all sides, rows upon rows of taupe houses visible in the distance. I took my portable CD player out of my backpack and put on the same ridiculous over-sized headphones I donned nearly six years ago, the first time I listened to The Smiths. It was embarrassing to have such an attachment to a musical group, but only when I allowed others' opinions to penetrate my mind. When I isolated myself, it seemed perfectly suitable.

I brought my player with a lone CD inside: The Smiths singles compilation, *Louder Than Bombs*. Adrian hadn't returned my albums to me, but it was okay. I figured he could keep them now. There was only one song I wanted. It was juvenile really, but that made it comforting. I missed the days when music was enough to sooth me. Morrissey was my most faithful of invisible friends, and I hoped his voice, so mixed up in the stew I called my own, would provide the final comfort and courage I desired.

I took the pills from my pocket. There were nine of them, blue. There's no use telling you what brand, but they were left from the days when I was over-medicated. They were old, but I don't believe stimulants expire. I knew that like James Dean, I would be sped up before the final crash, and that was how I wanted it.

Already shaking, I pressed play on my machine and skipped to track 23. Holding the mouthful of pills before me in my small hand, I prepared to swallow with dry difficulty; in my haste, I forgot a water bottle. The CD buzzed and whirred. I cranked the volume, waiting to hear the soothing sounds of Johnny Marr on the piano- waiting for Morrissey to sing me to sleep.

Imagine my surprise when the sound of a pompous, innocently pulsing guitar filled my eardrums. What the hell? I apparently hadn't memorized the album as closely as I thought. Ah yes. "Asleep" was track 24. Track 23 was "Unloveable."

I was about to press skip and carry on dying when Morrissey's voice sang in my ears, lugubriously proclaiming, after a series of melodic moans:

"*I knooooow I'm unlovvveable. Youuu don't have to tell me.*"

I couldn't help it. I smiled.

"*I don't have much in my life, but take it, it's yours.
I don't have much in my life, but take it, it's yours.
I know I'm unloveable; you don't have to tell me.
For message received, LOUD & CLEAR, LOUD & CLEAR
Message RECIEVED!*"

Something incredible happened. Words will fall short. The most I can tell you is this: I found myself giggling and unable to stop.

And so, abandoning the fastidiousness I acquired in my early twenties, I dug into the dirt with my nails, creating a shallow grave into which I dropped the last of those blue pills. I patted the burial ground firm and leaned back against the tree. I watched as the sun began to rise, the silhouette of the church steeple alight. Syracusans were now making their way to work, speeding down Route 11 in their variously colored SUVs, their minds occupied with thoughts of bills and meetings and Dunkin Donuts iced lattes. I was still listening to that silly song, grinning. Nothing could touch me, and yet I could feel everything. I was still a child, with all potentials intact. I could be both, I could be neither, I could be nothing, I could be everything. I was strange indeed; a danger to myself and probably society. But I know that you would like me, if only you could see me. Oh reader, if only you could meet me!

EPILOGUE

Dean sat barefoot on his roof, sipping seltzer and rereading a letter. The leaves on the trees glowed gold in the sunlight, and dead or dying bugs sparkled in the cobwebs. It was a warm October evening, and he had suburbia to himself.

The letter said:

Happy Late Birthday Dean!
I sent you your CDs of The Smith. Should arrive soon by mail. Sorry it took me so long. I loved it all so, so much. I want to discuss it more in person.
How are you? I don't know if Viv told you, but I got into NYU! I'm living with her and Sheila. We have an apartment in the Village. And guess what? I'll be 18 in December, and I'm starting testosterone therapy! Mom and Dad don't know, but I don't plan on going home any time soon. I'm so excited! Thank you for helping me along the way. I really couldn't have done it without you.
I hope you're OK. You really should visit soon! I can introduce you to some of the trans guys I met at college. Also, get a facebook account! I want to show you pics of my transition. And I won't have to write letters whenever I want to talk to you!
-Adrian

Dean pocketed the letter and leaned back, shielding his eyes from the sun with his hand. He frowned, thinking. An entire summer had passed since he'd socialized with anyone. He wasn't sure he remembered how.

He tossed the empty seltzer can through the window and stretched out on the shillings. The sun warmed his skin, and the breeze felt nice on his bare feet. He was starting to fall asleep when he heard a car coming around the bend. He assumed it was one of the neighbors, because his parents weren't due back for a few days. He was about to start listening to his CD player when he heard a faint knocking noise. He froze, straining to listen. There was more knocking, followed by the sound of the doorbell ringing.

He scaled the roof, crawling over the peak and down the other side so he could see the front yard. He stayed near the side of the house, not wanting to be seen. The porch roof blocked his vision of the front door. He cursed quietly and was about to go back when he noticed a familiar car in the driveway.

He moved as quickly as he could without falling, ascending the peak and scrambling back through his bedroom window, straining his groin in the act. He winced and hurried out of his bedroom, sliding his hand along the railing as he raced down the stairs. Reaching the hallway, he unbolted, unlocked, and opened the wood and then glass door.

Colin stood before him, rubbing his arm. His hair had grown out and was similar to his old style. He looked thin and pale despite the summer. Most notably, he was wearing a new tee shirt. It was white, with a bouquet of red flowers and said, in large black font: THE SMITHS. When he saw Dean, he grinned. "Dean! Surprise!"

Dean stood blinking, unsure how to react. Colin was always unfairly handsome and since his success, his confident presence was downright hypnotic. He was mature, successful and powerful, whereas Dean felt like the same bumbling idiot who answered the door two winters ago, unable to properly shake hands.

"Hey," he said. "Well, yes, this certainly is a surprise. Come in. Would you like some tea?"

Colin laughed. "No, thank you, it's late. You are so strange."

Dean winced. *No, no, no, no, no.* He pulled up two chairs, and they sat at the kitchen table.

"So," he said. "What brings you to the north?"

"To see you, of course," Colin said. "I told you I'd visit, didn't I?" There was a gleam in his eyes. Dean knew there was something more. "How are things with the band?" he asked.

Colin smiled. "Well that's actually what I wanted to talk to you about." He placed his hands palms down on the table and leaned in, with all the dramatic flair of a marriage proposal only seen in old movies. "Dean," he said, "How would you like to be our new vocalist?"

Dean stared without emotion. The words did not register at first. "I, uh, what? I'm sorry, come again?"

"The lead singer," Colin said, "and lyricist of Owl Eyes. What do you say?"

Dean felt hot and itchy all over. "I need some water," he said, and he hurried over to the sink, filling and then downing a glass in one gulp. He returned to the table, not feeling any better. He kept sipping the cool beverage, hoping it would help focus his thoughts.

" So what do you say?" Colin said.

Dean didn't know what could say. This couldn't possibly be happening. "But I can't sing," he said.

Colin laughed. "Of course you can! And we'll get you some lessons in the city just in case. I'd be more than willing to accommodate. Once the album is out you'll have more than enough to pay me back from itunes sales and touring and what not."

Dean still didn't feel well. His vision was hazy. "But no. I mean, really. I'm trash. People wouldn't want to listen to me."

"Cooper," Colin said, "begs to differ."

"What?"

"Well," Colin said, leaning back and folding his arms across his chest, "he's concerned about Craig's involvement. It isn't working for him. He said I was basically the lead man, and I might as well just sing for all that Craig was contributing. He was especially disappointed in our new tracks we recorded this summer. He said the music was great, but Craig had to go. And then he made this comment, in an email. He was saying how well the trans thing was helping with our popularity, and he said *if only we had another one of you who could sing*. And that's when it hit me. So out of curiosity, I emailed him the rough recordings of the songs you and I wrote over the summer."

"And?" Dean said. His blood pressure was elevated, pounding in his throat and temples.

"He said your singing does need work," Colin admitted, "But he also said the lyrics were perfect for our new image. And he said he remembered you from the show in SoHo, and that he was watching you, and you definitely have presence. He said the 50's, pompadour look is back in fashion, and that you're perfect. Bottom line, he wholeheartedly encouraged the switch."

Dean shook his head. He did not accept this was happening to him.

"Didn't you hear me?" Colin said, "Aren't you thrilled? Cooper knows his stuff, and he says you've got talent! He says you have presence!"

Dean didn't respond. He kept shaking his head, avoiding Colin's eyes.

"So you'll do it, right?" Colin said. "You can come back to Long Island with me tonight, and we'll write more songs together. We can do that thing where we sit in my room and then you go to the beach. It will be great; you and I always did mesh better. And then once we have a bunch of songs, we can get Jeff and Scot to come over and we can start practicing. By winter, we can start working on the album, and then tour!"

"Don't you have to have your surgery?" Dean asked.

Colin waved his hand. "My dad convinced the surgeon to let me stay on the waiting list, but to push it forward to next fall. This will give us time. I thought about it, and the music needs to come first. I've got my whole life to have surgery. This is a once in a lifetime opportunity."

"Then you can't marry Maggie," Dean said.

Colin shrugged. "Stop dwelling on technicalities. I'll get to that eventually, it really isn't important."

Dean certainly didn't think Colin should rush into surgery, but he couldn't help but wonder how Maggie would feel if she heard his words. He stared at his hands, silent.

"Come on," Colin said, getting inexplicably more hyper by the second, "Come on, Dean! Are you listening to me? This is your dream!

Fame! Half the reason people liked me on television is because I acted like you. You could be an indie and queer icon, basically over night. Please don't be shy, this is what you are meant to do. I mean, come on, you can't stay here forever, and you know it. We can really change people's perceptions. We were meant to do this."

Dean bit his lip, thinking. Then he asked the question he was putting off since the start of the conversation. "What about Craig?"

Colin sighed. "Oh Dean, what about him? I know, I know, he loves the band because it gives him an excuse to spend time with me. I've known that for a while. But, well, I don't care about him like I do you. And besides, he just isn't cut out for the artistic life. He's perfectly content working at some clothing store somewhere."

"I don't think that's true," Dean said softly.

Colin cracked his knuckles, barely considering. "Well, regardless, I'll make sure he doesn't hate you, if that's what you're worried about. If all goes according to mine and Cooper's plan, Craig will just quit soon anyway. I've been pushing him for awhile, purposefully leaving him out of the loop, being passively rude and stuff. I've known I had to replace him, though admittedly I never thought of you as the solution. Hm, that was pretty dumb, it's obvious now. Well, hindsight is twenty-twenty vision."

"You were doing all that stuff on purpose?" Dean said, "To upset him? But he's your best friend. He trusts you."

Colin sighed. "I know, I know. Don't think I don't feel bad, because I do. But it's business. It's not personal."

Dean buried his head in his hands for several seconds, thinking.

"So let's go then, shall we?" Colin said, getting to his feet, "It's a long drive, we'd better be getting back on the road before night fall."

Dean kept his face in his hands.

"Come on," Colin said, tugging him by the arm, "Don't be weird, Dean."

Dean stayed seated. "Is there any way," he said quietly, looking up, "Any possible way that Craig and I could both be the lead singers?"

Colin laughed and rolled his eyes. "No way, come on. Wow, you really know nothing about how the music industry works, do you? That's just weird and gimmicky, and we've already got enough strange points with two trans men. We definitely don't want to over do it; we're a quintet, that's what works. Plus, you two are completely different; it would clash. You'd over power him, and he'd just look like an idiot. Actually, maybe if we try that at rehearsals, he'll feel stupid and quit and we won't have to feel guilty."

"No," Dean said. It came out louder than he intended.

"What?" Colin said, "No what?"

"No," Dean said, "I don't want to."

He expected to feel awful, but instead he felt better. How could that be? Considering- well Colin put it best:

"But Dean," he said, "Think. This was all you ever wanted; you told me, don't you remember? I asked you what you want to be when you grew up and you said something stupid like *Morrissey, or a monk* or something to that effect."

"I didn't say a monk," Dean said, "Not that time. And yes, I did want to be Morrissey. But I don't see how this would qualify."

Colin laughed, rolling his eyes. "That's so typical, Dean. You idolize him, but if you knew anything about the music industry, you'd know everyone has fucked people over to get to the top. I mean, Morrissey is kinda racist, did you know that?"

"No he isn't."

"Well, did you ever hear about the lawsuit with The Smiths in the 90's?"

"Of course I did," Dean said.

"So you see? You've got to stab some people in the back… you've got to compromise your ideals every once in awhile. Otherwise, well, you'd never get further than your own bedroom."

"I have a nice bedroom," Dean said.

Colin shook his head, chuckling. "Come on, you can't possibly be serious. The artists you idolize, they're just regular assholes. You must know you're basing your decisions in life on myths."

"We all have our mythologies," Dean said, getting to his feet. He stood in the entranceway. "Besides, you're missing the point. This has nothing to do with Morrissey or monks, or you, for that matter."

"I know," Colin said, getting to his feet. "It's all about you, Dean. It's *always* about you." He chuckled.

"It's also about Craig," Dean said. "He's been a good friend to me. I won't betray him."

"You've got such a martyr complex," Colin said. "But you could make a *real* difference if you escaped this place. Is it really so bad to go behind Craig's back, it means you could save thousands of kids' lives? Think of the hope we'd give transgender youth. You'd be a real hero, and not just a rebel without a cause." He smiled lovingly and ruffled Dean's hair.

Dean didn't smile back. "You should go now," he said, staring into his eyes.

For the first time, it was Colin who looked away. "You've been in this house too long," he said. "I'll wait. I'll give you some time to think it over, change your mind. I'll wait as long as it takes."

"I'm not going to change my mind," Dean said, opening the door. "Now please leave."

Colin smirked. "But Dean, come on. Think of the money! You could live in the city and have all kinds of luxuries! I know how much you love clothes and books and records and crap. You can't pretend you don't. If you don't do this, you'll never be able to afford that lifestyle. You're going to have to get a normal job eventually. One that you hate."

Dean continued to hold the door open. "We'll see."

"What do you mean?" Colin looked panicked. He never expected this. "You--You have to come! If not you'll be stuck in this... this *nowhere*! What are you going to do? You're a *trans* man with a B.A. in *literature*. You're twenty-three years old for Christ sake, and you've never worked a day in your life! This is your one and only chance to be somebody. You have to!"

"I don't have to do anything," Dean said. He nodded towards the door, still holding it open. "Now please leave. My arm is getting tired and there are mosquitoes."

Colin shook his head and swore. He was out of ideas. Defeated, he finally walked out the door, his car keys jingling in his hand. Dean stood on the porch, watching him go. The sun was setting and a cool breeze made his mother's wind chimes clang.

Colin unlocked his car and paused before getting in the driver seat. He turned and looked over his shoulder, meeting Dean's gaze. "I really miss you," he said softly.

Dean sighed. "Good luck Colin. I really mean it. With everything."

Colin still didn't get in the car.

"If I don't hear from you," Dean said, "please send me an invitation to your wedding."

Colin snorted. "Really?"

"Yes," Dean said. "You have my blessing." The corners of his mouth twitched.

Colin's face changed. He looked on the verge of tears. "I wish you'd come with me," he said. "I really wish you would. It's not fair. I-" He seemed to be searching for the right words.

Dean knew without him saying. "Good bye Colin," he said. His throat hurt, but he was not sad.

Colin sighed, shaking his head. "Bye."

Dean stood on the porch and watched Colin's car pull out of the driveway and disappear around the curve of the cul-de-sac. He then sat on the step, staring across the street at a sprinkler. He stayed very still, with no concept of time, until a lone monarch butterfly landed on the walkway. His eyes snapped into focus. The insect flapped its wings, emphatically demure, then continued its migration south. Dean smirked. Over the hum of lawnmowers and distant traffic, he began to sing a strange, spontaneous song, keeping the beat on his knee. Hours later, when the stars were in the heavens and the mosquitoes were unbearable, he headed back inside.

About the Author:

Elliott DeLine (born 1988) is an independent writer from Syracuse, NY. He is the author of the novel *Refuse* and the novella *I Know Very Well How I Got My Name*. His work has been featured in several publications, including the *Modern Love* essay series of *The New York Times* (2011), *The Collection: Short Fiction from the Transgender Vanguard*, and a blog for the magazine *Original Plumbing (2012-present)*. Elliott attended Purchase College and graduated from Syracuse University in 2012 with a BA in English. Elliott currently lives in Syracuse, where he is involved with several local advocacy groups, volunteers at a queer youth center, and is hoping to one day open a used bookstore/cat cafe. He is the co-founder, promoter, and general coordinator of Queer Mart, an LGBTQ arts and crafts fair.

Visit elliottdeline.tumblr.com for updates, events, cats pictures, selfies, transsexual propaganda, and unpredictable miscellany!

I KNOW VERY WELL HOW I GOT MY NAME

A prequel to REFUSE

$12.00, Available @ elliottdeline.bigcartel.com

"... one of the most nuanced, well-written transgender origin stories on the market today, showcasing DeLine's impressive range as a writer. *I Know Very Well How I Got My Name* fearlessly re-enters the pain and confusion of childhood to tell a story that's at once specific to transgender experience and a universal exploration of how we come to form our identities, from the playground games insisting on "boys vs. girls" to the pitfalls and perils of first love. Though DeLine is only 24, with Refuse and I Know Very Well How I Got My Name, his is already a major contribution to queer literature. Like so many of the classic gay and lesbian novels from the earlier part of the 20th century, these works are sure, years from now, to enjoy wider readership and recognition as pioneering examples of transgender writing. Moreover, DeLine's well-crafted storytelling and skill at cultivating voice prove that, far from being a niche genre, transgender narratives by transgender authors are a welcome and still underrepresented presence in contemporary fiction today."

-Jameson Fitzpatrick, *Kirkus Reviews*

"*I Know Very Well How I Got My Name* seems to spit in the face of most traumatic renderings of a transgender experience. The book seems to say that, "yeah, I know things got kind of fucked up for a while. We're all really haunted by something in one way or another. But I'm going to take from it what I think is valuable and then write my story differently." ...We are not watching someone become reborn or rise up from the Phoenix flame as so many transgender narratives have described. Instead, we watch someone who has been silent, haunted, and abused, suddenly say "okay, yeah. That's enough. I'm done." and walk away. This is not the ending of a false life and the beginning of something true. This is someone getting fed up of other people defining them - and finding a voice, no matter what that voice is."

-Evelyn Deshane, *Prosaic Magazine*

"In his fiction he departs from conventional 'coming out' narratives of transgender persons — that the transgender character's story concludes when they outwardly identify themselves as existing outside the gender binary. Rather, DeLine represents transgender persons as more fully complex human beings wherein their identities are not wholly subsumed by their gender."

-Dr. Jeffry Iovannone. SUNY Fredonia, Women & Gender Studies professor

Printed in Great Britain
by Amazon.co.uk, Ltd.,
Marston Gate.